TO PLEDGE
Allegiance

"Once again, Robert W. Smith has written a winning, intuitive, and gripping historical novel, a sequel to his enduring A Long Way from Clare. Set in the early days of Chicago, Smith creates an additional character in the essence of a city bursting with life, the Chicago Newsboys, and the gangsters. One can imagine Jimmy Cagney and John Garfield, maybe even Humphrey Bogart stepping onto this canvas, not to mention Lauren Bacall. Smith's characters are that vivid, and his newsboys like the Dead-End Kids. This aside from the style of an author at the height of his game."

—**Robert Walker, author of**
Annie's War

"Smith breathes vivid life into the classic noir tale with his cast of cops, thugs, and one lawyer colliding in Chicago's gritty underbelly."

—**James Conroyd Martin, author of**
The Poland Trilogy

TO PLEDGE
Allegiance

by

ROBERT W. SMITH

Meryton Press

TO PLEDGE ALLEGIANCE

Copyright © 2024 by ROBERT W. SMITH

All rights reserved. No part of this publication may be reproduced, distributed, or transmitted in any form or by any means, including photocopying, recording, or other electronic or mechanical methods, without the prior written permission of the publisher, except in the case of brief quotations embodied in critical reviews and certain other non-commercial uses permitted by copyright law. For information: P.O. Box 34, Oysterville WA 98641

ISBN: 978-1-68131-091-6

This is a work of fiction. Names, characters, places, and incidents are products of the author's imagination or are used fictitiously. Any resemblance to actual events or persons, living or dead, is entirely coincidental.

Cover design by Janet B. Taylor
Front cover image: Alson Skinner Clark (1876-1945). *The Coffee House, Winter 1905-6*. Oil on canvas. 96.5 x 76.2 cm (38 x 30 in.). Gift in honor of Mr. and Mrs. Alson E. Clark. 1915.256. The Art Institute of Chicago, Chicago, IL USA. Photo Credit: The Art Institute of Chicago/Art Resource, NY

Back cover image: "Street types of Chicago – 2 newsboys" photo by Krausz, Chicago (1891). This work is in the public domain of the United States because it was published (or registered with the U.S. Copyright Office) before January 1, 1929.
Edited by Elizabeth L. Farlin
Proofreading by Brynn Shimel
Book layout and design by Chayseland Taylor

Published in the United States of America.

I dedicate this labor of love to the first true fans of my novels, Bill Closs and Thom Sheridan. Bill, I see that big, toothy smile every time I notice an empty barstool. Thom, you were one of the few guys I ever knew who figured out early that good parenting is a function of patience. Damn Agent Orange and thank you for your Vietnam service. RIP, my friends.

I didn't raise my boy to be a soldier,
I brought him up to be my pride and joy.
Who dares to place a musket on his shoulder,
To shoot some other mother's darling boy?
Let nations arbitrate their future troubles,
It's time to lay the sword and gun away.
There'd be no war today,
If mothers all would say,
I didn't raise my boy to be a soldier."

—**Lyrics by Alfred Bryan, Music by Al Piandatosi—1914**

Chapter 1

Chicago, March 3, 1917

"Extry! Extry!" called the youngster to the swarm of penguin-like men in mustaches and bowler hats celebrating another day's end over a beer at Manny's Saloon in the Monadnock Building. The lad navigated the wall-to-wall crowd of lawyers and businessmen like a little bull loose in a herd of cows. "War plot exposed," the boy bellowed. "Mexico to align with Germany, Kaiser promises Arizona and New Mexico as spoils."

The papers were calling it "The Zimmerman Telegram" after the German Foreign Secretary whose message was intercepted and made public by the Wilson administration. Germany had finally gone too far, Conor thought. It started a couple of years back with the Lusitania sinking, followed by the Annie Larson Affair and its endless investigation that exposed a conspiracy among the German Consulate, Indian nationalists and Irish republicans to ship weapons from American soil to India and the IRB in Ireland. The aim was to foment revolutions that would draw needed British troops from the continental war to protect the Empire abroad.

Conor hollered over the din of the bar, "Gimpy, Gimpy, over here, Son! The boy wears his street-given name in the way an old sailor wears a peg leg: a mark of survival, a sign for the world that the child had weathered its blows, endured its pain and cruelty. Gimpy was far from disabled, but one short leg caused a noticeable limp.

Gimpy's physical imperfections ended with the short leg. Big hazel eyes and a thick brown mane topped a matching set of dimples that would melt a glacier with the mere hint of a smile. It was said around the alley that many a spinster had stopped Gimpy on the street with an invitation to adopt him. He was bright and even tempered, with an ability to mediate the disputes that often arose within the newsboy community.

The boy's business partner was a slightly older lad called Toad, a strong, quiet Negro boy and Gimpy's self-anointed "protector," according to the newsboy grapevine. Together, the two friends were thought to earn a decent living. Both boys also held part-time jobs at Riverview Park, the wildly popular amusement park on the North Side. Conor's wife, Maureen, had fed them both on numerous occasions.

But what do the boys think about during a black winter's night lying on the hay-strewn floor of their shed in Newsboy Alley? What do they know of war and German submarines, of the ominous repercussions certain to come from this telegram? Hell, Gimpy isn't even certain of his own age; a fact he reluctantly admitted only last week. He looks no older than 14, but he knows that the worse the news, the better his income.

Young Gimpy was an entrepreneur of the purest variety and had become the lawyer's friend over the last two years. Along the way, the boy learned to read, likely through sheer willpower, and the daily newspapers gave him a rudimentary, if superficial, outline of the world order—or disorder. In terms of maturity, Gimpy was years ahead of his privileged contemporaries.

"Aye, Mister Dolan," replied the youngster, an extra-edition Examiner already folded in his ink-stained hand. This would be Conor's third paper of this late winter day. He didn't need the extra edition for its news value, and without his eyeglasses he couldn't get past the headlines.

But he gave Gimpy two nickels, twice the price of the paper, and opened to the sports page, squinting just enough to bring the headlines into focus. Now there's something to get excited about. "White Sox open spring training." The addition of "Shoeless" Joe Jackson last year should finally put the Sox in position to win a World Series in 1917. His White Sox had been bogged down in a generational slump.

Heading east toward the "L" train on Wabash, Conor spotted a dustup of some sort in the intersection at State Street blocking the streetcar tracks. Loud chanting caught his ear as flying rocks and bottles filled the air. Instinct told him to reverse course and board a streetcar on Clark, away from the chaos, but curiosity drew him closer to the mayhem that appeared to reach far beyond the intersection in both directions.

Crude signs sprang from everywhere among the crowd. End All War Now, To Hell with Britain, Bugger the King, Stop Arming England, even a personal proclamation regarding the monarch: Long May He Reign with Ass in a Drain. A dominant chant echoed and bounced from the canyon-like man-made walls of Marshall Fields to the north and the towering new Century Building to the south. "Not war . . . Peace not war." The protest stretched south from Jackson Street, at least down to Van Buren, with the demonstrators themselves under vicious attack from a seemingly organized group of crudely armed thugs.

The timing of the peace rally could not have been worse for the quickly shrinking anti-war crowd. News of the Zimmerman Telegram seemed only to have upped the volume and intensity of the war mongers. If this was the reaction in peace-loving Chicago, how would the rest of the country see it? Owing to its massive helping of German and Irish immigrants, Chicago still held the largest, if diminishing, concentration of neutrality supporters and a generous helping of Kaiser-loving Germans and English loathing Irish. The Irish would love anyone at war with England.

The Zimmerman Telegram was the most recent of Germany's provocations against the United States that began in 1915 with Lusitania sinking by a German submarine, followed by a growing roll of American dead in subsequent sinkings. This blatant conspiracy with Mexico to violate U.S. sovereignty might well prove the catalyst that drove the country to war against Germany.

Careful to dodge the violence, Conor made his way south to Harrison Street, around the mayhem, boarding a southbound streetcar and immediately spotted more trouble ahead blocking traffic in all directions. A group of thugs stood menacingly, armed with clubs and chains, intermingled with streetcars, pedestrians, wagons, and horses. On command, the gang advanced in an organized way into the crowd and began to beat protesters, mostly women, while shouting vile slurs. They seemed disciplined, with a leader hanging back from the fight, shouting orders. Curiously, they all wore American flag armbands.

Conor spotted a young woman bleeding from the head and stumbling aimlessly along the tracks toward the streetcar. He managed to step off the slow-moving car only feet from the helpless lass as the beatings raged on. He was fortunate the old Good Samaritan instinct hadn't landed him under the car. Just on the short side of forty, but still fit and lean, he swept the woman up into his arms and carried her briskly from the street, heading for cover. She seemed weightless in the moment and smaller than she had first appeared. He found shelter in a nearby doorway and sat her on a sheltered ledge. His handkerchief helped stem the blood from the graze above the woman's ear. With trembling hands, she grabbed his arm firmly but could not bring herself to speak as her blue eyes began to tear up slowly. The blue was subtle, lighter than his own Stars and Stripes shade, like that first sparkling hint of star-studded night sky that settles over an orange sunset. "You're welcome, Miss. Now we need to find a safe place for you."

But before they could move, an arm-banded man, slightly taller than Conor's five-foot-ten-inch stature, grabbed her by the hair as another swooped her up by the ankles, leaving her shoes flailing in the air in a most unladylike way. One of the laughing hooligans began to carry her like a side of beef toward an open wagon loaded with beaten and bloodied protesters as she fought and twisted and scratched.

Conor was upon them in a flash, grabbing the first scrawny "patriot" vigilante from behind and freed her ankles from his grip as a shabbily dressed goon wielded a baseball bat, winding up for a swing at Conor's head. Before the attacker could deliver a blow, a police baton came crashing into the side of his face and the man dropped instantly to the ground.

"Let's move, Conor," said his rescuer firmly.

Conor was delighted to see the stoic face of his long time friend, Lefty Hawk, the legendary child-labor organizer of the Chicago Newsboys turned, of all things, Chicago cop. Conor knew the story all too well and had himself played a significant role in the transformation. Lefty had always been grateful and to their credit, the Chicago Police had taken advantage of Lefty's unique experience and background by posting him permanently to the Newsboy Alley beat. Lefty was doing the work he loved.

The three made their way west toward LaSalle Street along Madison, away from the violence, then north toward the infamous "Newsboy Alley," known on the maps and street signs as Calhoun Place.

Within a few minutes, the three were safe in Lefty Hawk's world. Running east-west between LaSalle and Fifth Avenue, the legendary "alley" was tucked behind and between the once numerous newspaper buildings along Madison and Washington Streets.

"You're a gentleman, Sir. I'll be fine now. My flat is fairly close. I'll just rest a bit and catch my breath. My name is Viviana Bensini."

Around twenty-five, the woman was modestly if expensively dressed for civil disobedience in late winter. A velvet underskirt, deep burgundy, dropped to just above trim ankles. The matching top, long-sleeved and buttoned in the front, opened near the neck into a wide lapel and collar that dropped to mid-back and covered her shoulders. Sturdy, high buttoned shoes provided style and mobility, but her rust-colored hair, fashionably short, resembled a frazzled clump of dead tumbleweed. Her hat, if she had started the day with one, was lost forever.

Conor removed his Homburg to find it had been smashed in the fray. "Conor Dolan, Miss. This is Officer Hawk."

"Ma'am."

Looking at Lefty, she said, "You two know each other. How fortunate for me."

"Yes Miss," Lefty replied. "We're old friends."

The alley hadn't changed much since Conor's first chaotic days in Chicago back in 1903 but the tenants had. Nearly all the major papers once operated around the alley with loading docks and staircases where the newsboys would load up with wet papers and hit the cobblestones until the next edition rolled off the presses. On busy news days, the youngsters would often hawk the extra editions late into the evening.

But Chicago had become the beating heart of the Midwest, a city fueled by invention and technology and innovation and driven by ambition. As the city evolved and expanded, so did the newspapers. More readers meant bigger buildings and wider circulation logistics to meet the need. As a result, many of the newspaper buildings had fanned out up and down the river, newsboys in tow. But the old "alley" remained the beating heart of the newsboy community with four of the largest dailies still in residence. Lefty Hawk was known affectionately by the occupants, which included a few young girls, as "Da Earl of da Alley."

The alley was still electric with excitement, the exuberance of energy and youth on exhibit in half a dozen languages and a hundred smells. Wagons and motor trucks vied for space through the narrow passage, producing non-stop congestion and heated arguments. Polish, Italian and German streamed from every nook and cranny. Everyone appeared engaged in something frantic, if not illegal. Conor could see crap games with coins littering the cobblestones, penny pitching, animated arguments, banjo playing, even an older boy standing atop a crate giving a lesson in what appeared to be picking pockets. The alley still served the loading docks of some legendary Chicago papers, including the Herald and the Evening Post.

They stopped and Lefty walked over to a police callbox attached to a dilapidated, one-story brick façade under a hand-painted sign reading, "Newsboy Resort and Spa." After a brief conversation, he turned back to Conor and Miss Bensini. Motioning up the alley, he said, "Come on. Let's have a rest in my little office. You gotta wait 'til it's safe to walk the streets. There's three peace protesters dead so far on State Street."

Lefty's face was weathered by the outdoors, browned from the sun and prematurely wrinkled, but the protruding nose and deep-set, gray eyes helped give the raven-haired cop the look of a prowling wolf. His two missing front teeth remained a dominant and disarming feature that instantly morphed the wolf into a lap-loving puppy whenever it appeared. They'd never spoken of

Lefty's ethnicity, but Conor had always pictured him as a descendant of Lakota warriors. Lefty probably had no idea. He had started his life as a newsboy around the age of eight and his natural leadership qualities blossomed from day one.

The cop's "office" was an old kitchen table in a shed, complete with an obviously expensive but worn-out sofa, likely pitched into the street by one of the industrial barons on Prairie Avenue. The woman dropped onto the sofa with her last bit of energy as Lefty handed her a glass of fresh water. "Thank you both," she said while trying to assess the damage to her clothing.

"You had a close call," said Conor. "Better sit for a while 'til you get your strength back."

"I will."

Lefty handed her a moist towel and she dabbed it along her forehead and the back of her neck. "Were you marching in the peace rally?"

"No. I was on my way home from shopping and found myself caught up in it."

Two boys appeared in the doorway, obviously looking for Lefty. One was older than most, maybe seventeen, and politely removed his cap upon spotting a lady in the shed. A serious looking lad he was, lanky and rough but well-nourished with fair skin and ruby cheeks.

"Whatchoo need, Mumbles?" Lefty asked impatiently. "Can it wait?"

"We was just w-w-w-wonderin' how long dis ruckus on State Street gonna last? We ain't sold no p-p-p-papers since it started. We got rent t' pay, expenses too. Where da hell da c-c-cops at? Fuckin' thing been blowing up fer hours."

"Watch your mouth, Boy," Lefty growled.

"Sorry, Ma'am."

"I ain't got no clue when the streets will clear," Lefty admitted. "They already knew about it by the time I called it in, so they shoulda got wagon loads of cops in there two hours ago. Can't never know what's going on downtown." He motioned toward the door and added, "I'll find you in a bit."

Conor suspected what the comment about downtown meant but let the remark pass. Instead, he said, "I never saw that kid."

"He's been with us quite a while," Lefty replied. "Mother was a housekeeper at some brothel in the Southside Levee, died when Mumbles was six or seven. That's when he came to us. He left us a couple of years ago for a job running a carousel or something at Riverview Park up north. He came back last year but I didn't ask no questions. He'll tell us about it when he's ready. Good boy, but he sometimes keeps seedy company. I think he has another sideline."

"What does that mean?"

"His special talent is climbing up walls and drainpipes, squeezing through narrow openings. He's popular with some of the local boosters, burglars and such."

Conor said. "That's a risky sideline. By the way, who were the hooligans with the flag armbands?"

"I'll be looking into that," Lefty replied. "This is the second time they've attacked a peace demonstration near my beat and similar incidents have been reported around the country."

Chicago and the Midwest had long been the beating heart of the anti-war movement, with its many socialist-leaning labor organizations and the outsized presence of German and Irish immigrant communities. But the Lake Michigan wind was now blowing toward a dark and violent place, and today's events signaled an imminent crisis.

The administration was calling it the "preparedness campaign" and it was gaining steam every day. President Wilson was expanding the navy and proposing legislation for a national draft. Ever since the Lusitania sinking, the American people had been slowly piling on board the war wagon and it seemed Wilson himself, although officially still neutral, was at the reins. The sparks were everywhere. The submarine sinkings kept ticking up the death toll and the Russians were being routed everywhere.

The anti-war coalition, once led by the elite industrialists, was in tatters, to the point that support for neutrality had all but disappeared or was confined to the privacy of Irish saloons or whispered conversations among Marxists, Socialists, intellectuals, pro-German elements and conscientious objectors. Wilson had even formally rejected an embargo on arms sales to the Allies and the industrialists were cashing in. In the current climate, today's demonstration had been a bold and dangerous venture.

Before departing, Conor handed the woman his law firm's business card. "Well, under the circumstances, Miss Bensini, I think it prudent that I escort you home."

Lefty was having none of it. This was his territory. "Not necessary, Counselor. I'll grab a couple of the bigger boys to get her home safe."

Conor decided to take an indirect route home to avoid further incidents. Maureen would have learned of the Zimmerman Telegram by now and would no doubt be eager to express her opinions. He'd need to brief her on this most interesting day. There was a violent storm raging across the Atlantic and headed straight for his Bridgeport neighborhood in the heart of Chicago. But two questions burdened his thoughts on the ride to Bridgeport. Who was directing those thugs with flag armbands and where were the cops today while Rome burned?

Chapter 2

Conor hopped off the streetcar in front of the new First Lutheran Church as dusk was descending on the neighborhood. The dim glow of electric streetlamps lined Thirty-First Street. They were glass enclosed but seemed always to flicker, as if holding back a strong wind. A chill had descended from a cloudless sky carried by a cold lake breeze. The wind often proved a blessing that carried off the fermenting bouquet of rotten bovine carcasses from the nearby stockyards. Occasional stink was a fact of life here and a necessary blight on the city's ambience, but Lake Michigan was a nurturing force of life that helped maintain a tolerable balance.

The Dolans had done well, he thought, since those first chaotic months in the great city. In terms of status quo, Bridgeport was a middle-class community of mainly thriving German and Irish immigrants, seemingly a million miles from Mrs. Kaplan's boardinghouse in the old neighborhood. In truth, it was a mere forty-minute walk north to the scene of so much drama that first year in Chicago. The Dolans liked their home on Normal Avenue, one of the new bungalows springing up across Bridgeport.

To get home from the streetcar stop these days he had to zig-zag around the Lutheran church property, south down Canal then west to Normal. Until they built this huge church, he hadn't realized there were so many Protestants in Bridgeport, Germans mostly. As far he could tell, the only Germans in the Dolans' parish, Saint Bridget's, were of Bavarian ancestry.

He found the boys finishing their homework at the dining room table, as usual. It was an inviting room at the center of the narrow, elongated home, finely finished in dark, stained wood and a dull, orange wallpaper featuring a muti-colored, repeating floral pattern. This was where the Dolan family decisions were generally made.

"How was school, boys?"

Patrick, seventeen, did not reply, seemingly lost in a textbook. Their younger lad, Liam, said, "Just finishing up, Pa."

Conor mussed Liam's hair playfully. "Alright, fellas. Wrap it up for now. You boys can finish in your room after dinner." As a rule, he would hear Maureen preparing dinner in the kitchen at the back of the house. But not this evening. "Where's your Ma, boys?"

"We don't know," Patrick replied. "Haven't seen her since we got home from school. She must be at one of the neighbors'."

"Hmmm, that's strange. Did she leave a note?"

"No," said Liam.

"Well, maybe she ran down to the shops for something and started gabbing. It's early in any case."

Conor had just poured a Jameson when a knock on the door breached the silence. He opened it to find his friend Tommy Scanlon outside, wild-eyed and breathing heavily. "Conor, they took Maureen and a dozen or so other folks. I followed them to a storefront on Halsted."

"What? Who took Maureen?"

"The ruffians, vigilantes, whatever they are. There was a peace march downtown and-"

"I know all about it." A chill enveloped him; he could feel his hands shaking. He and Maureen had spoken about the current political situation as recently as last night and she agreed that her neutrality activities and open support of the IRB in Ireland were becoming increasingly dangerous and should be confined to their home. Conor was already reaching for his coat. "Come on in. I'll let the boys know I'm leaving, and we'll head over there. Wait. I'll telephone the cops and we'll meet them there."

THE LOCAL BEAT COP WAS ON THE SCENE when they hopped off the Halsted streetcar in the darkness. He was milling with a group of a dozen or so ruffians outside the storefront in the area of commercial businesses. The cop moved toward the two Irishmen instantly, palms raised and shaking his head back and forth. "Easy now, Gentlemen. Mister Dolan, is it?"

How in heaven does he know my name? "It is, and where is my wife?"

The goons behind the copper were quiet but grinning like the pickpocket who holds up your wallet to the window of a moving train just for a laugh.

Conor's fingers were no longer shaking but coiled, ready for whatever might follow. Scanlon stood at his shoulder but quiet as a dead pig in the bog.

"It's alright now," said the copper. "Just a misunderstanding. Your wife is on the way out here as we speak, and not a hair on her beautiful head harmed. I gave her a glass of water myself only a minute ago."

Conor, already heading for the door with Scanlon, did not reply, as the mob closed around the doorway. Then Maureen appeared like Moses parting the Red Sea, crimson hair loose and wild, green eyes raging like a great storm, but composure intact.

The smirks had vanished from the crowd of thugs and a taut silence thickened the evening air. Conor spoke first, addressing the cop while keeping his gaze fixed squarely on the thugs. "Who are these guys and why are they not under arrest?"

"Now then, I've spoken to the boys, and I'm satisfied it was all a misunderstanding. I see you're upset, but we'll have no more trouble here tonight."

The boys, is it? It didn't make sense. People were dead. This gang had kidnapped his wife, and the cop was making excuses for the criminals. "That's not good enough," Conor replied. "I want to sign a complaint. I want them arrested. Why are you the only cop here? I'm not leaving here until I get some answers."

A short, well-dressed man stepped forward from the group, distinguishable from the goons in work clothes, P-caps and worn coats. He looked to be in his fifties, with a trimmed beard and sporting a Bowler and cravat. The man extended his hand. "My name is Joseph Norton,

Mister Dolan, a retired U.S. Army captain. I'm in advertising now, and I also lead this group of American patriots. Please accept my apology for our mistake." Conor did not take the hand. Nor did he move or speak. "Your wife was in the company of subversive agitators this afternoon and some of my men mistook her for part of the disloyal element."

It was all too much to process on the spot. Ignoring the man in the Bowler, Conor said to the cop, "So are you going to arrest him or do my friend and I get the pleasure?"

Maureen chose that moment to whisper in his ear. "Please, Conor, let's just go home. You don't want to do this."

Bristling at the slight, the short man said, "The wind is changing quickly, Mister Dolan. You hyphenated Americans are in for a big come-uppins and it won't be more than a few days."

"Conor, please . . ." came the pleading whisper in his ear.

As the three backed away slowly from the scene, Conor took note of the officer's name badge and said, "This isn't over, Officer Larsen, not by any means."

BACK IN THEIR BRIDGEPORT SANCTUARY, with the boys down for the night, he poured them a whiskey and tossed a couple of logs on the fire. "First thing I'd like to know is did they hurt you? I mean did they touch or beat you?"

"Well, 'twas no fun being thrown over someone's shoulder and carted off like a lamb in a wagon, but no. They didn't hurt me. They questioned us—me mostly—I think. There were eight or ten taken in my load, mostly women, though I didn't know any of them. They knew full well who I was straight off. One of them said we are known Irish republicans with German sympathies, even said they have a file on us. They wanted to know what Irish organizations we belong to, how we feel about the Kaiser, and where would our loyalty lie when war is declared."

It was insane but starting to make more sense. Her questioning had been intended as a message to Conor as well—Conor in particular. Their information was accurate, although not up to date. Since 1904, they had both become well known inside the Irish Republican community, specifically the Clan-na-Gael, and active fundraisers for the Irish Republican Brotherhood in Ireland. But the Clan was on life support these days. Contributions had dried up, meetings gone unattended and support for violent revolution in Ireland gone underground. The driving force was fear of retribution and of being labeled a *hyphenated American*. "So, I thought we'd agreed you'd keep a low profile with all that's going on, Maureen. Is there something I don't know?"

Without warning, the dog launched himself over the coffee table onto Conor's lap, sending the whiskey glass into the air and the contents across the sofa. He'd forgotten to take the mut out for a walk. "Jesus, Dillon," he barked, "could you not wait five minutes?"

Dillon was an overweight, long-haired mut, black as coal and named after one of Maureen's great uncles, Byron Dillon, a martyr of the 1867 Uprising. Conor's old friend, the late, three-legged Dog, had brought the wandering hound over for dinner one night about four years ago and he never left. Frustrated and smelling like whiskey, Conor grabbed Dillon's leash from the hook and headed for the front door. Maureen was cleaning up the mess and said, "Ye had better wait, Conor. Sure there's more bad news."

With the leash still in his hand, he flopped back onto the sofa. "Alright then, let's have it."

"Patrick got sent home from school. I had to go there this afternoon before the peace rally," she announced. "Sure they suspended him for three days. It would have been more this time, but I'd say they didn't want to have to deal with you."

Conor could hardly belief he had the strength to summon a giggle. "What did he do now?"

"The usual. Ditching classes, faking teacher notes."

All Conor could think of was the new Selective Service Act. Wilson was increasing the size of the army with a national draft as war loomed. Conor forced himself from the chair and grabbed Dillon by the collar. Fastening the leash, he said, "That's enough information for tonight. It's late but I may stop at Scanlon's with Dillon on the walk to thank him. Don't worry. I'll deal with Saint Bridget's High School, and we'll continue our conversation about the Clan tomorrow."

With so much on his mind, the cold air and brisk walk helped clear his head. Conor still considered himself American but supported neutrality as much as his wife. Like most of the Chicago Irish-Americans, he bore no ill will toward Germany and retained a deep resentment for all things British. He saw no conflict in that complicated tangle of sentiments. Until recently, they'd both done their part for the IRB and the rebellion in Ireland through the Clan-na-Gael, but it was too dangerous these days and the pipeline had dried up. He hoped Germany would win quickly now with Russia in disarray and talk of the Czar's abdication. The Russians would surely capitulate in the coming weeks. Maureen might not. Her hatred of England ran deep and with good reason. But, if she couldn't keep her head down and her trap shut now, there would be trouble enough to go around.

He wondered sometimes if Maureen felt any spark of loyalty whatsoever to their adopted country. Before meeting Conor, she had known only poverty and injustice here since emigrating from Ireland under horrific circumstances about which they hadn't spoken in years; the elephant in the room.

It took Dillon forever to get down to business as they walked west on Thirty-Second Street, but he got the job done before they reached Tommy Scanlon's Saloon. The proprietor was a Clare man from Listoonvarna. Their kids often played together and Scanlon shared Conor's conflicted opinions war and about "God's one, true Church." The saloon keeper was also an executive committee member of the Clan-na-Gael, technically anyway, as the organization only existed in the minds of Irish-Americans these days.

Unlike Conor's old friend, Dog, Dillon didn't like saloons; maybe it was the smoke or the racket of fiddles and flutes; more likely he had no taste for beer. Still, the two had become attached, inseparable, the neighbors would say. Their common passion was music. Often, as Conor would unwind in the evening with a whiskey at the grand piano, Dillon would lie quietly at his feet listening, even piping in with a melodic harmony on occasion. Conor tied the mut outside and went in.

In a way, the news about Patrick's school trouble was the worst of the lot, especially in light of the changing political winds. Unlike young Liam, Patrick was his stepson, but he loved the boy as his own and had helped raise him that way. If war came, Patrick's wild streak and his lust for adventure could prove an existential disaster. The boy was too much like his mother. Patrick and his friends already talked about enlisting, going to Europe and finishing off the "Huns." Poor Maureen lived in fear of the ultimate nightmare. Conor had hoped that by now the lad would have expressed interest in becoming a lawyer like his old "Pa," but the boy was in transition to manhood, strong-headed and would need to find his own way.

Their youngest boy, Liam, twelve, would thankfully never die a soldier. The boy's Polio caused him to limp badly, maybe even require a crutch at some point, according to the doctors, but his mind was curious and his future bright.

He stepped up to Scanlon's bar and noticed the folded republican newspaper, The Gaelic American, on the bar. It was hard to get ahold of a copy these days as the paper had disappeared from the newsstands. The front page had nothing of the Zimmerman Telegram as it required a few days to ship from New York but could still be found in every Irish saloon in Chicago, a large number, indeed. The headline announced what might prove to be the last hanging execution in connection with the 1916 Easter Rising.

Conor could put a name to every one of the dozen or so night drinkers at the horseshoe-shaped bar, mainly Irish-born with a few Irish-Americans and Germans for variety. As he exchanged greetings, Scanlon placed a bowl of water on the bar as usual. "And how is our teetotaling Dillon tonight?"

"Don't ask and I'll tell you no lies. Quick stop tonight, Tommy. I wanted to thank you for your help today."

"Think nothing of it, my friend." While Scanlon poured drinks, Conor took the bowl outside for Dillon.

He stayed only long enough to down his drinks. There were dangerous days ahead—for Conor, for his family, and for everyone who openly rejected the clamor of fife and drum.

Chapter 3

March 20, 1917

The war was not looking good for the Allied Powers. With the Russian Revolution raging, Czar Nicholas II had abdicated only five days ago. It was difficult to believe the consensus of newspaper reports that Russian troops remained in the field on the Eastern Front. It was said the war effort was now being directed in large part by informal committees of enlisted soldiers in the field amidst a wholesale slaughter of officers. Conor had never been a soldier, but it didn't take a general to question how an army could be effective under such circumstances. If the Russians capitulated, hundreds of thousands of freed up German troops would join the war on the Western Front. How long could the Allies last under the weight of such force?

Conor arrived at the office at eight o'clock, as was his custom. "Officer Hawk is here to see you, Mister Dolan," Mrs. Schmidt, his secretary, announced matter-of-factly. He'd come to rely on her for her loyalty and organizational skills over the years. Thirteen years and Conor still addressed the old widow with the formal title. "I let him wait in your office."

"Thank you, Mrs. Schmidt." Lefty preferred the sofa over the two stiff client chairs, probably made him feel at home. "Didn't expect to see you twice in the same month, Lefty."

Lefty wasn't much for small talk. "Got a new case for you, Conor. That is . . . "

"You mean a new case for a newsboy," Conor teased. It wasn't the first time, but Lefty didn't make a habit of it. "Tell me about it, but first, how did it go getting that young lady home?"

"No problems. I sent Mumbles and Gimpy on the job. Not the biggest boys, but definitely the smartest. I think they brought Toad. The lady got quite the high-end flat on Randolph or somewhere. She took the boys for a good meal in a posh restaurant, but Gimpy said she wouldn't let them order a beer."

The door opened and Mrs. Schmidt appeared, placing two cups of coffee on the desk without interrupting the conversation.

"So, what about this new case?"

"It's Mumbles," Lefty replied. "He's the one you met in the alley that day, the little guy. He was shot in a burglary at some warehouse down in South Works."

"Where is he now?"

"He's at Cook County Hospital under guard."

Conor rolled his eyes. "So . . .we're talking about a free case, of course."

Lefty shrugged. "I guess. He ain't got nothing right now."

"Well, I can't waltz over to the Hospital and announce that I'm representing 'Mumbles'. What's the boy's name? How old is he?"

Lefty pulled out his cop notebook and found the page. "It took some investigating, but his given name is Jan Kazmirski, according to the detective at Harrison Street Station. I could get his birth certificate from the county, I think, but he looks around sixteen."

"Good idea. His age matters. The cops may just charge him without even finding out."

South Works, on the city's Southeast Side, was the Midwest's beating heart of industry. Tens of thousands of workers, immigrants from a dozen countries, toiled in the mills around the clock to meet the insatiable hunger for iron and steel as huge lake steamers waited ravenously for their booty at the docks and along the Calumet River.

According to Lefty, the police alleged that Mumbles and an accomplice were burglarizing a warehouse along the Calumet River when confronted. The case had generated little attention from the dailies. Lefty was emphatic that the kid was not armed during the incident and had just visited the hospital only to find the lad still unconscious.

The cop started to get up, then settled back down in the chair. "I'll try to find you some paying cases. You know, to make up for it. I . . ."

That was about as sentimental as Lefty could get. "Forget about it. I'm doing just fine. You and I are square. Let's let sleeping dogs lie. I did some things back then I'm not proud of, made compromises and such. I'm just happy some good came of it."

There was no point in rehashing all of it, even less point to telling Lefty the details, making him an accessory. Alderman O'Sullivan was a slimy, if successful, creature of a thoroughly corrupt city government. But the man always kept his word. Conor Dolan could have derailed all that after discovering the now Congressman's role in covering up rape and slavery evidence against one of Chicago's wealthy industrialists. The victim had been Nellie Finley, the immigrant girl accused of murdering her baby. But with Nellie acquitted and getting the mental health care she needed, Conor decided to essentially extort the alderman into a few charitable concessions, the first of which was to get Lefty appointed to the police department. Besides, someone had already put a bullet in the rapist's head.

With the basic facts about Mumbles reduced to paper, it was time to leave for the morning court calls. "I'll get over to the hospital after work, Lefty, and check in with you tomorrow."

The new incarnation of Cook County Hospital was said to house over two thousand beds and, following decades of decline and neglect due to political corruption, was now restored to respectability and widely acknowledged to be the nation's premier teaching hospital. Despite the overwhelming influence of graft in the city, reformers could still snatch a victory now and again on the back of public outcry. Such was the case with Cook County Hospital. Treatment at the facility was available to anyone and everyone. The new three-story main building along the 1800 block of West Harrison Street was said to be an elegant example of Classic Revival and reminded Conor more of a Parisian palace than a modern, urban hospital. The political leeches and connected alcoholic doctors had been purged from its employment rolls, replaced by competent, even cutting-edge medical professionals.

It was still dusk but the electric lighting around the facility bestowed a sense of majesty on the sculpted columns and arches, bolstering Conor's sense that this was a good a place as any to be sick or dying. Mumbles was on the third-floor emergency ward, not segregated but under a "no visitor" warning. A uniformed CPD patrolman sat beside the swinging door reading a magazine. Conor bypassed the cop and walked directly to the nurses' station, where two crisply uniformed nurses were locked in conversation. One was razor thin and short, the other middle-aged and of ample girth. From their animated expressions, Conor gathered the conversation was of a personal nature.

"Excuse me," he said.

The older one turned toward him and replied, "I'm Miss Poletti, the Charge Nurse. How may we help you, Sir?"

He removed his Homburg. "I'm an attorney, Conor Dolan, and I'm hoping to speak with Jan Kazmirski whom I believe is being treated in the ward."

The woman's eyes appeared to take his measure, top to bottom. "The short answer is no, Mister Dolan. Are you with the prosecutor's office?'"

"Lord no, Ma'am." Handing her a card, he added. "I've been retained to represent the boy. I'm a defense lawyer. Would it be possible for me to visit my client?"

"I'm afraid not. Jan is very popular. The detectives have been here the last two mornings demanding to question him."

"And did they? Question him, I mean."

"No. They couldn't have, even if the doctors had agreed. The poor boy lost a great deal of blood. Fortunately, it was a through and through wound, missing the major organs by some miracle. A year ago, he might have died from that bullet. If there is any upside to the slaughter in Europe, it's the advancements in medicine, Mr. Dolan, particularly surgery and infection control. Nitrous Oxide's effects sometimes linger for a day or two, so we'll be in no hurry to release him. I'm sorry. You asked about the detective. His name escapes me, but I found him annoying and rude. Don't come to a hospital and try to intimidate staff."

"Yes," Conor remarked. "I suspect you were well prepared to deal with that."

"I'm afraid you won't have any better luck than the detectives," she admonished. "He's not up to visitors but recovering well. God willing, he'll be out of here in a week."

He liked headstrong women. That much was obvious to anyone who knew Maureen, but one at a time was enough for any man. "I understand. Actually, at the moment I'm more concerned that the cops might talk to my client before I can interview him. Might I impose on you to witness my conversation with that policeman sitting at the door?"

"I don't see why not," she said, coming around from behind the desk. "It's certainly in the boy's best interest."

The cop still sat, arms folded, half-asleep. Conor held out an envelope and the man took it before having a chance to think. "What's this?" he grumbled. "Who the fuck are you?"

"My name is Conor Dolan, lawyer for that kid in the ward. I've handed you my card and a written instruction asserting my client's right against self-incrimination. I request that police not question him regarding this or any other criminal matter outside of my presence."

The cop was near retirement age and apparently happy with his current assignment. He tucked the envelope into his pocket and said politely, "Okay. I know how it works, *Counselor*. I'll pass it on," then retreated to his state of near slumber.

The nurse followed Conor to the staircase, out of earshot from the cop. He turned and said, "I'll push my luck and ask for one more favor, Miss . . . Poletti. Would you please, telephone my office tomorrow the moment I can speak with my client?"

He detected a softening in her expression, a glint in the recently sober amber eyes. "That's it then? You're leaving?"

Her comment momentarily unnerved him. Was the woman softening? "I don't understand. If I can't see my client, I have no further business here at the moment."

"You were born in Ireland," she declared. "I didn't detect an accent until just now. It's very faint."

"Most people don't notice. You'd have made a good detective."

"I was born in Italy. I know about accents—cops too." Her smile warmed. "Follow me," she instructed and led him around a corner to an unmarked door. Producing a key from her apron, she added, "Your client woke up earlier this evening. That blue hippo in the chair has no idea. We'll use the maintenance corridor to access his ward from the other side. Officer Sunshine won't be getting out of that chair until his shift ends. I can give you ten minutes. I'll bring the policeman a pastry and coffee."

Mumbles looked pretty good for a shot man—or boy. The kid was propped up in the bed and dozing with his eyes closed. They opened as Conor approached. The newsboys had to be notoriously light sleepers.

"Mr. D-D-Dolan," he said. "I remember you."

Conor pulled up the chair near the bed and sat facing his new client. The cheeks were no longer rosy. "I thought you'd look much worse. Lefty sent me over here to look out for you. You'll need a lawyer. You know not to talk to the cops, right?"

One eyebrow lifted, nearly disappearing into the brownish mop covering his forehead. "I ain't stupid. I'll be outta here in no time, but what am I looking at here, Mister Dolan?"

"Probably burglary. It carries a minimum of one year and a maximum of twenty. They're holding you on a huge bail. They told the court you have a felony station adjustment for burglary and battery when you were fifteen. The Court is not supposed to consider that. What was it about?"

"Long story. Once or twice a year I get a job offer that's too good to pass on. I have talents."

"So I hear. How old are you now?"

"Seventeen."

"How old?"

"Almost seventeen."

"You're not on probation, so I should be able to get you out of here."

The lad rolled his eyes. "Terrific."

"Okay. Is there anyone I can notify? Loved ones?"

"There's a lady named Bell who runs a saloon down in Pullman. I clean up for her on the weekends and when the news business is slow. She kinda looks out for me.

You know, beer and a good meal. Ain't had much time to give her lately."

"I'll tell her, Son. What's the name of the place?"

"Just Bell's Saloon. Her son claims to own the place, big talker and a bum. Can you help me, Mister Dolan?"

"We'll have to see how the evidence pans out, but who knows? Maybe we can beat it. So who was the other man?"

"Called himself Mister Graves. A real d-d-dude, he is. I met him at Big Jim's Backdoor Casino Number Three down on Eighty-Seventh Street. I got a second paper spot down there, a good one near the S-S-South Works' mills where I get the workers coming home from their shifts. It's way outta Lefty's territory b-b-but nobody gives me no trouble down there."

"What else do you know about him? Anything, nickname, description, clothing, physical characteristics."

Mumbles went on to describe a middle-aged aged man, slightly built, well-dressed with a fancy accent, short hair, as if he cuts it with a shears, and a ring on his right hand, a huge red stone. The kid thought it looked like a ruby, although he had never seen one except in a newspaper ad. "He just started being nice to me, you know? First, I thought he was a dandy-boy lookin' t' get his johnson polished, but no. Kept asking me about the South Works' warehouses."

"Okay, why would you help this fella break into a warehouse?"

Miss Poletti suddenly appeared with a tray of food that included an array of pills. "You'll have to wrap it up now, Mr. Dolan. The patient needs to eat and take his medications. Besides, that's quite enough stress for tonight."

"I understand," said Conor. "Just a few more questions?"

She put the tray down on the side table and said, "I'll be back in five minutes."

Mumbles resumed his train of thought flawlessly. "Everybody knows I gamble. I got into Big Jim for eighty b-b-bucks and his boys was puttin' da squeeze on me pretty good. They was pressing me t' give up my paper spot. Then Graves says if I get him into this warehouse, he'll pay off my debt to Big Jim. Sounded better than waking up with my d-d-dick in my back pocket."

"Did you tell him about the debt?" Conor asked.

"I ain't no Prairie Street pansy, Mr. Dolan. He didn't know nuttin' from me—but he musta asked around."

"Tell me about the break-in. Was this Graves one of Big Jim's guys?"

"Maybe. I ain't sure."

Conor decided to take a shot in the dark. "But you do jobs for Big Jim once in a while. Right?"

"Says who?"

"Never mind." The lad's answer was enough.

Mumbles explained that Graves was interested in a particular warehouse along the north bank of the Calumet River. The only access to the roof was on the east side of the building. A prowler would take care to avoid being caught in the open there at night. Whenever steel is poured at night, the glow from the stacks illuminates the sky in gold with the power of all the electric lights in the city, leaving any potential burglar exposed and vulnerable. Conor remembered briefly seeing the phenomenon himself on night walks along the lakefront. The "light show" had become a treasured spectacle on warm, clear evenings for lovers in Grant Park and along the beaches.

From below the window, three floors down, Conor could hear a big commotion with sirens and loud voices. Looking out, he could see a mass of newspaper reporters, a motor ambulance and a parade of cop vehicles. "Go on," he said to Mumbles.

"I got in through da the roof," Mumbles said. "Them roofs is all the same. There wasn't nobody around, so I let Graves in the little side door."

"What were you going to steal?" Conor asked.

The youngster shrugged. "Nothing, I guess. That's the thing. I thought it was strange that we went in on foot with no motor transport, not even a pushcart for booty and no helpers. Graves carried a small leather case. That's it."

"What kind of case?"

"Looked like a gas mask t' me and some other stuff."

"Well, why this particular warehouse? Do you have any idea?"

"Nope. I was just happy to be working off the debt. Graves seemed to know where he was going. He told me to keep a lookout through the window of the small door. I seen cops outside and yelled at him. When we got outside, the sky exploded with light. I told Graves to keep low, but the light from the stacks lit him up like a Christmas tree. I had no choice then. I stayed low and never saw Graves again."

Conor's five minutes were almost up when noise from the hallway invaded the room, followed shortly by Miss Poletti. "Wrap it up, Mr. Dolan. It'll be crazy around here for a while."

Turning back to Mumbles, he said, "Where was Graves when you came out of the warehouse?"

"I don't know. The whistles and sirens was already blowing when I tried to sneak out the side door. When I saw the cops, I tried to skedaddle. Don't know where he went."

"Where were the cops?"

"They was to the north forcing me toward the river. I thought I was running away from them, but at least one must have been on the river side 'cuz that's where the bullet came from. Hit me in the left side around my stomach."

Miss Poletti's patience had expired. She stepped between the patient and the lawyer with an expression that would send a drill sergeant running for cover and pointed to the side door. "Done. Out now."

"Okay, okay." Turning back to Mumbles, he said, "I'll find out who shot you—and who was behind it. I promise. One more question. Do you have any idea what Graves was doing there?"

"No."

"How did the pair of you get to the warehouse?"

"Graves had a Ford motor car. He parked outside a saloon about a mile away. I told him there was no way we could p-p-park a motor car at the warehouse." Conor saw Miss Poletti on the march and ended the interview.

In the hallway he said, "I only needed another minute. What's wrong? What happened?"

"Some bigshot businessman was shot tonight on the steps of his own home. They're bringing him in now. Apparently, it's very bad."

"By the looks of it," he said, "it must be Marshall Field himself."

"It's Clifford Wellborn. I never heard of him but apparently somebody has. Now go."

Chapter 4

Friday morning, March 30, 1917

The three morning editions on Conor's lap all bore nearly identical headlines, the substance of which was that President Wilson had asked to address a Special Session of Congress on April second. It didn't take a civics teacher to understand what that meant. Wilson was about to ask Congress for a Declaration of War against Germany.

It was hardly a surprise. National outrage over the Zimmerman Telegram had exceeded even the reaction to the Lusitania. And the newspapers appeared to be all in on the decision. By the time the "L" train stopped at his Jackson Street Station, Conor had devoured all three papers. What would happen to the country now? How would young Patrick react? And where would the Dolans fit into this rapidly changing political landscape?

From the office, Conor opted to make the twenty-minute walk north to the courthouse rather than use the streetcar. State Street would be a mess around nine-thirty. Besides, a good walk would clear his head on such a beautiful early spring morning. The Dearborn Street lift bridge was crowded all along the plank walkway and the sudden breeze tracking the river nearly sent his Homburg into the drink.

Virtually the only other substantive news that morning was the wide coverage of the Clifford Wellborn murder. The dailies uniformly described the man as a "major arms broker" to the Allied powers. The more salacious dailies openly suggested, without evidence, that German agents had murdered Wellborn. He could think about all that later because his business that morning was Jan Kazmirski.

Conor had come to think of the West Hubbard Street Courthouse as his primary place of business and was well known within its arched granite corridors. The Cook County Jail was next door and in between was the infamous courtyard and gallows where four of the Haymarket "anarchists" were hanged in what was now considered one of the city's epic miscarriages of justice.

The site of the gallows was an ominous reminder of even more violent and unsettled times in the great city.

"THE PEOPLE OF THE STATE OF ILLINOIS versus Jan Kazmirski," the court clerk announced to the nearly empty courtroom. Mumbles was scheduled for a preliminary hearing on a charge of felony burglary but still not released from the hospital, a fact that would force a continuance of the proceeding into next week. But Conor had also filed a motion asking the court to reconsider the boy's two-thousand-dollar bail.

After hearing a report of the defendant's condition, Judge Thompson continued the preliminary hearing until the following Tuesday, at which time Jan was to be present and enter a plea. Thompson also agreed to review the boy's bail immediately.

Conor then addressed the Court. "Your Honor, the defense is prepared to proceed on the bail issue by way of proffer if the court chooses."

With over thirty felony matters on the morning call, the young prosecutor did not object to Conor's summarizing his proposed evidence by way of proffer.

"Very well, Mister Dolan," said the elderly judge, Lawrence Thompson, "Tell me what new evidence or change of circumstances would cause me to modify the original bail order of a competent magistrate."

"First, Your Honor, I would point out that the original cash bail order was entered *ex parte*. My client was in the hospital at the time of the hearing and had not been afforded the benefit of counsel. I was not retained until after bail was set and, therefore, he was unable to present a case for bail."

"And you have now consulted with your client?"

"Yes, Your Honor, and there are mitigating factors of which I am now aware, facts not previously before the Court."

It would be a busy morning for Judge Thompson, and he clearly wanted to get on with it. Looking over at the young prosecutor, he asked, "Was there a gun involved here or was the defendant armed at the time?"

"No, Your Honor, but the defendant does have a prior arrest for burglary."

It was time to interrupt. "Jan has a station adjustment related to a burglary inquiry, Your Honor, when he was fifteen. No consequences were imposed and no charges filed." Mumbles was under the mistaken belief he served a period of probation.

Thompson glared at the prosecutor. "And was there a handgun involved there in any way?"

"I'm not certain at this time, Your Honor."

Conor saw his chance. "I am, Judge. That case involved no weapon."

"And you are making that assertion as an officer of the Court?"

"I am, Your Honor."

"Alright. I don't have time for this," Thompson grumbled. "Mister Dolan, can he post twenty-five dollars?"

"Yes, Your Honor. Thank you."

The prosecutor handed Conor a thin packet of materials and managed to get a word in. "For the record, Judge, I have handed counsel a packet of preliminary discovery including a sketch of the crime scene, the incident report of the responding officers, and the clear and close report from the detective assigned to the case."

"Noted. Clerk, call the next case."

Jan would be out of the hospital tomorrow and free to return to the relative comfort of Newsboy Alley instead of the Cook County Jail. For Conor, it had been a simple court proceeding, but one with a happy outcome—for now.

LEAVING THE BANK ON MICHIGAN AVENUE after lunch with twenty-five bucks in his pocket, Conor hopped a westbound streetcar on Harrison for the short ride to County Hospital. Mumbles would sleep better knowing he'd avoided a stint in the county jail—for the present. The lawyer would stop at Newsboy Alley on the way home and arrange for one of the kids to post the twenty-five bucks down at the jail. Lawyers were not allowed to post clients' bail. Conor wouldn't get paid for the case but at least he would get his money back when it was over. It was a simple case. Mumbles didn't hurt anyone and no property was missing. Worst case, he figured the kid would get off with some period of probation.

The war mongers in Washington D.C. and the industrialists of Astor Street had plans for boys like Mumbles, plans that would not be upset by a felony conviction or two. The newsboys were generally clever, tough and resourceful, but ignorant or callously dismissive of their own vulnerability, in other words, perfect fodder in war. Mumbles was no exception. Maybe it was a simple-minded, misplaced faith in humanity, an innocence that clothed these lads with a false air of nobility. Or maybe they just reminded Conor of Ireland and of his beloved, if complicated brother, Kevin, the Lord rest his soul. In any case, the newsboys might soon pay a high price for their virtues in the trenches of Europe.

FROM THE TOP OF THE THIRD-FLOOR staircase, he could see the nurses' station down the hall and recognized Miss Poletti holding a tray of medications and cups. He could see distinct redness around her eyes, smudged makeup and sloping shoulders. As their eyes met, the tray and its contents crashed and shattered across the floor and Conor knew that Mumbles was dead. *But how? Why? He was supposed to be released tomorrow. He was getting out on bail.* He hardly knew the boy. They were not friends. There was no reason for faintness, for loss of breath, yet . . .

"I'm sorry," she whispered in a halting voice. He could see her small hands cupping his palm, thin fingers with the broken, jagged nails of a working nurse . . . squeezing, yet he felt nothing but forced himself to speak. "How?"

"Infection is the diagnosis. He passed early this morning."

"But you said . . ."

"I know. It was unexpected. The doctors thought the danger had passed. It doesn't happen often anymore. We're getting better at controlling it, but it sometimes gets the best of us. I'm so sorry. I routinely see death in this job, but someone so young . . ."

ON THE "L" RIDE TO BRIDGEPORT HE removed the discovery envelope from his case and placed it on his lap. There was no point in reading it now. The strength or weakness of the evidence against Mumbles no longer mattered. It would be like watching a moving picture of last year's Kentucky Derby. Pointless, meaningless, a sinful waste of time and effort. You had money on the loser. Forget the last race; move on to the next. Judge Thompson would simply dismiss the case next week and Mumbles would be a memory in a pauper's grave. But a memory to whom? According to Lefty, the boy had no family. *Wait. What was the name of the old woman he told you about? It might have been Bell.*

The meaningless envelope on his lap started to gnaw at his curiosity. There were facts in the case that didn't fit the standard burglary pattern. This Mister Graves sounded more like a big time criminal than a burglar. They had no means of stealing more than they could carry away. From a warehouse? Who was Graves? Where was he now and, more importantly, what was he doing in that warehouse?

He opened the envelope and removed the thin stack of mimeographed sheets. They were smudged, as usual, but legible. The one-page incident report of the responding officer topped the stack. According to the report, the cops stumbled into this burglary during a routine patrol.

About two in the morning, they left the patrol vehicle some distance from the warehouse, making their way on foot to an old marine junkyard near the warehouse. The absence of a horse wagon or motor vehicle near the warehouse reassured the cops until one of the officers noticed a moving light through the small window of a side door. As they moved in to investigate, the sky exploded in a golden light of fire from the stacks. Within a minute, they spotted two figures exiting the side door as the light cast their outsized shadows across the side of the warehouse as in a moving picture show. When the figures ignored commands to stop, the officers opened fire, apparently wounding one as the other escaped. The report contained no description of the second offender. Conor nearly missed his trolley stop but managed to secure the file and hop off at the last moment. He arrived home early to an empty house and decided to take Dillon for a walk to Scanlon's. He made a pointing of taking the briefcase.

With Dillon tied up outside, he dug into the file over a Jameson and a beer at the bar, pulling out the report of the primary detective. The Close as Clear Report, or "C & C" as they called it, was a summary of the evidence at the close of an investigation. In some cases, like Mumbles's, it came quickly, maybe too quickly. In others it could take years.

He was into the second page of the three-page narrative when it snared him like a mouse in a trap. *"The single bullet removed from the body was fired from a pistol of 'undetermined' caliber."* The cops had fired eleven rounds total, all from standard issue .38 caliber revolvers. But a single 9mm cartridge was recovered from the scene near the river bank some fifty feet from where Mumbles fell. Because revolvers do not discharge spent cartridges from the weapon, all the .38 cartridges were retained in the police pistols and submitted in evidence. The report concluded that the spent 9mm casing had most likely been fired on a different occasion and was not related to the burglary.

Conor was no ballistics expert but his experience in criminal trial work had taught him that police do not use 9mm ammunition. It was primarily used by European manufacturers, specifically in the German Luger, the official pistol of the German Army.

The conclusion drawn by the detective from the report was that Jan Kazmirski was shot by a "non-specific" police weapon as the cops on the scene did not observe either defendant holding a pistol.

Part of him wished he had never opened the damned file. "Likely?" Maybe, but "conclusive?" Hardly. He could hear the voice of young Mumbles whispering in his ear. *There's a one in twelve chance Graves shot me, hell, killed me. Don't let it go, Mister D-D-Dolan, please.* Conor spread the remaining reports and sketch of the crime scene across the bar for review and said to Scanlon's bartender, "Give me another beer, Mack. I'm going out to get Dillon before he freezes to death." He would still be home in time for dinner.

AFTER DINNER, CONOR HEADED FOR NEWSBOY Alley to deliver the word to Lefty before he heard through the grapevine. He found the cop there three hours after his shift ended, as expected, but the news had preceded Conor. Nothing happened in this city outside the earshot or view of the newsboys. Lefty was expecting him and had gathered a box of Mumbles's belongings. A toothbrush, a small mirror, a deck of cards, but not a single memory of his mother or family. At the bottom of the small box, he found a stack of postcards, all from Bell addressed "care of Newsboy Alley" and all greetings to Mumbles in celebration of Christmas or Easter and particularly his birthday.

Due to the lateness of the hour, he grabbed a cab for the trip down to Pullman, an entire community built for and by The Pullman Company as envisioned by its deceased owner, George Pullman, until a series of strikes and economic conditions reduced demand for the iconic Pullman rail cars. In recent years the pullman houses had been sold off by the city and now comprised a distinct middle-class neighborhood on the South Side. Bell's Saloon was prominently located in the heart of the residential neighborhood on 105th Street.

The saloon was a tiny place on the corner but packed solid with local patrons when Conor arrived at around eight o'clock, asking the driver to wait. He found the proprietor behind the bar, eased himself into a spot and placed the box on the polished hardwood surface. The woman was at least in her sixties, strong and heavyset with constantly searching dark eyes. Nothing would happen in the place that escaped her notice. "You bring me a present, Mister?" She asked in an unmistakable Chicago accent, as dimples formed magically below rounded, red cheeks. Conor decided he liked her. "What'll you have?"

"Schlitz, please. Actually, I came to give you this. It's from a kid you knew. Seems he considered you next of kin."

"Knew?" she asked matter-of-factly, almost like she'd been expecting it. "Jan, right?"

"Yes, Ma'am."

"Something involving violence, most likely."

"Yes, Ma'am. It was."

"Don't tell me the details. I don't want to know." Her lack of emotion was more telling than a bucket full of tears. This woman had lived a hard life, likely a life peppered with pain, loss and deprivation. Who could tell what else?

She took the box and stowed it carefully under the bar. Conor said, "I should tell you I went through it. Not much there. It's—"

"I'll go through it later." She drew a beer and poured a generous shot of whiskey. "The drinks are on me, Mister."

"Dolan, Ma'am. I was his . . . friend." The woman expressed no interest in the details.

Bell leaned forward, head down with her palms on the bar, like she was gathering thoughts or deciding whether to speak. Then she looked at Conor and said quietly, "Jan didn't know his own birthday. I couldn't believe that, Mister Dolan, even here in Chicago. I gave him a birthday and we celebrated it every year."

"I know, Ma'am. The cards are in the box."

"Thank you for that, Mister Dolan. Jan didn't know he was going to inherit this business, the building, everything. Only thing I asked in my will is that he keep my no-account son employed and fed. He'd have done it too. There's a good side to abject poverty, loneliness, and rejection, Mister Dolan. Sometimes it filters out the pettiness, idle temptations, and vices, if you will, of men who have too much and give too little. This can be a mean city. I won't forget Jan, ever."

On the ride back to Bridgeport, Conor wished he'd gotten to know Mumbles better. It had been an eventful Tuesday. Jan's burglary case was closed but there might be a murderer out there thinking he got away scot-free. The truth might have died with Jan Kazmirski. Time would tell, but Conor Dolan was a long from admitting it to himself—or to Jan's memory.

Chapter 5

Sunday, April 1, 1917

The month began in grand fashion with a beautiful, clear morning, arranged largely by an April breeze. After mass, Maureen and Conor decided to take young Liam on a day excursion to Riverview Park, Chicago's most popular carnival attraction. Patrick had apparently outgrown such family outings, preferring the company of his neighborhood mates. The couple agreed to take Liam's friend, David, from down the block as company for the boy.

On the Halsted streetcar ride up to Belmont Avenue, Liam and David sat together pretending not to know the "elderly" parents, giving Conor and Maureen a chance to talk.

Conor watched the two lads laughing and joking from their seat near the front of the car. To a twelve-year-old boy of means, Chicago was a wonderous playground of thrills and excitement in 1917. But a dark reckoning was looming overhead for everyone. "I'm worried, Maureen."

She turned her head to face him and squinted. "About what? War?"

"More than that. Last Thursday a group of men flashing badges barged into a lawyer's office on my floor. His name is Gunther Meuller. They searched his suite without a warrant, removed a trove of documents and carted him off to Lord knows where for 'questioning.'"

"Well, we certainly know about that. What kind of badges?"

"That's the worst part. His secretary said they called themselves the American Protective League. The badges identified the organization as 'Auxiliary to the Department of Justice.' There is no such organization at Justice."

"Well, apparently there is now. 'Tis hardly a surprise to me after what happened at the peace rally only a fortnight ago."

"There's a big difference between a bunch of screaming vigilantes and warrantless searches and seizures under color of law. I think this finally tells us who kidnapped you and carted you off from the rally that day."

At Belmont Avenue, the family transferred to a westbound car for the short ride to the park. They all had to stand as the car was packed with the expected Riverview crowd, especially on such a glorious day.

Secured by the leather hand grip overhead but squeezed like a sardine in a tin, Conor said, "I hope nobody has smallpox. We have enough problems at the moment."

Maureen scowled. "Hush your mouth, Conor Dolan. Yeer embarrassing us both."

He shrugged. "Sorry."

"Listen, Conor. Sure I'm not ungrateful for what I have, but this country is not exactly the Kingdom of Heaven. Do I need to remind ye of that?"

"Of course not, but I'm a lawyer and keenly aware of how a democratic society functions. We all have a duty to see it function by the rules."

The scowl returned but more as a snarl. "And I am what exactly? An eejit?" *When in doubt, keep your mouth shut.* "Justice is something to fight for, Conor, and it doesn't exist here. You, of all people, know that. If it did there would be no homeless children and the jails would not be filled with poor, immigrant colleens from Ireland whose only crime was to seek a better life. Homeless men would not be sleeping in the basements of police stations. Sure ye have a short memory, Conor. Do ye not remember that poor Nellie Finley whose case you handled years back?"

He did remember Nellie Finley and would never forget her, the girl who jumped off a bridge with her newborn to spare the child the suffering that lay ahead. She'd nearly been convicted of murdering the child until Conor found the baby alive.

In the intervening years, Nellie's mental illness had been brought under control to the point that she had regained custody of the child some eight years ago. Things were slightly better for the immigrant women now but there were still too many Nellie Finleys in the streets and the brothels. Jane Addams' Hull House was making a bigger impact than ever. The Chicago Welfare Council, established in 1914 to coordinate and focus efforts of the many private aid agencies, had helped to some extent with training, housing and medical care, but with the exception of Cook County Hospital, the government had yet to step up to its social responsibility to care for the poor.

Fortunately, the streetcar stopped in front of the great arched entranceway into Riverview Park, saving him from Maureen's trap, and the group headed into the crowd toward the ticket windows. The buoyant crowd was not unexpected. The nation was coming to a boil and folks were craving a distraction. Following a fifteen-minute wait in the ticket line, Conor led his little delegation into the park. Beyond the archway, they entered a different world, a world of bells and barkers and bangles; a world encased in a dome of organ music, of bearded ladies and a horse the size of a cat. The earthy aroma of the carnival assaulted their senses, a mixture of burnt sugar from the cotton candy, popcorn oil, grilled onions and sauerkraut. For a day at least, the problems of the world and of Normal Avenue would disappear into a chorus of laughter and fun.

The two boys had already found their way to a nearby cart vendor. "Pa, can we get a frankfurter?" Liam pleaded.

The old man behind the cart snapped, pointing to the sign over his cart. "What are you, kid? A Kaiser lover? These here is hot dogs, not frankfurters."

Conor literally bit his tongue. "Two *hot dogs*, please." Then he turned to Maureen. "Sorry, do you want one?"

She shrugged. "I may as well. We'll see if a *hot dog* tastes better."

The rollercoaster was undeniably the most popular ride or attraction at the park, and Liam and David headed straight for the entrance line down on the west end of the park near the river. The boys were already advancing in the long line when Conor and Maureen arrived at the ticket window. "You want to have a go?" Conor asked his wife. She laughed. It was her first of the day and it warmed him.

Looking almost straight up at the crest of the wooden structure, she said, "Once was enough for me, Conor, and ye know it."

They found a nearby bench from which to watch the boys slowly climb each peak, then drop nearly vertically at breakneck speed, all the while screaming like banshees. She said quietly, "I never saw polio as a blessing until all this talk of war, Conor."

"I know what you mean."

"What will happen to Patrick if they declare war?"

"We'll have our hands full keeping him from enlisting. As of now they're not going to draft seventeen or eighteen-year-olds. That may change. I just don't know."

By late afternoon, the boys seemed finally to be breathing heavily and ready for the ride home. On the way back to the entrance they would have to pass the park's second most popular attraction, the one Conor always took pains to avoid. As they neared the interactive booth, he avoided staring and tried to distract the boys from the sight. "So, boys, would you like to stop for ice cream on the way home? Ma doesn't like you to have it before dinner, but I'll use my influence, if I still have any."

It was too late. Both boys were transfixed by the action and the chants of the crowd, all centered around a booth under a large banner reading, *Dunk the Nigger*. At the far end of the booth, a young Negro boy sat perched on a plank over a large tank of water.

"Pa," Liam began, "We've never tried that. Can we do it now? Just once?"

As they passed, the crowd's chants grew louder and Conor walked faster, all to no avail. Liam and David stopped momentarily. "Dunk that nigger. . .Drop that nigger to the bottom. . . Drown that nigger!" The increasingly vile chants seemed to ignite the frenzied crowd into a satanic horde as they plunked nickels onto the counter. United in common malevolence, this was an eclectic mob of poor people, Bridgeport folks, Astor Street hobnobs and all manner of good citizens in between. *They could end homelessness with a coalition like this, but nothing unites people like hate.*

When one of the thrown balls hit its mark squarely, the plank collapsed, sending the youngster into freefall some ten feet and into the tank with a splash. The crowd erupted into laughter and jeers.

"Move, boys," Conor commanded. "We won't be stopping here."

As the young boy began to climb up the ladder, Maureen gasped. "Conor, that's your friend, Toad, the

Negro boy who does errands for us. The Lord have mercy on us."

It was Toad, alright. No denying it. He knew the boy had a part time job at the park. "There's nothing we can do, Maureen. He's doing this by choice. They pay him. We have to stay out of it. The boy is a survivor and knows what he's doing."

"Feck sake, Conor. Ye can stay out of it. I'll match whatever these monsters pay him to degrade himself."

She was already quick marching toward the booth. Conor grabbed her by the arm. "Maureen, it's complicated. He doesn't see it as degrading, please."

Her face turned red as a June apple. "Does he not!"

And it was on. Without releasing his grip, he turned to the boys. "Go to the entrance and wait outside the gate, please, boys. We'll be along."

With the lads out of earshot, he said, "Maureen, get hold of yourself. When his shift is over, he goes home to the alley. His life isn't that bad."

Shaking free of his grip, Maureen turned to face him, chin high, nostrils flaring. "Listen to me, *Mister Dolan*. I shouldn't need to remind ye I understand hatred and ethnic abuse in this fine city, and I'll not turn my back on it."

With that, she marched directly to the booth's side entrance to the dismay of the barker on duty. Standing directly beside the tank, she hollered to the boy just as he reached the top of the ladder while pointing to the ground. "Get down here this minute, young man!"

The wild-eyed crowd of around forty began jeering and swearing. "Bitch, slag. . ." As the boy descended the ladder, they began throwing baseballs at Maureen, then stones from the ground.

As Conor rushed in, a sharp stone caught the side of his head, staggering him. In the mayhem, he reached for Maureen who was holding Toad firmly by the collar. By some miracle the trio made it away from the crowd to the park exit.

With the five safely aboard a homebound streetcar, Toad spoke for the first time. "Now I ain't got no side job, Miss Dolan. That fella was payin' me two bucks a week fer only seven or eight hours."

Maureen replied in a quiet voice. "Ye have a new side job now, Toad, and Gimpy as well. I don't even want to know what *he* does for these beasts. Ye work for us. Same hours but the pay is two and a quarter."

The boy's eyes narrowed and became distant for a minute. Then he said, "Doing what?"

"Whatever we ask ye to do. Don't get all rebellious with me. Whatever it is will be legal and won't subject ye to vile indignities,"

"To what?"

"Never ye mind."

The corners of his mouth turned up halfway to his ear lobes and the boy shrugged. "Well, you n' Mista Dolan gotchoo a regular errand boy, Miss Dolan."

Conor chimed in for the first time. "I think I have the perfect work for you guys."

The two other lads had the good sense not to say a word as Maureen tended to the cut on Conor's head. He sensed a silent agreement to never speak of the matter again.

AS THEY MADE THE STREETCAR TRANSFER at the bustling corner of Western Avenue and Thirty-First Street, Conor noticed a group of newsboys hawking extra editions. It was not a regular spot for the newsboys. The papers were flying out of their hands. As they approached the intersection, he could hear the familiar cry. "Extry, Extry. . ."

Managing to fight his way to the front of the crowd, he heard what he had prayed never to hear. It was a certainty now. "Extry, Extry. . .Wilson to ask Congress for Declaration of War on Germany!"

"Damn," said Toad. "I thought it was finna be a slow news day. I'll see y'all later, Mista Dolan. I gotta find

Gimpy. Still money t' be made tonight." And the boy was off.

He didn't get far. Stopping dead in his tracks, he turned to face Maureen, tipped his trademark newsboy cap and said, "Thank you, Miss Dolan, for the new job. We'll stop over soon as I can, but this war news is the best thing could happen for our business so it might be next week."

Conor watched as Maureen willed the corners of her mouth upward in the shape of a smile, a gesture of kinship for this wayward soul. To someone who truly knew the woman, it was a remarkable and courageous act. She waved in Toad's direction and said in a deadpan voice, "So happy for ye, Toad."

THAT NIGHT, IN THE BUNGALOW ON Normal, they made love like wild animals late into the night and for the first time in weeks. For Conor, it was like discovering the real beauty of his wife for the first time. Her breasts were more ample now and less disciplined but seemed to cover his chest like a warm blanket in winter, giving his tongue more secret places to explore. He sensed that Maureen knew their lives were changing and the lovers were planting an anchor to hold them steady and together in the coming months.

Chapter 6

April 10, 1917

Despite the virtual collapse of the Russians in the East, the Canadian Corps had launched a successful offensive at the town of Vimy Ridge in Northern France. While the battle still raged, the Canadian breakthrough was swift and relentless. On April 6, Congress declared war on Germany.

The global order had now been shaken to its core and Chicago was a city at war. Recruitment posters decorated virtually every building and lamp post. The war in Europe was a world war and the United States was in it to win it. Young men flocked to the recruiting offices, not all eligible men but many. Factories tooled up for war production, from large manufacturers to textile mills to little family businesses that produced buttons. Patriotic organizations sprang up nationwide overnight, none bigger or more influential than the familiar American Protective League, a literal army of volunteer vigilantes operating in the open across the nation and backed by the Department of Justice. APL agents already saturated the American workplace, universities, local government offices, even the Boy Scouts. Neighbors reported neighbors for negative comments about the war. The League routinely searched homes and businesses of suspected "alien enemies" without warrants.

The APL was no longer a shadow organization. Now they all carried—even displayed—law enforcement-type badges as described by the German-American lawyer in Conor's building. The newspapers had themselves jumped on the war wagon, praising the APL and running non-stop editorials in support of the war. "Slacker" was the instant term for any man of military age not in uniform. Every house was expected to fly the flag from its front porch. Any home not in compliance would receive a visit from the APL.

Speaking against the war had become a dangerous endeavor that could get someone arrested and questioned. APL factory workers regularly reported their co-workers for "un-American" statements. Germans and German-Americans became by definition "suspected enemy aliens." Even the Irish and Irish Americans had to take great care in their speech and activities. The term "hyphenated-American" assumed an even more vile meaning than before. Any open expression of support for Irish republicans could be considered treasonous as rebellion in Ireland would directly diminish the British war effort.

Within this war-driven environment, the Dolans tried to keep their lives as normal as possible. Conor's criminal law business continued to thrive, although the virtual disappearance of the Clan-na-Gael left his political influence considerably deflated. He could no longer broker jobs or influence the Irish voting block as before. But on the positive side, his establishment as one of the city's top criminal defense lawyers had relieved him of the sleazy concessions he'd been forced to make in the early years, like paying the ward heeler ten percent on cash bond fee refunds. He liked his life; he loved his family, but a voice inside kept telling him, *Brace yourself, Boy. There's a storm brewing.*

On the way to the office, Conor held off buying a newspaper at the Jackson Street "L" station, expecting to see Gimpy at his regular spot outside the Monadnock Building. The lad did not disappoint. "Mornin', Mista Dolan," said the boy. "Examiner and the Herald?"

He handed Gimpy twenty cents for the two dailies. "Morning, Gimpy, anything to report?"

Following the Riverview incident, Conor had made Gimpy and Toad his part-time private investigators. The more he thought about it, the more he regretted not doing it two years ago. The cops . . . well, Lefty anyway, had been using the newsboy network for all kinds of investigations including missing persons, fugitive hunting, even surveillance of potential criminal locales.

It was a great investment for Conor. For two and a quarter a week he got at least ten hours from Gimpy and Toad. On occasion, they would subcontract work to other boys on the cheap. It was a win-win for everyone involved. Nobody knew the city better than the newsboys, the good, the bad and the ugly.

"I think I got something for you," the boy replied.

"Good. I have to be at Hubbard Street at nine but I'm free after the morning calls. Can you stop in the office around noon? I'll have sandwiches for us."

"MISTER TITUS FREEMAN IS HERE TO SEE you, Mister Dolan," announced Mrs. Schmidt, standing just inside the office door.

"I don't know anyone by that name, Mrs. Schmidt. Besides, I already have a noon appointment. Ask if he can come back."

"Oh, I think you'll want to see him, Mister Dolan."

"Alright then. Show him in, but tell him I can only give him a few minutes . . . Oh, Missus Schmidt, does he look troublesome?"

"Very, sir."

A few moments later, Conor was looking across the desk at a new incarnation of his old friend, Gimpy. The boy still wore the standard overalls over a wrinkled, cotton shirt, but the newsboy attire ended there. A white necktie hung prominently from the stained gray shirt and a spotless brown Homburg topped the ensemble. "Well, this is a surprise, Gimpy. Won't you have a seat?" he added, pointing to the sofa.

Gimpy removed the hat like the proper gentleman he had become. "Thank you, but when I'm on my private investigator job, better you use my real name. It's Titus Freeman."

"Yes. I heard something about that. So, tell me, G . . . Titus, what have you on this Graves?"

Conor couldn't get Mumbles off his mind and had assigned Gimpy—Titus to have some of his boys stake out Big Jimmy Ruffulo's common locations keeping eyes out for a man fitting Graves's description. It was a longshot, but Conor figured the information about Mumbles's debt to Ruffulo had to come from within the organization, maybe even from Ruffulo himself.

It would be impossible to surveil all Ruffulo's casinos, brothels and saloons, so Conor and Gimpy concocted a plan to cover the most logical spots like the South Works Casino where Mumbles first encountered Graves. The Forest Park casino was the biggest and a must on their stakeout schedule, as was Ruffulo's home out in River Forest, a risky but essential target. The final locations were two of Ruffulo's favorite restaurants, Luigi's on Eighteenth Street and Henrici's in the Loop on Randolph. The surveillance had been ongoing for about two weeks.

Titus said, "We don't got Graves yet, but you remember that lady me n' the guys took home after the peace rally?"

"Of course."

"Well, sir, yesterday she got out of a fancy Ford motorcar with Big Jimmy Ruffulo himself and went into Henrici's Restaurant on Randolf, same place she took us. All the boys know Big Jimmy. Sometimes he gives a boy half a dollar for a paper."

"Was anyone with them?"

"Just the man's driver and chief enforcer. Name is Mickey Lucchesi. He's a mean one."

Was it possible? Conor didn't see that pitch coming. The woman he rescued didn't fit the profile of a gangster's crumpet, but the conclusion was obvious. Maybe Ruffulo liked the shop girl type. "Any chance you could be mistaken, Titus?"

"I'm telling you, Mista Dolan, it was that Miss Bensini. Ain't no doubt about it."

Mrs. Schmidt chose that moment to enter the inner office with a tray of sandwiches and two bottles of Meister Brau beer. "Are you gentlemen ready for lunch?"

Titus gave his best facial impression of a lawyer accustomed to being served lunch by an employee. It would need work. The face looked more like a fox stalking eggs in a bird's nest. "I guess I could be tempted. What's in the sandwiches?"

"Corned beef, Mister Freeman," the secretary replied.

"Just put the lunch down, Mrs. Schmidt," Conor said hurriedly. Then he turned back to his young investigator. "You're telling me this woman is Ruffulo's girlfriend? Did you see them holding hands, kissing, anything like that?"

"Nothing like that. They had a driver but Ruffulo himself helped her out of the car. It ain't no mistake. I remember that lady real good. She was a mighty pretty lady and Mumbles was stuttering so bad he could hardly get a word out. He really liked her. I remember how good she smelled too. It was her. I seen her myself from not twenty feet away."

Being Ruffulo's girlfriend didn't make Viviana a bad person. Conor hardly knew the woman, but her best qualities were immediately obvious. She was sincerely grateful and felt obliged for the kindness Conor had shown her at the rally. Beyond his character observations, Conor had found her socially adept and not a gaudy or fancy dresser. The lawyer himself found the woman attractive. Why would Big Jimmy not? Maybe she needed the mobster's money, but wore no furs, no jewelry, nothing that would associate her with that lifestyle.

Titus Freeman was gobbling down the last of his corned beef and had started on the second bottle of beer. "Hope you don't mind, Mista Dolan. Figured you'd have more beer. You looked like you was doing some thinking anyhow."

"Indeed, Titus, indeed. Do you remember where you took the young lady that day? Her flat I mean?"

Sure. I remember exactly. I mean I know the building but not the apartment number. It was the Sherman House Hotel on Randolph Street, even has a head man and bellboys outside in spiffy red suits. We know them all."

By that the lad meant that the newsboys had some side deals going with bellboys in the posh hotels. "But we don't know if she lives there. They do have residential flats so keep digging. If she lives there, I want the room number. Add a few more boys if you have to. Oh, you say she took you boys to Henrici's that day. Did she take Toad too?"

"Sure did, and nobody said nothing, I mean about Toad being a Negro. It was a little strange. You know, all the rich people. She nearly had to force us to go inside, but the food was great, and nobody bothered us. She seemed to like Mumbles the best. Only thing is she wouldn't let us have a beer."

Titus made no move for the door then stopped, looking at the other sandwich.

"Take it if you want. . .and good work, Titus Freeman," Conor said. "Good work."

At least Titus was standing. "One more thing, Mista Dolan. Can me n' Toad have some business cards? You know, 'Titus Freeman, Chief Investigator.' Toad would be just 'Investigator'."

"Sure. Talk to Mrs. Schmidt on the way out. And Toad? Does he have a name?"

"Ah . . . actually his name was Titus Freeman, but he never liked it. Thought it sounded like a slave name, so he let me have it."

"Of course. Why didn't I think of that? Have Mrs. Schmidt wrap up the sandwich. And remember, she's your boss too if I'm not around. Oh . . . and please don't wear the Titus Freeman outfit while you're on duty as a sleuth. Your *modus operandi* is to blend in and go unnoticed."

"What?"

"When you're poking around as an investigator, try not to look like one."

"Got it, Boss."

Apparently, Conor had a new name as well.

Chapter 7

With no court case on the afternoon schedule, Conor hired a taxi for a trip down to the South Works, specifically to the warehouse where Mumbles was shot. He brought the case file that included the detective's sketch of the crime scene. He figured walking the crime scene and speaking with the workers might turn up a new clue or reinforce an existing one.

The spacious industrial section was an area of unrestricted access, except for high, gated and fenced enclosures around each individual mill or smelting operation. As a first-time visitor to the South Works, Conor saw at first only an eyesore; a massive, apocalyptic conglomeration of spartan brick buildings with rows of smokestacks, stained and streaked with soot; bare steel towers; and bridges, fences, and cobblestones in general disrepair.

Whistles and bells and horns bellowed out a steel symphony from all directions. Because of the time of day, the driver explained, the areas outside the mills and factories hosted little traffic, motor or pedestrian. But two hours from now the shifts would change, and all at once a great upheaval of overall-clad humanity would blanket the area, lunch pails in tow.

Outside the ring of industry, they entered an area of warehouses along the Calumet River. From there, the cargo was floated upriver and loaded aboard huge vessels for the voyage to Europe or beyond.

The Ford Taxi wound around the property until finally reaching its destination, Warehouse 47. Conor requested the driver wait while he began his investigation. The place lacked security of any kind. Looking through the wide-open massive side-by-side doors, he could see a crew of workers engaged in various tasks. The first things Conor noticed were large windows along the roofline, that Mumbles likely used to gain entry the night of the burglary.

Using the hand-drawn crime scene sketch, he walked toward the river through an area of tangled weeds and low brush until coming to the place where police had recovered the 9mm casing. There appeared to be a passable, if difficult escape route along the riverbank in two directions. The east route, toward Lake Michigan, dead-ended less than a quarter mile ahead. Graves must have escaped to the west as it was the only way to avoid entrapment. Was it possible that Graves fired the shot that struck Mumbles?

"Excuse me, sir. Can I be after helping you?"

Conor turned to find a brawny, middle-aged Irishman, hands on hips. "Oh, I'm just looking around." Extending a hand, he added, "Conor Dolan. I'm a lawyer looking into that shooting that happened here a few weeks ago." The man looked familiar, but he couldn't place the face.

The worker's eyes widened, and he chuckled. "Do ye not recognize me then?"

Conor shrugged. "Sorry. You do look familiar."

"I should, indeed," the big man replied. "Tommy Rafferty. And didn't I pour enough money into the cotters at yeer dear wife's Friends of Irish Freedom picnics and dances and such? Sure ye'd want to be alone in a field these days t' mention Irish freedom or, God forbid, the Clan-na-Gael."

"That's the truth of it," Conor replied.

"So, what is it ye're doing here, Conor Dolan?"

"Are you the manager here, Tommy?"

"I am that."

"Do you have an office or someplace we could talk?"

Tommy had a proper office all to himself, but for a secretary who seemed never to look up from her typing or filing. The man produced a bottle and two glasses from his desk and poured. "Joanne, will ye go out and compile those inventory lists for me?"

With the woman gone, Tommy said, "And what can I do for ye, Conor?"

"Well, for starters, who owns this warehouse?"

"I wouldn't know that. I work for the exporter, Riverside Enterprises. They lease the warehouse. Feck sake, maybe they own it. I don't know." Tommy slid forward in his chair, placing his glass on the desk. "Now Conor, I won't lose my job for this or anything. Will I? We have those APL feckers right in this warehouse."

"I give you my word, Tommy. Nobody will know we spoke."

"Well, they act like they own the place sometimes."

"Do you have any idea what the two burglars were after that night, Tommy?"

"No."

"Is everything here on the up and up?"

"Far as I know, it is. What is it ye're getting at?"

"Nothing, Tommy. Just trying to understand what happened. What kinds of things are stored here?"

One of the warehouse workers chose that moment to enter the office. The door was closed, but he did not knock. Ignoring Conor and the manager, the man began going through a file cabinet against the wall. Tommy called out, "What do ye need, Lou?"

The man turned to them and smiled. "Oh, I'm looking for the bill of lading for that new shipment we took in this morning. Looks like there may be a discrepancy."

"I'll be finished here in a few minutes. Go back to work, and I'll find ye."

When the man had gone, Tommy said, "That's one of the feckers, right there. Anyway, I was saying it's mostly shipments bound for France. War related stuff. It's all packed and crated except for large machinery and things. I keep the records carefully, bills of lading, everything that comes in, where it's going and when it leaves. Everything we get goes overseas."

"Did you discover anything missing or damaged after the burglary?"

"We did, actually. It was very minor and maybe an accident. It's probably not worth mentioning."

"Please. Go ahead. Anything at all."

"Well, there was a shipment of barrels heading for France. In the inventory, we found a small hole punched in the top of one of the barrels. We called the brokerage and they took the barrel away. We have protocols for leaks and spills and such."

"What does *punched* mean? Could rough handling have damaged it? Maybe it fell into something."

Tommy shook his head. Then he reached into the desk and produced a pen and a sheet of paper. He drew a circle about three inches in diameter and pushed the paper across the desk to Conor "Like this. It was perfectly round, maybe a three-inch diameter, like it was done with a drill or a press. Take that paper with ye, please, Conor."

"Did you report it to the cops?"

"Above my pay grade, but I doubt anyone reported it. Most likely it arrived that way."

"What was in the barrel?"

"I'm not certain. There were fifty barrels in all, as I recall. They were marked 'Poison.'"

ON THE TAXI RIDE BACK TO THE OFFICE, Conor went over his notes, comparing them with the detective's narrative and considering the possibilities. Looking at the narrative, he noticed that the condition of the spent 9mm casing was not described in any way. Surely, the condition of the casing would be relevant to the analysis. *Was it rusted? Badly? Slightly? Was it still sharp and polished? Why was the information not included?* He needed to see the casing. Finally, *what would the autopsy show regarding Mumbles's death? Was it infection? Or something more sinister?*

With the information he had now, Conor felt confident he could get the cops to open a proper investigation and decided to pay a visit to the reporting detective, Giovanni Gianelli, at the Harrison Street Station, a place in which Conor was very well known.

The desk sergeant sent Conor directly upstairs where the detective squad worked on solving serious crimes. He found Gianelli was in and was allowed to enter the familiar room upstairs where the detective squad worked on solving serious crimes. Even on the second floor, Conor could detect the pungent odor of unwashed humanity in the large, smoke-filled space, no doubt emanating from the basement, two floors below. The basement hosted the station's jail cells, a series of eight or ten units along the north and south walls. Each night, especially in winter, the center walkway between the rows of cells became a flop house for homeless men, a longstanding practice repeated daily in all manner of city and county government facilities, even in City Hall, where extra sanitary attention was applied every morning to battle the inevitable stench.

Despite his name, Gianelli was a Chicago boy, most likely from Little Italy on the near Southwest Side. The man was easily into his mid-fifties, a fact that seemed to temper the instinctive defense mechanisms so common to Chicago cops. The two men were well acquainted; not friends, more like mutually respectful adversaries. Besides, Gianelli was a close friend of Conor's old mate, the retired Detective Eammon Flynn, with whom he had butted heads during the Nellie Finley affair and during the last chapter in the life of Conor's late brother, Kevin.

It seemed detectives never conversed with lawyers without their feet on top of the desk. The habit had likely been taught and handed down as a means of intimidation. *You can stare at the soles of my feet, pal. That's all you'll get from me.*

But Gianelli was too old and savvy for such nonsense. At this point it was just a bad habit. Still, it was hard not to notice the tangle of black hair swarming the cop's shins between the top of his socks and the bottom of his pants leg. It was bushier and thicker than the matching crop on top of his head--and equally unkempt. The small talk didn't last long and no wonder; the stack of case files on the man's desk was nearly tall enough to block his torso from Conor's view.

"The warehouse thing, huh? Yeah, I remember. What about it.?"

"Well, I represent . . . did represent the kid who died, Jan Kazmirski," Conor said to the filth-stained soles of the cop's scuffed shoes. "I have some question about the discovery and was hoping you wouldn't mind . . ."

Gianelli interrupted. "Going over some things? No, I don't mind. I have a few minutes. But if the kid's dead, why do you even care? I mean, why waste your time?"

Conor shrugged. "That's kind of what I wanted to kick around with you. I've learned some things about the break-in and about Jan's death."

Thankfully, Gianelli removed the feet and the undergrowth from the desktop and began sorting through the stack of files. "Ah, here it. Closed out and ready for the dead files." He opened the folder and moved the chair up close to his desk, withdrawing his eyeglasses from the front pocket. Conor noticed that the lenses were reading glasses, thicker than his own, maybe a glimpse of the near future. "Shoot, *Counsel.* I'm ready."

Conor gave a short recitation of the questions and issues raised by his recent visit to the scene, including the single 9mm casing, the chemical barrel, Graves, and the casino. Then he said, "I'm hoping that's enough for you to open an inquiry."

Gianelli made a point of slowly laying his pen down onto the note pad. "An inquiry into what? I'm sorry about that kid, Mister Dolan. I really am, but . . ."

"Nothing makes sense. According to Jan Kazmirski, they had a car and parked it a mile away. They couldn't have stolen much there. Why were they there and who was the second suspect? I don't have to tell you there are German agents all over the city. You can't walk half a block in the loop without seeing some poster warning people to look out for German spies. You must know about the recent sabotage incidents in New York and Seattle. I was in South Works today and must have seen a hundred of those posters. Isn't it enough to at least find out what was in there that was so important to this Mister Graves?"

Gianelli removed a single sheet of paper from the file, handing it to Conor. "Mr. Dolan, Jan Kazmirski never told us anything about meeting a Mister Graves at Ruffulo's casino. He told us nothing because you told us not to speak with him. You're giving me worthless hearsay, not evidence. I would love to hook Big Jimmy Ruffulo up for murder. Give me something I can use. The city won't finance espionage cases, Mister Dolan. Those are for the Department of Justice."

"Alright. You recovered a 9mm casing from the riverbank. You have to know that suggests a German pistol."

"I'm not stupid."

"You must have seen the casing up close. What was its condition? Was it rusted?"

"I don't remember."

That wasn't good enough. "Well, can you get it out of evidence and look? You don't need an open case to do that."

The cop's shoulders drooped. His eyes trained on the floor like he was searching for cracks. "Look, Conor, I can't help you any further. It wouldn't matter to my investigation if the casing was rusted or not. I'm not asking you to stop investigating this. Follow up and see where it goes. If you get something solid, come see me." Gianelli stood and offered his hand. "Good luck. You can see yourself out."

Chapter 8

Wednesday, April 18, 1917

Chicago's Eddie Cicotte had thrown a no-hitter on Sunday in St. Louis as the White Sox crushed the Browns 11-0. Things were finally looking up for the Sox who had started the season 2-0 with their new outfielder/slugger, "Shoeless" Joe Jackson. The war news never stopped, and the action wasn't confined to France. According to the Evening Herald, Vladimir Lenin had returned to Russia earlier in the week from exile in Switzerland. It was reported that the Germans had aided Lenin's return with the expectation that he would restore order and sue for peace. But the week's most interesting war-related event was on the home front where, in Eddystone, Pennsylvania, a munitions factory exploded in a massive disaster that claimed one hundred thirty-three lives. Sabotage was suspected. Conor had already resolved not to raise the tiresome subject of war when he arrived home from the office.

"WHAT DO YOU MEAN, 'HE'S ENLISTING IN the army?'"

"He made the announcement this afternoon after school, even brought a permission statement from the recruiter for us to sign since he's not quite eighteen. Says he's leaving when school is out next month. He can't enlist unless we sign it, right?"

"Technically, yes, but . . . where is he?"

"I threw a fit, and he walked out. Said he would be back for dinner." Turning her back, she added. "Our lives are going to hell."

Conor hung his hat on the rack, poured two Jamesons, and followed her into the kitchen. "Hopefully he'll come home for dinner. What else did he say?"

She slammed a slicing knife down on the empty cutting board like it was a sledgehammer. "Jesus, Conor, it wasn't exactly a fireside chat. I said no, he said yes. I yelled like a banshee, and he told me he would enlist one way or the other. If we didn't sign, he'd enlist in another state and lie about his age. He can't do that, can he?"

He tried to calm her down. "Let's try not to let it get that far, shall we?"

By now her face had gone beet red. "I didn't ask ye to placate me. Did I? I asked if he can get away with it? I don't want our son in anyone's army. But especially not an army fighting on the side of the bloody Crown."

"I'm certain he can . . . but there may be another way."

A stranger might have thought Maureen was threatening to disembowel him with a large kitchen knife. He knew she was merely emoting demonstratively. "Another way, is it? Ye mean like the top half in the army and the bottom half not?"

He knew what drove her loathing of war in general and of all things English specifically. Maureen had endured life in its worst form. She was forced to leave Ireland alone years ago with her unborn child rather than face the inevitable shame of unwed motherhood following a brutal rape by three Crown constables. It was a cross she bore silently every day until it became more a blessing than a horrible memory, a blessing named Patrick. She'd spoken of the assault to Conor only once in the fourteen years since they'd met, and Conor had never again broached the subject.

When she stopped and turned, he saw the eyes clearly, framed by the sun through the window. They could play Chopin, those eyes, or part the Red Sea if they chose. The only thing they could not do was lie. "Conor," she said, "I know ye're trying to help and I'm grateful."

How much cruelty and abuse is *enough* to justify hate for the abuser? Conor's memories of Ireland and his first days in America were unsettling but less than traumatic, never a threat to his capacity to love or feel or reason. His family's efforts to minimize and disguise the brutality and the danger allowed Conor to thrive and grow unburdened by the limitations of fear, retribution, and guilt—of hate.

Although young Patrick knew nothing of his unholy conception, the incessant bad behavior and acting out often made Conor wonder if the boy sensed something was afoot, off kilter. Maureen had told him his real father died of fever on the trip over. For a good while after their marriage, the little boy would ask questions about his father and Maureen would stick to a simple, carefully crafted script. "He was a wonderful man, second son of a farmer always destined to seek his life across the water." A pre-marital pregnancy with the love of his life expedited his emigration and landed them both on an ocean-going steamer, accompanied by one cloth bag and an unborn child.

The story seemed to be the right mix of confession and pride. Lying was the wrong word for it, but he couldn't think of a noun for a falsehood reflective of the good intentions and compassion that crafted it. She maintained the lie to spare Patrick the great burden of the truth.

Was it so different from what his own mother and brother had done for little Conor back in Ireland? Even the worst memories of his family's cruel eviction and the long journey to America were less than traumatic. His mother and brother, Kevin, had made certain of that by absorbing the pain and suffering to shield little Conor, to preserve and nurture the most important attributes of his humanity and spare him the curse of growing up in the shadow of hate and anger. Even in the most horrific moments of uncertainty and pain; the torching of their family cottage, the bitter cold and dark nights in the hole of a filthy ship, Kevin lied over and over. Their lies protected the boy from the invisible damage that hardens hearts and fosters enmity. An umbrella cast in unconditional love. *Where is the evil in such lies?*

He felt better when she put the knife down onto the board. Resting her palms on the counter with his back to him, she said. "I understand."

With sloped shoulders, she walked over to him and plopped down on the other chair. Any other woman would have cried. But, raising the glass, she gave a miserable impression of a smile and said, "*Sláinte.*" With that she downed the entire two fingers, slapping the empty glass onto the table.

"I'll have a talk with him tonight after dinner, Maureen. But I'll need to make a telephone call now and clear my schedule for tomorrow morning."

"WHAT WILL YE HAVE, PATRICK?" SCANLON asked.

"A beer, I guess."

As Scanlon drew the beers, Patrick turned to Conor and said, "So Ma asked you to bring me for a beer and talk me out of enlisting. Right?"

"Nope. This was my idea and I'm not here to talk you out of anything. I know you can do this if you're determined to. I'd just like you to explain to me why you have to do it now. They won't be drafting anyone under twenty-one for now."

Scanlon put the two beers on the bar, followed by a bowl of water. Conor said, "Why don't you grab us a quiet table while I take the water out to Dillon?"

He gave his son a minute or so to gather his thoughts before joining him at the table. "Okay, I'm all ears."

"All my friends are enlisting. I don't want to be the only one at DePaul University while the other guys serve. It's unpatriotic. The Huns are murdering Americans on the high seas. Hell, they want to give Arizona to the Mexicans."

"Who's enlisting and exactly when are they going?"

"I know what you're doing; you're being a lawyer. That drives me crazy. You know none of my friends have signed up yet, but they will. Even if they don't, I don't want to have to tell my own grandson one day that I was a slacker. I let other boys do the fighting."

"Alright, but why the army? Why not the navy? Have you ever thought of being an officer? My point is that if you're determined to serve, you have many options."

With the ice broken, the conversation began to flow more easily. They talked about the war. Conor was hardly surprised that Patrick kept so well informed. Over a second beer they began to recount old family memories and funny stories. Patrick had already answered his question and a solution would depend heavily upon the strength of the bond between them. As they left Scanlon's for the walk home with Dillon, Conor said simply, "We'll talk again tomorrow or the next night."

THURSDAY MORNING

Congress was back in session after the Easter recess, but Conor's old acquaintance, Congressman O'Sullivan, former First Ward Alderman, was known to sneak home on the train nearly every Thursday for the weekend from Washington, D.C. Conor's appointment at his local office was for 9:30 a.m. He arrived five minutes early.

O'Sullivan did not keep him waiting. The secretary escorted him directly into the Congressman's sanctuary where he found the old politician waiting just inside the door, hand extended. He must have been seventy-five, but still the dapper, charismatic, clear-eyed alderman Conor remembered. "Wonderful to see you again, Conor. Come. Sit and we'll talk, catch up on old times." That was typical O'Sullivan. Over fifteen years, their relationship had been driven by mutual contempt, extortion, bribery and other disreputable factors. Yet the man could sit there and pretend the two were long lost brothers.

The Irish-born O'Sullivan, until recently, had paid regular dues to the Clan-na-Gael, although he didn't know Padraic Pearce from Parnell. In years past, the old Alderman O'Sullivan would have converted to Judaism if it meant votes and the Clan-na-Gael was nothing if not a source of votes. As a U.S. Representative, he'd been *incognito* in D.C. these last ten years, no doubt enjoying the perks in anticipation of his double pension.

"Tell me, how is ah. . .Maureen, is it?" The man not only knew Maureen's name but detested her. Conor had come here to maneuver and negotiate with one of Chicago's longest-standing political gladiators and would soon learn if the old hole card could still win a hand.

O'Sullivan had to know Conor wanted something. Self-preservation was the last political instinct to surrender to senility and the alderman exhibited no diminished capacity. The two men had never been friends, so there could be no other reason for the visit.

O'Sullivan had clearly dialed back his anxiety over the years, especially since the statute of limitations had expired on the most recent of his miscreant activities. But somewhere in there was still a master politician, the same O'Sullivan who'd been constantly cloaked in a veneer of pleasantries through every conversation of their long association, like the hyena smiling disarmingly at its prey until the moment it strikes. *Let's play it out and see.*

The small talk didn't take long, for the men had nothing in common but for their Irish ancestry and the large sledgehammer always looming above the congressman's head, the handle never far from Conor's grip. Finally, O'Sullivan asked, "So what brings ye back to us today, Conor?"

"It's my son," Conor replied, "Patrick. He's seventeen. The boy is very bright, and his mother and I have been fussing about his future."

O'Sullivan nodded but the smile remained frozen, like a photograph. "And how is it I might be of help to my favorite constituents in this regard?"

Conor had patiently withheld employing his leverage over the man in recent years, preferring to use it only when necessary and never to benefit or enrich himself. Now he wondered if he had waited too long. In fact, he thought, the last time he had called in a chip on the congressman was getting Lefty Hawk an assignment to the Newsboy Alley beat. It had proven a solid strategy and Conor was ready to call in the house today for Patrick. "The boy is graduating high school. He's very bright, like his mother."

"Like his mother, of course," O'Sullivan said sarcastically. "I remember. Go on."

"Well, the lad's a bit rough around the edges, but a good boy. We think he'd make a fine naval officer."

"Would he indeed now? Well, a first-class education is just the ticket for a lad like that—especially a free one." Then he delivered the kicker. "Sure I'm certain ye haven't considered it, but it would also be an effective means of keeping him out of a war, I mean in that unfortunate circumstance—at least out of the trenches."

Yes, Conor thought, O'Sullivan was still in there and still in the game. "I had considered that, actually," Conor admitted.

O'Sullivan leaned back in his chair. "Ye are aware, of course, Conor, that my academy appointments are extremely limited. I already have requests from a former governor and two former mayors. I would have to disappoint more than one of them. Shall I go on?"

This was all part of the dance, Chicago style, and probably a lie, just like the part about people questioning the Dolans' patriotism. But the politician had to negotiate the value of this favor before the trade, and he was aiming for the mountaintop.

O'Sullivan understood the family dynamics involved. This was personal, a life-or-death request worth more than all the jobs and contracts a corrupt politician could barter and both men knew it would level the books. The story about the alderman's involvement in the Nellie Finley murder case in 1903 would die forever. Only three specific words were required from Conor to seal the deal, delivered directly and succinctly. Loathing the very sound of his own voice, Conor said, "I understand, Congressman."

O'Sullivan leaned back in his chair looking like he'd just destroyed a young opponent in a primary. "Do you reeeeeeally?" He asked rhetorically, with just a hint of amusement in his predatory eyes.

Conor was stumped, and being a lawyer, wasn't about to answer until he could identify his ground and assess the risk. So, he just sat there quietly and let his confusion show. *They can't use a facial expression against you in court.*

"Here's a little secret for ye, Conor Dolan. People are asking questions about ye, questions ye wouldn't like. Oh, I told them all there was no reason to question yeer patriotism. Still, 'twas a great favor for me to even meet with ye today." Conor had almost forgotten the nuances of the game. *Always keep your opponent off guard, worrying.* The old man seemed to be playing his own hole card. "I'll say no more about it, but there are certain activities the government will frown upon going forward. I say that only for yeer benefit, Conor." *Sure you do.*

"I thank you for that, Congressman, and I'll act accordingly." *But you're not going on the defensive here, Conor. Nice try.*

The secretary entered, placing a tray of coffee and pastries on the desk. She didn't speak.

Pointing to the tray, O'Sullivan said, "Help yeerself, Conor. Anyways, getting back to the subject of yeer visit, despite all the global upheaval and the uncertainty about the future of our own nation, what do you think causes me the most annoyance? I mean what is the number one petition overwhelming my Congressional time and staff?"

"I'm sure I have no idea."

"It goes like this. 'My son or my nephew would make a wonderful Naval or Army officer, Congressman.' It's a real *craic* because five or six years ago only a select few people wanted to find their destiny in uniform. Now, the requests pour in faster than votes on election day. Dozens three months ago and more every month since. 'Tis a shame I don't have the power to anoint priests. Why do ye think that is the case?"

There was nothing to say, not yet. *Better to remain silent and be thought a fool than to open your mouth and remove all doubt, Pa used to say.*

"I have two appointments every term," the Congressman continued, "and over a hundred requests for appointment to the next term, but I'm going to appoint your son to the Naval Academy, Conor Dolan. Oh, and I couldn't give a shite if you broadcast everything you know about. . .well, let's leave it at that. I never meant for any of that to happen and I think you know I had no idea what that poor child went through. I'll be retired soon. My starred agenda items include doing whatever I can to make things right, to fix my mistakes before I take the last rights. There just may be a hell and I'd prefer to avoid it, if possible." *In a pig's eye you do.*

"I don't know what to say."

"Say nothing. I'll need to make some calls, but I'll leave word at your office. When we first met, I gave you a month before this city would make road stones out of you, but you proved a most resourceful young man and, despite all your annoying maneuvers over the years, you never asked anything for yourself—until today."

Chapter 9

The giddy lawyer couldn't wait to get home that night. It wasn't a done deal yet, but the hope might temper Maureen's growing anxiety over recent developments. As for Patrick, if the boy wanted a uniform and some status, who could argue with an appointment to Annapolis?

He found his wife in the kitchen and told her about his interesting visit with O'Sullivan. Her whole body seemed to deflate upon processing the news. She laid the dish cloth on the counter and sat down at the little table. "I'll say this to start. If there were ever a snake in Ireland after Saint Patrick cast them out, it was O'Sullivan. I know ye mean well, Conor, but what are we doing? Bargaining with a weasel over our son's life. Planning our future, protecting our children with political calculations, backroom deals. It's hypocritical, to be sure." Then her shoulders started to droop, eyes cast down at the table. After a pause, she added. "Still, if it keeps Patrick out of that fecking war, I'd gofer it. The question is, will he?"

"We'll talk to him. It would keep him out of the trenches and hopefully satisfy his childish need to be a soldier."

"Sure 'tis worth a try. But what happened to him along the way? We didn't raise him to be a soldier, especially on the side of the bloody English."

"He's not like us, Maureen. He only knows what we told him about Ireland. He's never seen it, felt it in his bones like we have. The boy is what we made him, American, typical among his peers, hypnotized by the spread of war fever and itching for a great adventure. We'll let him have one."

He poured. She downed it instantly, then stared into the empty glass until it rested on the table. Half a minute passed before she said, "What if he doesn't like it?"

Conor shrugged. "That's the gamble. I don't deny the boy's wild, but he has a curious mind, sharp and gifted in mathematics and history. When they put hands on him at Annapolis, they won't want to give him up. They'll challenge him and he'll get his taste of military life without fighting in the trenches. I don't know what else we can do."

"Alright then, give it a go and see how he takes it. It's certainly a great opportunity for a first-class education."

FRIDAY, APRIL 27

Back at the office in time to review Monday's files, Conor encountered a beaming Mrs. Schmidt holding a telephone message. There was little in the Dolans' lives that Mrs. Schmidt was not privy to. "Mrs. Schmidt, tell me you're holding the message I was hoping for." But her glow had already made the announcement. The words were mere details:

Annapolis appointment confirmed for fall term. Contact admissions office to arrange for family orientation in May and obtain details for transcripts, medical exam, security clearance, etc. O'Sullivan.

This would be the night for his talk with young Patrick about the Naval Academy. If the boy was willing, they would all visit Annapolis next month to get acquainted with the facility in advance of the family orientation in May.

Dinner on Normal Avenue that Friday was uncharacteristically quiet. With no time for a private chat before dinner, Conor conveyed the news to Maureen with a wink and a smile. There would be no visit to Scanlon's tonight. This was a matter for the entire family and Conor launched into it over coffee after dinner. "Well, I have some news for Patrick."

Maureen sat motionless, eyes cast down on the empty plate. "About Annapolis?" Patrick asked matter-of-factly.

"Yes. You have secured an appointment to the incoming September class, should you choose to accept it."

Patrick leaned forward in his chair, palms on the table, eyes wide. "You're doing it to keep me out of the war."

"If I really had a choice, I'd be pushing you into law school. You have a great talent for the courtroom. How does it matter why we're doing it? I'll give you the facts. You can accept the appointment or not."

Still nothing from Maureen. Patrick nodded. "Alright. Let's hear it."

"You would start eight weeks of basic training in July and begin classes in September. You'd need a medical exam, oh . . . and a vision test if you are interested the naval aviation program."

"What? Flying airplanes?"

"Not immediately, according to the admissions officer I spoke with today, but the Navy is in the process of quadrupling its size. There will be a great need for hundreds, maybe several thousand intelligent and daring young men to fly the thousands of planes now being manufactured. There's a need now to hunt German submarines along our coastline and most of the new ships will be equipped to carry a small reconnaissance plane."

Patrick sat back, looked over at Maureen and said, "I could go for that, but the war will probably be over in a year."

Maureen stood abruptly and said in a hurried voice, "Sounds marvelous. I'll get dessert and more coffee." Conor figured she was trying to keep the conversation going.

Young Liam chose that moment to intervene. "Patrick, if you don't want to go, I'll go in your place." Conor knew he was teasing but, well aware of his own limitations, Liam was encouraging his brother to accept.

"Patrick, I don't know how long the war would last, but I did confirm that the flight training program begins in freshman year."

He seemed to perk up even more. "It does? You mean I could be flying a plane next year?"

"I know nothing about the program, son. I'm certain there will be some interaction with the airplanes, but there's a lot to learn before you take to the air. I don't guarantee you anything, mind you. You'll have to apply and be accepted. That will be up to you. And there are always other, fine opportunities in the navy."

Maureen chose that moment to return. She had been listening from the kitchen through the crack in the door. "Blueberry pie, lads," she said, feigning ignorance. "How is the discussion going?"

"Can I think about it?" Patrick asked.

"Not more than a couple of days," Conor cautioned. "It's a last-minute appointment that fills an unexpected vacancy. I have to get back to them Monday."

He could almost hear Maureen praying. The thought of a son going to war would terrify any mother. But Maureen was not any mother, and Patrick was not any son. Maureen had carried him safely in her womb alone and penniless across an ocean of endless waves, fear, doubt, and uncertainty. At the cost of her own pride, she willingly became the mistress of an abusive man back in 1903, Conor's own departed brother, submitting to the indignities and the pain, only that the child might live another day.

Now, for the first time in her life, this woman was powerless in an existential crisis, a frustrated and angry passenger, watching helplessly as her broken ship slipped slowly under the waves. At last, a glimmer of hope. He could almost envision her praying through the sweet aroma of blueberry pie.

Chapter 10

Wednesday, May 2, 1917

The Russians had just celebrated the first national May Day holiday. Millions of people across Russia had turned out to pat themselves on the back without a thought of what comes next. It still wasn't clear to Conor who was governing the country. In St. Petersburg, the Winter Palace and buildings around Palace Square were plastered with banners, slogans of the revolution. In Petrograd, it was reported that German prisoners of war marched hand in hand with Russian soldiers. The Czar and his entire family were being held prisoner by whomever was governing Russia at the moment. The Russian army was still in the field but being mercilessly hammered everywhere. Soldiers were routinely shooting their officers. Entire divisions had now surrendered authority to the "soldiers' councils," groups of elected enlisted men entrusted with the authority to plan and execute strategy.

On the Western Front, the vaunted Nivelle Offensive was faltering, sparking wide-spread mutiny among French troops and causing massive French casualties as the French struggled desperately to restore order to its forces and hold the line.

But the news was not all bad. The White Sox had just split a two-game series with Detroit and were off and running with a 10-6 record. Only last week, the Cincinnati Reds had purchased the rights to Olympic hero Jim Thorpe from the Giants. Thankfully, the Reds played in the National League and could not face the White Sox during the regular season.

Conor was late to the Jackson Street "L" platform that evening, held up until nearly six by a meeting with Titus Freeman, whose new business cards read, "Titus Freeman, Chief Investigator, The Conor Dolan Law Firm." There had been no sign of Graves anywhere, but Viviana's connection to Ruffulo nagged at Conor like a sore toe.

He looked at the evening newspapers on his lap as the car began to move out from the Jackson Street stop. Nothing but war news. He would find no distraction in the papers. Instead, he opened the window and surrendered to the warm breeze and the creaking melody of modern transport lulled him into a pre-slumber state. A woman took the seat beside him on the aisle. He had smelled that perfume before. Conor paid her no mind until he heard a familiar voice. "Good evening, Mister Dolan." He turned his head to find the darkly angelic face of Viviana Bensini, the woman he had saved during what had come to be known as Chicago's last peace march. She was dressed much as before, modestly but with a sense of elegance and style. His mouth was open. He could feel the weight of his lower jaw, wordless and frozen. "I imagine you're surprised to see me."

He finally managed to say, "Do you?"

Her focused stare unsettled him, piercing his consciousness like a bullet, searching the archives of his soul through the mosaic of pale blue eyes. She said, "I could pretend this to be a coincidence, I suppose, but you wouldn't believe that. Would you?"

He was beginning to recover. "I don't know, Miss Bensini. I've been taken in before. It's kind of a habit. Still, I have a feeling this is going to be a memorable encounter. Tell me what's going on because I don't know the game."

"Your newsboys," she replied matter-of-factly. "They are monitoring my comings and goings, one boy in particular. I'd like it to stop now, but first, please explain the reason I'm being watched."

If nothing else, she was direct. He couldn't think of a single response that would not compound his predicament. His own lawyerly advice to a client in these circumstances would be to remain mute but respectful.

Viviana exhaled audibly and leaned back in the bench seat. "If you're looking for a girlfriend, this is not the way. Your actions are most unseemly, and I won't have it."

What? "Oh. . . no, no, no. I wouldn't do anything like that. I mean . . . I have a wife. I'm normal for Christ's sake."

"Ha . . . of course you have a wife. Most perverts do."

She was baiting him, and he'd nibbled. *Who in the name of God is this woman?* He decided to take the lawyer's advice. "I don't know what you're talking about."

She folded her arms like a man, eyes forward. "I'm twenty-eight, single. Yes, I find you mildly attractive. At least I might if you could convince me you're not a predator. I recall a gentleman named Holmes from some years back, a Chicago pharmacist who stalked and murdered a number of young women around The World's Fair. Please convince me you are not mentally deranged. Why are you doing this to me?" *Talk about an investigation blowing up in your face.*

This woman was literally making fun of him. She had to be. He hadn't been this awkward with a woman since Rebecca Fletcher back in 1903. The beautiful Jewish matron tutored him well in the ways of love and guided him down the pathway into a woman's mind, but the sum of her delicious efforts had not altered the nature of his personality. The great criminal lawyer felt like a twelve-year-old in Viviana's presence. "Who are you, really?" He asked, trying to change the subject.

She still had not turned back to face him. "None of your affair, Mister Dolan. And since we are dancing around each other, I'll ask you directly, do you find *me* attractive?"

The conductor appeared, bellowing in a loud voice, "Twenty-Second Street next. Twenty-Second Street!"

As the passengers shuffled off and on, he thought about lying to her. Then he thought about telling her the truth. Then he decided that this woman might be smarter than he. It was no mark of shame to admit it. A really good trial lawyer has to develop an effective defense strategy against smarter people.

"Well?" she asked again. "Do you?"

This had been a planned attack. There was a serious reason why she had trapped him like this, and she was not about to tell him, not now anyway. If Conor had learned anything in this ambush, it was that Viviana Bensini was nobody's bimbo. He would retreat to live and fight another day. Rising from the window seat, he said politely, "Excuse, Miss Bensini. Mine is the next stop."

In a bold response, the woman refused to let him pass. After gaining his full attention, she looked directly into his eyes and said in a calm voice. "Stop what you're doing, Conor—now. You have no idea what you're getting mixed up in."

"Is that a threat?"

"You saved my life. You think I'm here to threaten you? If we are seen together, it might be bad for both of us."

"How? Why does this always happen to me?"

"Maybe you're just irresistible."

ON THIS NIGHT, WITH MAUREEN AND THE kids in bed, Conor treated his anxiety with three after-dinner brandies and sat at the grand piano for the first time in weeks. Viviana's visit had raised alarming possibilities, most of which he had not been able to process or identify yet.

He played the old Irish ballad, "Galway Bay", ever so softly. He had played the song for Maureen one night at Mrs. Kaplan's boarding house many years ago and hadn't played it in years. The song distracted him, if only briefly, with good memories, a few bad ones as well, regarding his brother Kevin's involvement in the plot to kill the Prince of Wales. He thought about his poor mother in Ireland, sentenced to death by circumstance and starvation in a mud hut. *It's no wonder your brother turned cold and hard in his feelings about the English, Conor. It was Kevin who had to leave her there, knowing full well what she faced, and he did it to save you.* Everything was on the line now, not just for Conor, but for the whole family. Conor wished the old ballad held a hundred verses. Then he could sing through until morning without a thought of tomorrow—or of Viviana Bensini.

What was Viviana's game? Did she know Graves? Did she play a part in Mumbles's death? Was she a spy? If so, on which side? *If we are seen together . . .* a voice inside told him, *let it go. You have a good life. No need to take risks like that.* But the other voice, the troublesome, obstinate voice that had plagued him since childhood, offered different advice. *Conor, you can't turn your back on this. You have to see it through. Mumbles deserves justice.*

What tormented him most was Viviana's intuitiveness. It was almost predatory but not cruel or mean spirited. *Do you find me attractive?* She had asked him, as if she had reached into his mind, digging at will into his most private thoughts. Thoughts he would never share and desires upon which he could never act. *Do you find me attractive?* Indeed.

He would sleep on it, think about it, analyze all of it until it made sense. But it would never make sense if he walked away from the investigation. He didn't give a sow's ear whether unlocking this puzzle would win the war for America—or lose it. Nor did he care if the answers would rescue the British Empire from the scrap heap. Global politics and world order were existential issues for other men to fret over.

Maureen had once told him that his determination never to run for office came as a relief to her and that if he ever succeeded in changing the world, it would be one pitiful client or stray dog at a time. There was nothing pitiful about the dead newsboy, but he hoped Maureen would write that epitaph on his tombstone one day—after he found Jan Kazmirski's killer.

Chapter 11

The next morning, Thursday May 3, 1917

The Nivelle Offensive that began on April 16th along the Western Front, was collapsing and, according to the newspapers, doomed to failure. Robert Nivelle, the French general after whom the offensive was named, had been sacked and replaced by Phillip Petain. French units were engaged in mutinies across the front, undoubtedly dashing hopes for a decisive Allied victory that might end the war.

With no morning cases on the docket, Conor knocked out three client visits at the county jail and filed some pre-trial motions with the Clerk of Court, arriving at the office ten minutes early for his meeting with Titus Freeman. The lawyer found Gimpy—Titus—already waiting in the reception area. "Why do you always want an appointment at lunchtime?" Conor teased.

"Mornin', Mister Dolan," the boy replied, ignoring the question.

"You have good instincts. You'd make a better lawyer than you do a private investigator."

"What?"

"Never mind. Come on in," Conor said, grabbing his mail from the desk. "Good morning, Mrs. Schmidt."

The pint-sized investigator made himself at home on the sofa. He'd come up with an old briefcase somewhere, placed it proudly beside him and produced a notebook. "Got that information you wanted, Mista Dolan."

"Let's have it."

"Viviana Bensini has a resident flat at The Sherman House, number 302."

"What about the corporate search, Titus?" The young private eye handed Conor a two-page report from the Secretary of State. "Well, I'll be damned. Registered agent is a lawyer in this building and the largest shareholder is another corporation."

"What's that mean, Boss?"

"Maybe nothing. Maybe someone is trying to conceal his ownership. I doubt the cops even followed up on this. I'll give it to Eammon Flynn and see what he can dig up. Nice work, Titus."

"Hey, Mista Dolan, we goin' out t' lunch someplace?"

Conor settled back in his leather chair, doing his best to look serious. "You mean like Henrici's? What do you have a taste for? Dover Sole and a nice Chenin Blanc maybe?"

Titus shrugged. "Sounds good to me."

"Well, you'll have to settle for a sandwich and a bottle of beer again. You're right about it being a *rich* hotel. They use half of it as apartments for people with money, but you're still a horseshit detective."

The youngster's eyes narrowed, lips pursed. Conor had struck a nerve. "Whatchoo mean, horseshit detective?"

Mrs. Schmidt made a timely appearance with their lunch tray, giving Conor a minute to decide how best to repair the damage to Titus's newsboy ego. "I mean Viviana *made* you first day on surveillance. Then she spotted the other kids you sent over on shifts."

Titus shook his head. "Wasn't her. It was Ruffulo's guy, Mickey Lucchesi. We seen him hanging around the hotel and I think he recognized me."

"So Ruffulo is keeping an eye on his girlfriend. That's interesting. Is it because he's protecting her or suspecting her? What does this Lucchesi look like?"

"That's the thing, Boss. He looks like a lawyer, like somebody who works in your building. Nice suits, nothing flashy. He ain't big neither. Just ordinary."

"Still, I guess you're doing pretty well for a new man. Try not to look obvious. You still have the place covered?"

"'Course. Even the bellboys is watching her comings and goings."

Conor reached into his wallet, handing Titus a five-dollar bill. "You and Toad can't show your faces there anymore. Use other kids and hire a cab driver when you need to. Follow her when she goes out. This should buy you four or five trips around the area. See where she goes, who she sees. Make sure they wear decent clothes."

"I'll need another two bucks for all that, Boss."

Conor warmed instantly to his use of the term boss. Reaching for his hat and coat, he said, "Jesus, I'm surprised you don't charge me travel time for the walk over here. You'd better hit the road now. I have things to do."

Where but from Ruffulo would Viviana get the dough to live in a posh place like the Sherman House? No matter how much he wanted to think better of the woman, she was likely Ruffulo's evening distraction after all and tipped Conor off to repay a debt. The other possibilities were equally terrifying, so it wouldn't hurt to keep an eye on Viviana and to do a little digging into the big gangster himself. Come to think of it, an ambush could work both ways.

With Titus on his way, Conor telephoned the Sherman House, asking for Miss Viviana Bensini in Room 302. A woman answered almost immediately. "Miss Bensini? It's Conor Dolan."

"Well, you don't give up easily, Mister Dolan. What do you want?"

"I admit you caught me off guard on the streetcar. I'm hoping you might have time for a chat today. I got the impression you were warning me off my investigation in good faith. Let's say I didn't want to leave it like we did. Rest assured, I will cause you no trouble."

"You never answered my question, Mister Dolan. Why were you having me followed?"

"A friend of mine was murdered. Big Jim Ruffulo's name came up in the investigation. But I think you already know that."

A protracted silence followed the revelation before she said, "Meet me over at the new Municipal Pier in an hour."

The Municipal Pier on the lake in Streeterville was quickly becoming one of the city's premier attractions, despite having opened to the public only last July. Originally designed by famed architect Daniel Burnham, the pier was built primarily as a dock for freighters and passenger ships, but the plan had evolved to include indoor and outdoor recreation areas, parks, even an exposition center. The pier offered a perfect neutral meeting place on a warm May afternoon.

Conor was waiting at the main pier entrance when Viviana arrived. This time she looked more like a gangster's distraction, dressed fashionably in a wraparound, calf-length tempered pink skirt and white silk blouse with a v-neckline and wide collar. Something resembling a thick necktie framed the v-collar and dropped to her waist. The net effect was nearly heart stopping.

They walked out along the pier past the tourists, the travelers, the day trippers, and a large steamship, to a bench near the far end of the pier. On the stroll, they talked about little things. She was born in Chicago. Her parents were both alive and lived on the West Side somewhere. He was not surprised to learn she graduated from Northwestern University. She didn't let him off the hook by volunteering an explanation of her domestic arrangement. On the bench, the time seemed right for a meaningful dialogue. "I should tell you that someone involved in my investigation saw you going into Henrici's with Big Jimmy Ruffulo."

"Ah, so that's what started all this. What of it?"

"You warned me off this investigation. I appreciate the gesture, but you have to know I have no intention of letting this go. I had no idea about your connection to all this until my investigator saw you with Ruffulo, and it's important for me to understand why you sought me out. Believe me, your personal relationships are of no interest to me."

She rose from the bench and walked close to the edge, just beyond the narrow walkway, her back to him. He could almost feel her words, even with her face turned away. "Please, Mister Dolan. I can hear the condescension in your voice. Don't offend the gangster's girlfriend, the tart."

"It's not like that, Viviana, but I did need to know because Ruffulo is connected to my investigation." He didn't want to disclose too much. She might still go back and tell the gangster. "Now, I answered your question. Will you answer one for me?"

She walked back to the bench. The wind had picked up and Conor wrapped his coat around her shoulders. "Alright. What is it?"

"You know Mumbles? One of the boys you took to lunch?"

"Yes."

"He's dead. His name was Jan Kasmirski, and he was shot during a warehouse burglary. I have reason to believe Ruffulo was involved."

She nearly leapt from the bench, spun around to face him and said, "Conor, you don't want to take this any further. Trust me."

"Why?"

"Because he is a very dangerous and vengeful man."

"That's not good enough, Viviana. I have to know if he sent you there to warn me off." She turned away and started to walk briskly back toward the entrance, some half-mile away. He kept up with her and pressed for an answer. "Did he send you to threaten me?"

She stopped abruptly and turned to face him. The sun had given way to dark clouds from over the lake and Conor could hear the rain drops on the brim of his Homburg. She said, "No. He did not. I came because you were kind to me, and I don't want to see you hurt."

"You mean Ruffulo would hurt me? Why?"

"There's nothing else I can tell you, Mister Dolan. I'd like to go home now."

CONOR DECIDED TO CATCH A LOOP-BOUND streetcar to the office. Leaving the pier, he replayed their conversation in his head. If Viviana had been a mystery to him yesterday, she was now a complete enigma. The news of Mumbles's murder had not shocked her. The woman hadn't even feigned surprise. *Why? Why had she even agreed to meet him? What was her agenda?*

At some point in his musings, Conor quit being aware of his surroundings. As he reached the mouth of an alley along Illinois Street, two men grabbed him violently by the arms and swung him around, smashing him up against a brick wall. A third man rifled through his pockets, even going so far as to check his trouser cuffs. The two men brought his arms together at his back as the third slapped handcuffs on him. An unnoticed fourth thug threw a black sack over his head.

"What is this? What the fuck do you think you're doing?" Conor's shouts were unanswered.

They pushed him into the back of a delivery truck of some kind and drove off. Conor had seen the truck waiting in the alley. *It must be the same one.*

Straining to retain his wits, Conor tried his best to mark time and listen for audible clues about their direction or location. The vehicle had started out traveling west. He heard a train whistle about seven minutes into the trip and tried his best to mentally record the turns. Echoes told him they passed through a tunnel moments later. He made the lapsed time at fifteen minutes before the truck stopped.

They were inside a garage of some kind. He heard traffic outside and the sound of electric streetcars. They were in the city somewhere, but it might not matter any longer. *He was about to die. These animals were about to murder him, like a rat in an alley, where no one would see or hear the vile deed.* Through the paralyzing fear, he thought only of his family, his own selfishness for pursuing this quest. But he didn't want to die, not only for his family, but for himself.

He could hear the men whispering outside the van, writing the script that would transform Conor Dolan into an instant cadaver. The whispering stopped. The end would come quickly now, but he wouldn't make it easy for them. Hands and feet still bound, he managed to lift himself into a crouching position facing the door. It would come quickly now. They would dump the corpse into a barrel, then onto a boat for transport to his final resting place at the bottom of Lake Michigan.

With sweat pouring from his body, Conor steadied himself as one of the men began to turn the door handle. As the door moved, Conor launched himself like an arrow, head-first into man's belly. Kicks and punches rained upon every part of his head and torso.

He woke up in excruciating pain tied to a chair with a sack over his head, but almost instantly grateful and overjoyed to have awakened at all. If they hadn't killed him already, he would live. It was enough for now. Conor figured they were on the North Side, maybe Halsted Street. He remembered being dragged up a flight of stairs and through a creaky door.

"You're in a lot of trouble, Dolan." The voice presumably belonged to one of his three captors. It was calm and reasoned with no hint of panic or hatred, a measured tone that did not belong to Norton from the Halsted Street APL headquarters. *No, but I think you are.* Conor had no experience in being kidnapped, but if they'd wanted him dead, he'd already have an answer to the existential question of the ages. Is there a heaven? He decided not to play their game and remained mute.

"You and your wife are enemy aliens. We have a thick file on your activities for the Clan-na-Gael, a revolutionary society whose goal is to divert British men and war materials from the European front to defend the home islands. That's treason now that we're at war. Don't bother denying it."

"I won't and you're a fucking eejit. That's not their goal and Ireland is not their "home island."

"You should know we're working under the authority of the Department of Justice. We have eyes on you."

They were bragging about it "So you're with the APL, the American Protective League. Right?" His anger was nearly enough to loosen the rope.

"We're simply concerned patriots."

"Well, the Bureau of Investigation doesn't put sacks over suspects' heads or hide their identity."

"You really think that? Our Republic is in danger, Dolan, from sabotage, from spies, and from enemy aliens like your kind who suck up the benefits of a free society but won't lift a finger to protect it. Personally, I hope they charge you under the new Espionage Act and put you away where you belong, but that's not up to me. Be warned. Cooperate with us or face the consequences."

He wanted to tell this thug to go fuck a woodpecker, but they still might break his leg for fun—or worse. Good sense prevailed.

"We're not going to harm a hair on your head. We're Americans. We don't do that, but other people might. Help yourself, Dolan. Tell us who hired you to represent Jan Kazmirski. Who was the other burglar? Who paid you? We know you're in the Clan-na-Gael. Tell us what you know and prove you're not an enemy alien."

Why would the Department of Justice "authorize" this gang of thugs, even give them badges, to do their extra-constitutional dirty work and not keep them accurately informed? If this eejit was on the level, he knew even less than the cops. "I have nothing to say." Conor sat there, alone in the dark in pain and tied to the chair for two, maybe three hours in dead silence before they loaded him back into the truck.

From the eerie silence along city streets, Conor figured the time to be around one in the morning. With the hood still covering his head and hands tied behind his back with rope, he felt the vehicle pulling to the side of the road as though parking on a residential street. They had given him food and water during the ordeal, although he was exhausted from lack of sleep.

Silently, two men led him by the arms to a porch with cement stairs and seated him carefully on the second step. Not a word was spoken. For a moment, he wondered if they had been lying and were about to shoot him in the head like the arms broker. He heard fading footsteps before the engine rumbled and faded into silence. He would live another day.

Conor felt his way up the stairs, six, same as the Dolan Bungalow. Making his way up beside the front door, he found the address placard and ran his fingers over the numbers, one by one. Home. Knocking on the door with his head, he could envision Maureen's reaction to the hooded intruder and steeled himself for her response.

"It's me, Maureen," he? hollered through the locked front door. "Don't be afraid. I'm alright."

She opened the door, ripping the hood from his head and embraced him, kissing him with tear-stained cheeks. "They've been here as well, Conor."

Chapter 12

Tuesday, July 2, 1917

June had been an eventful month, not only in the Allied struggle but on the home front as well. With Lenin back in Russia, the country had exploded into all out civil war. The Bolsheviks were said to be desperate to withdraw from the conflict and were willing to sacrifice large swarths of territory, if only they could gain control of the government. The first-place White Sox had lost two in a row to the Indians and would play today to halve the series. The dreaded Espionage Act had become the law of the land and makeshift camps were springing up all over the country to hold draft evaders. On June twenty-sixth, the U.S. First Division became the first combat troops to land in France and on June twenty-eighth,

George M. Cohan released his instant classic recording, *Over There*. It had been a week since Conor's kidnapping and the Dolans had been lying low ever since to let tempers settle. Conor figured it was time to pick up the pace again.

With a clear schedule, he decided to track down his old friend, Detective Eammon Flynn. Flynn was retired but maintained strong friendships in the current detective squad and up the ranks. Conor grabbed an umbrella as the sky was overcast and promising a spring downpour to purge the atmosphere and drive away the creeping stink of the Stockyards. Flynn could always be found at Big Jimmy Ruffulo's Forest Park Casino on Tuesday afternoons. *You never know. Graves might have shown his stubby head at more than one casino.* He hopped a Lake Street train for the ride out to Harlem Avenue, only a short walk from the casino.

Thankful he had thought to grab an umbrella, Conor was only slightly damp as he found the retired detective on his usual pilgrimage to Ruffulo's illegal casino on Madison Street. Oddly, the place was prominently situated in a warehouse behind a Chinese laundry, just down the street from the police station. The casino occupied at least four thousand square feet of storage area with no visible windows and was accessible only through the laundry. Ruffulo didn't charge a fee for entry but required every gambler to deposit at least one dirty shirt or other item for laundering as a condition of admission. The place was considered Ruffulo's "flagship" establishment and the boss himself could often be seen greeting players. The casino was nameless because, officially, it didn't exist but was known affectionately as the "cleanest gambling joint in Chicago," despite the fact that it was well outside the city limits.

No fewer than forty motor cars and a dozen horse carriages surrounded the bustling laundry business, including two local police vehicles. Conor was glad he remembered to bring an old shirt for the proprietor.

The casino was dimly lit by electric drop lights in the ceiling. A series of trap doors on the sloped roof provided ventilation, aided by four large ceiling fans. The interior offered bare brick walls covered with cheap paintings, mostly women in various states of undress. But the place was surprisingly comfortable and smoke free. Making his way through the maze of poker and crap tables, he spotted old Flynn standing in the bar at a table along the back wall.

The retired sleuth was starting to look his age, which Conor pegged at north of seventy. Flynn spotted him and said, "Well, if it isn't the pillar of Irish-American society. Drink?"

Conor had already signaled the bartender. "Jameson," he said, "two."

"I thought I'd find you at the poker table, Flynn. Hell, you can drink anywhere."

"I tapped out early today," Flynn confessed. "Just waiting for them t' press me shirt. So, what brings ye way out here from Bridgeport, Counselor?" When they'd first met, Flynn used the word "Counselor" as an insult and pronounced it slowly with a dose of sarcasm. It was the same word these days but had become a term of affection.

"Bridgeport works for us."

Flynn chuckled. "A far cry from Mrs. Kaplan's old boardinghouse."

They talked about the White Sox and Flynn's well-known obsession with Charlie Chaplin, the rage of Twentieth-Century film comedy with appearances in some twenty films in 1914 alone. Then Conor asked, "Where are you living these days?" The man's wife had died only two weeks before Conor and Maureen's wedding back in 1904. He battled the grief by working another five years, but the drinking and gambling recently drove him closer to Mount Carmel Cemetery every day. Conor suddenly regretted having never invited Flynn for dinner.

"The Plaza Hotel in Oak Park," Flynn replied. "I have a nice little room there in exchange for hotel security duties."

"Well, that explains you hanging out in Forest Park. You can walk home from here."

Flynn smiled and quipped, "Or stumble." Flynn raised his glass and they toasted. "*Sláinte*. Now suppose ye tell me what's important enough to justify this trip to the outlands?"

"The warehouse burglary down at South Works, the one where the newsboy was shot. It's part of that corporation business I asked you to track down," Conor declared.

Flynn's gregarious façade appeared to dissipate before Conor's eyes. "Oh, Dear Conor, you picked a hot p'data there. Ye might say it's the favorite late-night topic of discussion and gossip in the copper saloons. Talk is the deputy Superintendent himself lifted the file from them only a week ago. It's being handled at command level on the hush-hush—or not."

"Why?"

"The dicks think German agents murdered that kid to hide any connection to the Wellborn murder. If it's true, then the Department of Justice is handling the case now—or sitting on it. The detective who had the file isn't too happy about losing his case."

"Gianelli?" Conor asked.

"Yep. Spoke to him about it meself after a copper's funeral out at Mount Carmel Cemetery."

Conor signaled the bartender for another round and said, "Let's sit at a table. Bartenders have big ears."

Secluded at a corner table, Conor said, "I'd like to know where this Clifford Wellborn fits in. I've been reading his name a lot in the papers. They're saying he was an arms broker to the Allies." Up to now he had only given Flynn bits and pieces.

Flynn shrugged his shoulders. "He was shot dead on his front porch only a couple of nights after your warehouse burglary."

It hit Conor out of the blue. "Of course. I was at the hospital when they brought him in. I didn't know anything about him brokering arms for the Allies until I read it in the papers."

"It wasn't a secret. I hear our guys were looking for the connection when the hammer dropped on both investigations."

"Interesting." Conor took his cue to bring the old detective up to speed on his own investigation, including Viviana Bensini, Ruffulo, and Graves, and the details of the warehouse incident, carefully explaining the suspected connections. "Ruffulo has to be involved because of Graves's appearance at the casino to court the newsboy,

Mumbles. The whole thing smells like dark shadows, secrets, alleys, and sharp blades to me."

Flynn was old but still a quick study. The old man took a stiff swig and leaned back in the chair. "Sure it strikes me ye're about t' open a very deep hole, Conor Dolan."

"Let's put that aside for the moment. I just spoke with Detective Gianelli about the case, and he didn't mention German agents or command interference or even Wellborn. I don't know if he's lying, but he did encourage me to continue my inquiry and that was odd."

"Why in the name of Jesuse would he blab to a defense lawyer, Conor? Detectives are not so different from yeer lot in one way. They like to bounce the ball off one another to see if they missed a clue or failed to check a lead. He and I are friends, worked cases together. Ye might say I trained him. Doesn't surprise me one bit that he wants ye t' keep digging. He knows full well there's a connection. He may have been muzzled, Conor."

"Why?"

"Who knows? Maybe Gianelli has his suspicions about the German saboteur theory. It's too obvious and pure speculation, just a wild conclusion being pushed by people in power. It's convenient."

"What people?"

"Maybe that's what Gianelli would like ye t' find out."

"Will you help me, Flynn?"

"I think ye should let it go, Conor. The lad is dead and ye can't bring him back. This has the markings of a high-level operation, maybe even international. It won't end well for ye."

"That's not what I asked you, Flynn. Will you help me?"

The old man shrugged his shoulder. "I suppose I could squeeze a few sources and put me head into it for ye. It'll do me good t' cut down on the gambling."

Then Conor remembered his other investigators. "Oh, I'm sure you know Lefty Hawk over in Newsboy Alley. He's in the loop too and will help if you need him. You'll have an assistant, my current investigators, Titus Freeman and his friend, Toad. Toad's a Negro lad and can go places we can't. You'll meet him soon."

"Good. Lefty's a good man. That makes the job easier and not so lonely. I don't know Freeman. An ex-copper?"

"Ahh . . . no, but you'll find him capable and . . . unique. Let's just say he can open doors off limits to a former city detective." Handing Flynn Titus's business card, he added, "You can find him through Lefty."

"Fine by me. Now then, is there anything ye left out?"

Conor remembered the casing and recounted small details about Graves, the man with the cropped hair and ruby ring. Flynn had no recollection of ever seeing a man fitting Graves's description at the Forest Park Casino or anywhere else. The detective had never been to Ruffulo's casino on Eighty-Seventh Street. Then he added the mandatory addendum. A lawyer would call it the *hold harmless clause*. "And Flynn, you already know this could be very dangerous."

Flynn's overgrown eyebrows began to wiggle over a wide grin. "I wouldn't have it any other way, Laddy."

ROBERT W. SMITH

Chapter 13

Friday, July 5, 1917

It had been an eventful and important Independence Day and the papers were all red, white and blue with a thirst for Hun blood. American troops were arriving in France by the hundreds of thousands. Many were still untrained, under-equipped, and would not be battle-ready for months, but Pershing was expecting to command an army of more than two million men on French soil by end of year.

The French population bubbled with support for their new American allies. The Herald recounted how the U.S. 16th Infantry Band marched and played through the streets of Paris and down the newly renamed *Avenue du Wilson* on July Fourth to throngs of Parisians. American flags were still on display from nearly every window. It was reported that the entire city of Paris had turned out to cheer the Americans, the "Doughboys" on parade.

In the afternoon, Conor paid a visit to Detective Gianelli at Harrison Street. The detective turned a deaf ear to his information concerning the kidnapping and search of Conor's home. "You made a report of both incidents, Mister Dolan. We have protocols and procedures. You, of all people, should understand that. Both cases will be reviewed in the normal course and assigned to a detective if warranted. There's nothing I can do at the moment."

"If warranted? What the fuck does that mean? I handed your cops the hood they covered me with. There may be clues to where it came from. For Christ's sake, Gianelli, they told me who they were, that they were working for the Department of Justice before threatening me if I didn't come clean about what I knew. That's how brazen they were. What more do you need?"

Gianelli rose from his desk and spoke quietly, with no hint of anger or annoyance as would be expected. "This is as far as I can go with you now, Mister Dolan, unless and until I get the assignment. I hope you understand."

Conor did understand. The detective might as well have spelled it out. Somebody had declared this case off limits to the Chicago Police. In a strange way, this was

Conor's most revealing bit of evidence since day one. The rumors about this APL were all true. In the interest of "national security," the police were instructed to allow the APL to act *carte blanche* in the city.

"Yes, I think I do understand, but let me ask one more question. I came away from our last meeting with the distinct impression that you wanted me to keep investigating these cases. Was I wrong?"

The detective's eyes shifted around the cavernous room. Then he spoke in a low voice, offering his hand. "If you pursue this, Mister Dolan, please be careful. I sincerely wish I could be of more help. Aside from official policy and rules, every man has to walk his own road."

On the walk to the streetcar, Conor considered the detective's last remark. It sounded like an apology. These goons had kidnapped him off the street and held him overnight while their "associates" invaded and searched the Dolan home, terrifying his family. Fortunately, all Conor's notes and documentation were locked in the office safe.

Was it possible the Wilson administration was facilitating the intentional violation of Fourth Amendment search and seizure laws, even tacitly authorizing illegal arrests and detentions without warrants or probable cause? The implications of such governmental overreach was mind-boggling. Where could one possibly go for redress of grievances if the government itself was behind the lawlessness? If it were true, any conversations considered critical of the war effort or the APL must be confined to the most private places, like kitchens and private offices. Conor would never have believed it would become dangerous to hold and express opinions in the United States of America.

But he was still far from convinced that the administration itself, either on its own or in concert with Allied authorities, sat atop the plot. Conor wanted to believe the U.S. Government would not abet the murder of a citizen or knowingly trash the Constitution. There were still holes in that theory.

The APL goons who kidnapped him knew virtually nothing about a larger conspiracy. Their questions were sophomoric within the larger picture, indicating ignorance of both the players and the game. *Tell us who hired you to represent Jan Kazmirski. Who was the other burglar? Who paid you?* If Conor's kidnapping was at the direction of the Bureau of Investigation, the kidnappers would have been better informed. Try as he might, Conor could not reconcile that distinction.

He opted for a short detour to Newsboy Alley and an audience with its resident earl. To his surprise, he found Lefty in his alley "office" conversing with Gimpy, or Titus Freeman, depending on the nature of the conversation.

"Ahh, speak of the devil." Lefty declared. "We was just talkin' aboutchoo."

"Flattering, I hope."

"Your investigator here, Mister Freeman, has compiled quite a book on Viviana's comings and goings. I think he might have run over budget. He was just asking my advice on how to tell you."

Looking at Titus, Conor asked. "How much?"

"Two bucks would cover it."

"Never mind. I haven't eaten lunch. Busy day. How would you both like to join me for a sandwich and a beer? The evening editions won't be out for a couple of hours yet."

He knew neither the man nor the boy would decline. "Let's walk over to Murph's Saloon in the old neighborhood," meaning down the street from his former bachelor residence on Fifth Avenue.

"Great," said Titus. "Just gotta run over t' my storage shelf next door and grab my Homburg n' tie."

"Of course," Conor replied.

TO NO ONE'S SURPRISE, TITUS LIKED THE roast beef and was pleased that Murph stocked Schlitz on tap. "So, what's our young lady been up to?" Conor asked.

Titus was sporting a new item to his detective outfit, a slightly used and oversized black striped vest. He reached into the pocket and produced the treasured notebook. "First thing is that she has a job. She's an actress or a dancer. She goes five times a week to the Majestic Theater on Monroe and leaves around ten at night, goes straight home.

"Let's see here. Day before yesterday she spent the afternoon at Lincoln Park with two ladies. One was older, the other around the same age. My man say she rode the streetcar and the 'L' straight back to the Sheridan House. Next day she walked down to the grocery store."

"Visitors?"

"No, but she made one more trip the same day out to Big Jimmy Ruffulo's house in River Forest. Toad followed her in a cab. Didn't stay long. She left about twenty minutes later."

"Not much of a distraction," Conor mumbled.

"What?" Lefty asked.

"I said that doesn't give us any traction. How did she get there?"

"Lucchesi picked her up."

Conor signaled Murph for another round of beer and he mapped out the case for his two investigators. The Germans, he postured, were still suspects, considering the Luger, the involvement of the APL, the kidnapping and the fact that Wellborn was a major arms exporter to the Allies. Curiously, the APL goons never warned him to stop investigating. Instead, they warned him to "cooperate." There had to be a significance to that difference that would expose a wide gap in knowledge between the APL and the DOJ.

Maybe the German Luger was too obvious. Blowing up one shipment of explosive chemicals might have some psychological or propaganda value but would hardly affect the war effort. He recounted the single hole punched in one of the barrels. If it wasn't accidental, what did it mean? Maybe blowing it up was not the objective. The pieces were not fitting together. Conor needed more.

His juvenile detective seemed to be reading his mind. "Can we find out what happened to the barrel with the hole punched into it?"

Titus's insightfulness hardly surprised him by now. The kid was smart and might be the most politically informed and well-read fourteen-year-old in Chicago. "I thought of that, but Riverside Supplies, the warehouse management, removed the barrel and God knows what they did with it. The cops never even saw the punch hole."

Lefty had been taking it all in quietly until now. "But why would the APL be so hell bent on finding out what you know?"

"That's another part I can't figure," Conor confessed. "The questions were fundamental, information that the cops already had. I got the impression the APL thinks the Germans were behind it all and they want payback, like they're out of the loop." It was the perfect opportunity for the government to warn Conor off the case, but they didn't.

"Not necessarily," Titus piped in.

Conor did his best impression of being annoyed. "This better be good. You're getting expensive."

"What if the right hand didn't tell the left hand what it was doing?"

He had Conor's attention. "Explain."

The boy told them about the time some big guys tried to move in on his Jackson Street newspaper spot. Gimpy hired a couple of big bruisers to work the spot for a week or so. He told them he was going on vacation but didn't tell them anything about the interlopers. Said he'd give them a bonus if everything went smoothly. The bad guys made a play to take over the spot and Gimpy's boys beat them senseless.

This kid was a diamond in the rough, Conor thought. "So go on. Play it out."

"It's the same thing, Mister Dolan. President Wilson ain't gonna tell these APL guys the whole story. They're just day helpers but he wants them shaking the trees.

What if the government fed this APL with a horseshit story about the operation? I'm betting the real story would be a pretty big secret. Right? What if the APL is just acting on the version the Justice Department gave them? They're like two trains running side by side but never touching. One's going to the station, the other toward a cliff."

Lefty smiled. "I practically raised this boy."

Conor nodded. He'd figured the government was keeping them out of the loop but had not considered it might be part of a larger plan. "I get it. Just give them enough information to stir the pot. It's possible. At least that would leave open other possibilities, beside the Germans."

Or maybe the Bureau's cleverness was just eluding him. He tried to think back to his interrogation by the APL man. Was there deception in the line of questioning? Was there one question in that barrage for which the government did *not* have an answer? Not likely because the APL was not that sophisticated, its agents were not trained, but vigilantes, civilians running around like kids with badges. Sure, the DOJ was behind them, but only as mindless windup toys to keep the populus in line and suppress all opposition to this war. More likely, the APL knew nothing really important, and the government wanted it that way.

Murph suddenly appeared with another round. "On the house, boys."

They clicked glasses and Conor offered his customary toast. "*Sláinte*, lads." With that he pulled a five-dollar bill from his wallet, setting it in front of Titus Freeman. "Here's the overtime for your employees—and a small bonus. Now, Genius, how do we find out what Graves was after in that warehouse?"

"Well," began the pint-sized investigator with the prodigious intellect, "if they didn't want to blow them up, could be they wanted to do something that would make them useless."

Lefty said, "Contaminate the chemicals somehow so they wouldn't explode. I like it. So how do we find out?"

Again, Titus was quick with a suggestion. "Newspapers is what I know. Reporters is always digging up dirt the government don't want them to. Maybe see if them artillery shells wasn't blowing up lately. Look through the old newspapers. What do you think, Boss?"

"That wouldn't cost much, and you never know. If this is a deeper conspiracy of some sort, it wouldn't be just one shipment. It would be a big operation that included multiple shipments. There might be a pattern in newspaper reports. French and British soldiers are notorious complainers. It would be time consuming but might show a pattern."

Conor remembered the big dustup recently when thousands of French soldiers refused to fight, essentially calling a strike. They just camped on the side of the road for a couple of weeks and refused to move. Drove the command nuts. The papers had a way of getting important stories out to the public, regardless of official secrecy. There was also an incident where the Germans and British in the trenches just quit fighting for the weekend at Christmas. They all met in the middle and swapped food and wine.

"Good idea," Conor replied. "I just need to find someone smart enough to do the research at the library, someone with the time to spare. Flynn can't do it. He doesn't do well in libraries unless they serve Jameson."

"What about Missus Dolan? She's a real smart lady." Titus suggested.

"Never gonna happen, Titus. She hates the English. If she even suspected the possibility that she was helping the English--"

Titus shrugged his shoulders and interrupted. He was gaining steam like a train engine. "Maybe you just don't tell her everything and she will *protect your spot.*"

Back to the wallet. It was well worth another dollar. "Don't start thinking you'll get a bonus every time you come up with a good idea. It's your job and I'll be expecting it from now on. But I have a new assignment for you. It might take you a month and there's no hurry, so I want you and Toad to handle this personally, nobody else."

"Sure. Name it, Boss."

"This Graves has a weakness. He likes nice clothes and probably expensive hotels. I'm going to make you a list of every high-end hotel in the city. There isn't a bellboy or a desk clerk in this town that you or Toad haven't done some kind of business with. Talk to every one of them individually. Find out if they've seen a man matching Graves's description, the ring, everything. Find out what they know and have them contact you if he comes back to town. If he works for Ruffulo, this wasn't the first time."

Chapter 14

Thursday, July 19, 1917

The Kerensky Offensive, a desperate effort of Russia's Provisional Government, was on the verge of collapse with the Bolsheviks becoming stronger each day. It seemed only a matter of time until a Russian surrender of some sort. On the other side of the world, a dashing young British officer being called Lawrence of Arabia had led a makeshift Arab Army in the shocking capture of Aqaba, a major port in Jordan, on July 6.

Despite the time pressures of the Mumbles incident, business for the criminal lawyer kept churning. Thursday was Judge Thompson's day for picking juries and Conor had received the notice last Monday that the judge's scheduled jury case had pled out, advancing Conor's armed robbery case up for trial from its previously scheduled date in August. There was no chance of reaching a plea agreement as the defense was misidentification. His client, a Polish immigrant named Stanley Bona, stood accused of robbing a street vendor at gunpoint and would never plead guilty because someone else committed the crime. It wasn't a complicated trial, and the lawyer was planning to put the jury out for deliberation by Tuesday.

Conor was sitting on a bench in the hallway going over his juror questions when Eammon Flynn took the seat beside him. "Good morning, Flynn. Mrs. Schmidt tell you I'd be here?"

"She did. I have a report to make. First off, ownership of Riverside Enterprises is a dead end. The registered agent is a lawyer. It's privately owned by a foreign corporation."

"No surprise there."

"I also have a few tidbits on the elusive Mister Graves, if ye'd be interested."

"Shoot."

"I started hanging out at Ruffulo's South Side Casino for a few evenings last week. Different times each visit. Mumbles was apparently a Blackjack player, so I kept an eye on the comings and goings at the tables. I saw no one matching Graves's description, but I did reacquaint meself with a former police associate, retired and working security for Ruffulo. A nice fella he was."

"Brilliant, so what did he give you?"

"This Graves just showed up one night before the burglary. He'd come in nearly every night and developed an interest in Mumbles and started hanging around the Blackjack tables."

"Interesting."

"The South Side casino is a bit more relaxed than the fancy place in Forest Park. No ties or cravats, mostly mill workers and locals with gambling problems, so most people wouldn't notice. Anyway, near as I can figure, Graves disappeared right after the burglary and Wellborn's murder."

"What about Ruffulo?"

"Easy, Conor. I can't go waltzing into Ruffulo's place asking questions about the man. I'm in good health at the moment, and I'd like to see eighty candles, if ye don't mind."

A bailiff chose that moment to interrupt their conversation. "Excuse me, Mister Dolan. Judge Thompson is ready for you. We have the venire on the way upstairs."

"Alright. I'll be right in."

Turning back to Flynn, he said, "That helps a lot. It tells us Graves is probably not local. Somebody hired him to do a job, two jobs most likely, after which he left town. It doesn't help identify who hired him. Did he see Graves talking to Ruffulo or one of Ruffulo's high ups?"

The old man shook his head. "Not once. Nobody bothered him. . .Wait, there was one strange thing. The security man told me Graves hardly ever gambled at all. He mostly hung around watching and talking to people. That's strange because you'd think someone like that would draw suspicion. My man said he included his observation about the man in his daily report a few times, but nobody ever instructed him to take action."

"That's a connection to Ruffulo."

"But here's the thing that will interest ye most. I hear in the copper saloons that there's a department-wide verbal directive to lay off anything involving the APL and the Wellborn murder."

"I suspected as much."

CONOR HAD A JURY PICKED BY FIVE-THIRTY that evening but decided to stop at the office on the way home to grab his messages and mail. Mrs. Schmidt would be gone, and he could call Maureen to hold the dinner.

With the heat letting up this week, it seemed everyone wanted to be in the streets, at the lakefront, and in the outdoor cafes. The "L" train was crowded but he managed to find a window seat. In these soothing downtimes, he liked to take in the urban sights, enjoy the breeze, and let his thoughts wander.

It was a sure bet now that someone brought Graves in from out of town to get into that warehouse for an unknown reason. He recruited Mumbles through Ruffulo for the newsboy's savvy and intimate knowledge of the South Works complex. In all likelihood, Graves also shot Mumbles. With the cause of death listed as "Infection," Conor could rule out a murder in the hospital. Going forward, he would proceed on the assumption that Graves murdered Wellborn to shut his mouth and to cover up the true purpose of the burglary.

THE FIRST PIECE OF MAIL ON THE NEAT PILE was a sealed envelope without a postmark from *Congress of The United States, Office of the Hon. Brendan O'Sullivan, Congressman, First Congressional District of Illinois*. Congressmen were exempt from paying postage but there was no exemption stamp, indicating the letter was hand delivered from O'Sullivan's local office this morning.

Ignoring the rest of the pile, he took the reading glasses from his desk and opened the envelope.

Dear Conor:

I regret to inform you that the Naval Academy has today rescinded the appointment of your son, Patrick Dolan to the Class of 1917. The action is beyond my control and taken for the reason that the Bureau of Justice has declared Patrick a security risk. Background checks are required for all incoming cadets and all admissions are subject to security approval. I am deeply sorry for this decision and the stress it will undoubtedly cause your family.

Sincerely,

Brendan O'Sullivan

Congressman

It had to be the damn APL. Conor watched the paper shaking in his right hand as a knot began to form deep in his gut. *Maureen will be devastated. What will happen now? You are to blame, Boyo, you alone.* Patrick had trusted him, gone along with his solution, agreed to his compromise. Even worse, Maureen had trusted him. Now it wouldn't happen. Beyond that, young Patrick had been branded a "security risk," akin to an enemy alien and not by his own doing. Disastrous scenarios swirled around in his brain.

This could destroy Patrick's future. What would the boy do now? He could still get into a college, but the stigma would remain, maybe forever . . . unless . . .

He tried to perish the thought. Sweat poured from his brow. The room began to close in around him. He opened the window behind his desk to inhale the fresh air but, in the process, knocked Mrs. Schmidt's plant to the floor where bits of dirt and ceramic carpeted the hardwood. Only one move could clear his son from suspicion. Would his marriage even survive the suggestion? But he wouldn't have to suggest, just tacitly agree or submit and sign the permission one morning when Patrick inevitably placed the dreaded document on the kitchen table. To purge this branding forever, Patrick would have to join the army.

Conor withheld the letter until the boys were down and the couple was alone in the living room. He simply told her he had received bad news from O'Sullivan earlier and handed her the envelope. She took a long time to read the letter and even more time to consider her response. No outcry, no fit of temper, and not so much as a tear. After all these years, he still underestimated Maureen from time to time. Finally, she turned to him and said, "We'll send him to Ireland, to my sister. They won't get him there."

Conor shook his head. "He won't go. You know that. Besides, if he went to Ireland he'd be in the British army in a week. It was my fault, my stupid idea."

"There's enough blame to go around, Conor, but we have to stop him from enlisting for as long as we can."

"Well, for now, we'd better tell him as soon as possible and be prepared for his reaction. He'll resent us if we delay. Whatever we think, the bat is in his hands, Maureen."

She leaned forward on the sofa, eyes narrowed. "Meaning what exactly?"

"I think you know what it means. You know Patrick better than anyone. He's exactly like you, right down to the red hair and sloped nose. In the end, he's going to tell *us,* and we'll have to listen. If it means he's enlisting, we can't stop him. If we refuse to sign, he'll leave and enlist in New York or somewhere and lie about his birth date. Then he may not even write to us. We don't want that."

"We don't want him back in a shoe box either, Conor." She was quiet for a minute with a blank look on her face, like her mind was someplace else. Then she added, "There has to be another way."

"Why don't we sleep on it?" He said, rising from the sofa. "I'll walk Dillon and join you in bed in an hour." He grabbed the leash and a jacket from the coat rack and Dillon came running.

"Say hello t' Scanlon for me," she said, giving a miserable imitation of a smile.

With Dillon leashed, he turned back to her. "Come with me. Dillon likes to shit in that big lot next to Scanlon's. You haven't seen Scanlon in a while. Besides, a couple of drinks will do you good. There's something else I want talk to you about."

"I don't have the strength tonight for any more disclosures."

"I won't take no for an answer," he declared, holding out her coat. "And it's nothing bad."

She didn't take the coat immediately. "Tell me what you want me to do first."

"Library research and nothing more."

It was a pleasant, late July evening, warm and windless but hardly oppressive. Conor held the leash tightly as Dillon took the lead. "I want you to join my team, Maureen."

"Oh Jesus, Mary, and holy Saint Joseph, just who plays on this team?"

"Lefty Hawk, old Eammon Flynn, the retired detective, and a very gifted young investigator named Titus Freeman."

"The usual suspects. At least they're not expensive."

"You'd be surprised."

He didn't lie to her, not exactly, but downplayed the leading theory that the Germans had killed Mumbles as a warning to other American brokers eying massive profits from the Allies. In that case, Maureen's efforts would not conflict with her . . . *sensibilities* regarding helping England. He gave her details about the burglary and Mumbles's shooting. He told her about the connection between Graves and Ruffulo's casino, about the fired German Luger cartridge and Wellborn's status as one of the biggest exporters of explosive chemicals to the Allies. He had to tell her about his suspicion that someone might have tampered with the chemicals, considering she would be looking for evidence of that very fact. Still, it was a plausible theory, he explained, in light of the small hole punched into one of the barrels and one they needed to eliminate.

At the bar, with Dillon's needs met and him tied up to the lamp post, they made some small talk with Scanlon, mostly kids, social events, school. But Conor could see her mind running on another track. When Scanlon had moved down the bar she got right to the point. "So, if we find Wellborn was sabotaging shipments to the Allies, then we'd be helping t' bail out the king's arse."

Although she'd never before shown an interest in becoming involved with his work, it appeared she had the aptitude, not surprisingly. "You can quit any time you like.

I don't know where this is going, Maureen. We're all at war now, and everyone will be shipping arms to France. Remember we're doing this for Mumbles, not for any government. Until we find out who Graves was working for or what he was doing there, we'll never solve this puzzle.

"There's evidence that points to the Germans; there's evidence of a direct connection between Ruffulo and Graves. It could have been Ruffulo for some reason unrelated to the war. That hole in the barrel is a key to this case and we need to find out what it was. Maureen, this isn't about taking sides for me. It's about a newsboy who didn't deserve to die. I don't care where it leads. It's my case and I'm going to solve it. Will you help me?"

"Certainly I'll help. But I think ye're asking the wrong questions."

Of course, you do. "What do you mean?"

"First of all, how do ye know the bullet that killed Mumbles didn't come from a police pistol? You said the bullet wasn't recovered or wasn't identifiable. The shooting might have been justifiable and the bullet from a police pistol."

He was ready for that one. "I don't, but all the suspicious connections exist independent of that issue. If the cops killed him, there's no murder, but there's still a conspiracy. We need all the answers to draw that conclusion."

She appeared to think for a minute, then nodded. "That's logical, but here's another one. Maybe somebody tipped off the cops and the detective lied when he said it was *routine* patrol. It's possible they want to hide that information. That name will open the tap and yeer answers will pour out like a bucket of milk. Now, drink up and let's go home."

His first reaction was to defend his investigative abilities. After all, he'd been working on this case since just after the burglary and made good progress. He'd glossed right over that question. "It's possible, very possible." For whatever reason, Conor did not mention the name Viviana Bensini.

ROBERT W. SMITH

Part II

Chapter 15

Sunday, August 19, 1917

August had been relatively short on war news. As Russia sank nearer to collapse, the war kept expanding. African countries like Liberia had declared war on Germany. Even China had joined the fray on the Allied side. The White Sox, meanwhile, had beaten the Phillies yesterday, boosting their record to 71-44, seemingly cruising toward a World Series. Conor would have time for details later.

He hated Mass. His four years of Latin had shed absolutely no light on the jibber jabber spewed out from the altar on Sunday mornings. Oh, he knew a few basics, like *mea culpa* and *Confiteor Deo* and *Sanctus, Sanctus, Sanctus*. Other than that, Mass was an opportunity to analyze cases, plan defenses and occasionally wallow in his sorrows. It was also hard on the knees, but Maureen never allowed him to slip off his knees onto the bench between the consecration and the end of the communion service.

This Sunday, Maureen suggested they break in the family's new motor car with a trip to Saint Michael's Church on the North Side to visit their mutual friend, Father Brendan White, for Mass. Patrick was off somewhere with his mates. He was getting too old for family day trips anyway. Maureen thought they might convince the overworked cleric to accompany the Dolans on a picnic to Lincoln Park where they could relax, sit on the beach, even take a boat ride. It would be the first real family outing in the new Ford. Conor suspected there was more on Maureen's menu than chicken and it most likely involved the old, trouble-making priest.

They met Brendan outside the church after the noon Mass and waited until the priest had greeted the last of his homebound church goers. Like Conor, the priest was looking older, maybe fifty-five with less hair to comb, but had stayed fit and very much the shepherd of his flock with a direct line to City Hall. "Well," said the old priest, "if it isn't me own surrogate family. And where is Master Patrick on this fine Sunday? I hope he went to Mass."

Conor was relieved when his wife decided to ignore the question. They exchanged hugs and made some small talk before Maureen made her pitch. "Sure we're taking our new car up to Lincoln Park for a picnic and thought we might talk ye into taking the afternoon off."

"Oh, I'd like nothing better, Maureen, but I've a full day ahead of me yet. Two baptisms this afternoon, then a round of visits at the hospital, but I wouldn't mind a dinner invitation to Bridgeport one of these days."

"Yes, it's been too long, Brendan. Ye shall get yeer invitation."

The priest had been Conor's guide into the deceit-filled cavern that was Chicago politics back in 1903. Under Brendan's tutorship, the young lawyer had managed to survive and ultimately thrive in the snake-filled political arena.

A most unusual Catholic cleric, Brendan's forte was Jesus at the retail level, roaming as needed throughout the city to solve individual problems and right small, personal injustices. The priest's naïve, altruistic habits had once landed him in hot water with the local archbishop, who proposed to ship him from his ministry to a monastery in remote Wisconsin, thus depriving the local down-and-outs of their treasured champion. The move would also have left Father Brendan's long-time girlfriend in Chinatown a virtual widow. Had Conor not intervened on

Brendan's behalf, the red-clad tyrant would have labeled the priest a thief for using dedicated diocesan funds to help the poor.

With Detective Flynn's help, Conor had uncovered a long-suppressed police report documenting the archbishop's arrest for child sex offenses years back and confronted His Eminence with the evidence in a bid for some *quid pro quo*. The startled bishop was happy to let sleeping dogs lie and keep his foot off Brendan's neck. Brendan had his suspicions but was grateful that Conor had spared him the details of the extortion in an effort to preserve the good father's standing with Jesus. The archbishop had not bothered Brendan since that day.

From Saint Michaels it was a short drive east and up Lake Shore Drive a couple of miles. It would be good to see Maureen relax for a change. Truth be told, the Dolans were excited about the new 1917 Ford Model T, a shiny, black machine with a back seat for two and a soft top that could disappear in summer, bathing the occupants in the sounds and sights of the open road.

On the drive with the top down, an animated Liam waved and shouted to nearly every pedestrian along Lake Shore Drive. Conor parked his new prized possession along the curb on the Outer Drive, a perfect spot with the beach on their right and the lagoon and park on the left.

Only the street and a line of maple trees along the park side separated the park from the beach.

Liam dragged them for a boat ride before setting up the picnic. At the boathouse, no fewer than a dozen small rowboats lined the pier and the three were free on the water within a few minutes. Liam assumed the oars and declared himself captain. People who would otherwise ignore a passing traveler waved and called out good wishes. Even Maureen seemed to have a genuine glow of happiness, if only for an afternoon—or the length of a boat ride—under the protection of her best umbrella.

After docking, Conor retrieved the picnic things from the Ford while Maureen and Liam found a good spot on the lawn. For a couple of hours, they laughed, drank, reminisced, and told jokes under the shade of an old oak tree. The afternoon reminded Conor of their first happy times together following those turbulent days in 1903. With the sandwiches eaten, the wine drunk, and the cake devoured, Conor and Liam played catch on the lawn as Maureen poked fun at her husband's geriatric attempt to simulate a fly ball to the outfield.

Later, when Liam ran off to play with a group of kids, Conor settled into the portable camp chair and started into the Sunday Herald to bone up on the big story of the day, maybe the biggest story since Congress declared war. Details of the new Espionage Act continued to emerge, confirming Conor's worst fears. Wilson's government had touted the Act as a patriotic shield protecting Americans from German spies and saboteurs. The Act had become law in June, and the vague language of the Act had troubled Conor from day one. It was now a crime "for any person to convey information intended to interfere with the prosecution of the war effort or to promote the success of the country's enemies." The language allowed wide latitude for abuse and all the outpouring of assurances from the administration did little to address Conor's worst fears.

Now, The Herald reported that in these first weeks, thousands of Americans had been arrested just for speaking against the war. Everyone who bothered to care foresaw the danger. The APL thugs had even threatened Conor with the Act before it became law. The new internment camps were filling up faster than they could be built. Virtually any criticism of the war effort or expression of sympathy for Germany could land an American citizen in one of the camps without charges or due process. Even silence was no guarantee of safety from the long arm of these "patriots." Simple failure to fly an American flag in front of the house could subject the owners to questioning and persecution. To Conor, it was pure insanity.

What would this war do to his adopted country? When individual rights are trampled, do they ever return? Was it like a rubber tire that retracts back into its resting position when the stress is lifted? Or is it more like losing a finger? You can learn to live with the disability easily enough, but the hand will never be the same. What about two fingers or three? It hadn't taken long to appreciate the danger of this newest threat to democracy. It was something out of a futuristic novel or a throwback to medieval times.

"Maureen," he said, reaching across to touch her arm. She was holding Patrick's letter, reading it yet again, looking for something between the lines that might change its meaning, reduce its toxicity, temper its horrific possibilities.

"Yes, Conor."

"Oh, it's nothing. I've forgotten anyway."

"Ye know, Conor, there may be a chance he'll stay at Camp Logan when they deploy the regiment. Sure they'll need soldiers there t' keep the camp running. Don't ye think?"

She was grasping at straws, but Conor saw no need for cruelty. "You never know, I suppose." By now, Conor could recite last week's letter by heart:

Dear Ma and Pa,

I can announce with pride that your oldest son is now a soldier. Our platoon will have group and individual photographs taken in uniform next week. I shall post it to you promptly. My uniform fits perfectly and I cannot wait to finish the basic training course. I am allowed to say that infantry training is a possible next step but will know more about my assignment as we draw closer to graduation. I may be assigned instead to the Artillery Corps or some other area of specialty.

Rumors abound that the regiment will be deployed soon into the regular Army as part of the 33rd Infantry Division. We will certainly give the Hun some hell when we get over there.

I hope all is well at home, especially with Liam. I will have to go now as we are minutes from "lights out." I love you all. My postal address is on the envelope. Hope to see you all for my graduation.

Your loving son,
Patrick

Showers were gathering over the lake, signaling an end to a good day. Conor started gathering up their things. He said, "I forgot to tell you I invited Eammon

Flynn for dinner. He wanted to meet, so I'm guessing he found something."

"Why don't you ring that hotel where he lives and leave a message for him to come around six?"

"Alright. We'd better head for the car before we get soaked."

The war had come to America, to Chicago, to Bridgeport, and now into the comfortable little Dolan bungalow on not quite so Normal Avenue.

FLYNN ARRIVED AN HOUR EARLY FOR cocktail hour, armed with a pint of Jameson. "You didn't have to do that, Flynn," Conor said.

"Ah, sure I'll drink most of it meself in any case. 'Tis cheaper than drinking in the hotel bar and sure the company's better."

With two fingers of whiskey each, they settled in the living room for the talk. "It must be important for you to come all the way out here. I have a car now. I could have come to you."

"Sure if ye insist, I may let ye drive me home. But 'tis important enough. Seems Riverside Exports has filed for bankruptcy. According to my sources, Riverside is the second largest exporter of arms and chemicals to the Allies. But that's not the good part. All contracts with the

Allied countries and the U.S. are being handled in the Receivership but the bankruptcy file has been sealed."

"I thought synthetic chemicals were produced almost exclusively in Europe," Conor pointed out.

"As did I, until I did some detective work." Flynn explained that the basic dynamics of the ammunition and chemical export business was no secret and had been widely reported. The Europeans, particularly the Germans and the French, had always been at the cutting edge of synthetic chemical innovation and production as well as arms technology. But three years of war had exhausted their resources and capabilities. The Allies were desperate now for ammunition of all kinds, even for the chemicals needed to make various explosives and gases in an industry dominated by the major warring powers since the late Nineteenth Century. DuPont and other American companies had adjusted and begun producing the European chemicals in mass quantities, even struggling to keep up with Allied demand to prop up their depleted stocks. Just another example of how the titans of industry had abandoned their neutrality support a couple of years back when they discovered the obscene profits to be made in the field of mass murder."

Flynn apparently wanted to increase the tension, like a drum roll before the trapeze artist prepares to dive. He downed the whiskey and retrieved the pint bottle from his breast pocket. Filling both glasses methodically, he announced. "Two years ago, this Riverside was capitalized at a hundred grand and exporting pottery and construction equipment. Last month the stock value was over two million bucks."

"Do tell," Conor mused. "It's possible Wellborn just had vision. Maybe he switched to explosive chemicals at the right time. It's no secret the Allies' supply of ammunition and chemicals is severely depleted, and production can't meet the current need. Right place, right time."

"Maybe," Flynn conceded, "but maybe he had backers, dark money and influence that wanted this man in this position at this time."

"Right, like from one of the warring powers. But that still doesn't tell us which side acquired his services and skills."

Flynn raised his hand. "I vote for Germany."

"It's starting to move in that direction."

As a major exporter to the Allies, Wellborn was in a position to influence the upcoming spring offensive by the Germans. Everyone knew it was coming early next year. It was the only chance for Germany to win the war before the Americans got into the fight and tipped the balance. Russia's war effort had collapsed since the Czar's abdication, and they were desperate to find a way out of the conflict. With no more war in the East, the Germans would free up dozens of divisions to throw at the West. A stockpile of dud weapons would help the Germans break through the stalemate. Once they mastered the system and operational details, they could expand the operation to all the ports of export.

Maureen chose that moment to enter the dining room with a large pot of lamb stew. Her timing told Conor she'd heard every word. "Dinner, gentlemen. Conor, would ye fetch Liam from his room?"

The old detective ate like a child of the Great Famine and stayed for an after-dinner brandy as they filled Maureen in on their recent discoveries. Conor passed on the brandy as he faced a forty-minute drive each way.

On the drive out to Oak Park along Washington Boulevard, Flynn said, "Ye know I can't get any deeper into Riverside's financials."

"I get it, but at least we're moving in the right direction. Wellborn came into a lot of money quickly. We can't get to the records without a subpoena, and I can't issue one without a criminal or civil case opened and filed. I can hardly sue him for Wrongful Death since Mumbles was breaking into his warehouse. The bankruptcy doesn't stop me filing a lawsuit, but I can't in good faith think of one right now. I'll give it some thought—Wait. That may not be necessary."

"Why?"

"Well, with all that's been happening, it might be wise to talk to that Irishman again, the one who manages the warehouse. He had access to the paper trails and might be unhappy with the current situation. I'm thinking recent events might loosen his tongue. He'll be easy to find. It's all in my notes."

They still didn't have a breakthrough, but the investigation seemed to be running on two tracks now. Track one was still sketchy and featured Wellborn and one or more of the Allied governments. It was starting to look like Wellborn was indeed engaged in some nefarious activity on behalf of the Germans. At this rate, the war might be over before Conor solved the puzzle, but he was still relatively young and determined to bring Mumbles to justice, however long the trail.

Track two was becoming clearer and involved Viviana Bensini, Big Jimmy Ruffulo, and the elusive Mister Graves. Viviana and Graves were each linked separately to Ruffulo, but Conor still had no direct link between Graves and Viviana. Except for Viviana's strange visit on the streetcar, he would have dismissed suspicions against the gangster's girlfriend by now. The answer had to lie on one track or the other as there was no connection whatsoever between Big Jimmy Ruffulo and the warring powers.

Chapter 16

Wednesday, September 19, 1917

The Sherman House Hotel was strictly for the Astor Street crowd, commanding the streetscape at the corner of Clark and Randolph, no doubt rebuilt for at least the third time after The Great Chicago Fire of 1871. Rust-colored brick distinguished the roughly twelve-story façade over hand-carved sandstone around the first and second levels. He could see a parade of stone-carved animal heads or angels across the top of the tower. They had names for the city's many architectural styles, but damned if he knew any of them. In addition to being the city of hogs and miscreants, Chicago was an oasis of fine architecture, and the recently deceased Daniel Burnham was the Architect Mayor *Emeritus*.

As Conor reached for the massive bronze door on LaSalle Street, an impeccably dressed porter—an older gentleman—said, "Good morning, Sir. You'll want the main entrance around the corner on Clark. This entrance is for ladies traveling and living alone. May I help you with anything, Sir?"

"Thank you. I'm having lunch with someone at the College Inn."

"Perfect, Sir. Around the corner, take the main staircase to the second level. You will find the *maître d'* there, Sir."

The lobby was strictly posh *du jour*, red scarlet throughout and a marble staircase guarded by polished brass railings. The *maître d'* stood his post like the King's Guard at Buckingham Palace. He was at least fifty, slick black hair and a tummy pouring over the belt buckle, no doubt fattened on a diet of dollar bills.

He'd only asked the woman for an interview, but she insisted on lunch. The meeting was strictly business. He should have done it before, he thought, weeks ago. For some reason, his eyes panned the massive space for any sign of an acquaintance, a familiar face.

Behind the palace guard, he could see directly into the famous restaurant. She was waiting for him and waved from a corner table beside the windows as he presented to the *maître d'*. She was alone, a practice frowned upon in high society. The place was crowded, of course, forcing Conor to traverse the length of the establishment, eyes fixed forward, to reach her. It was an ordinary business luncheon, he reminded himself, but no reason to draw attention. "Miss Bensini, I'm so grateful you agreed to speak with me."

She motioned him into the chair across from her. She wore less makeup than last time, a touch of rouge on the cheeks and lips with dark smudges along the eyelids. No guilt could attach from admiring such a face. It was a new and exciting look for Viviana that included a calf length dress with a V-neck.

They tried to make small talk, but quickly realized the two were virtual strangers with nothing in common. "You must be wondering why I asked to meet you."

"The question crossed my mind."

"I'm here primarily to seek your help in my inquiry." *Primarily?*

She rested an elbow on the table in a most unladylike manner and leaned forward. "I doubt that very much."

He ignored the remark. "You warned me to back off my investigation of the warehouse shooting. I believe you did so sincerely and in good faith and I couldn't care less about your relationship with Big Jimmy Ruffulo, whatever it might be. Best leave the judgment business to judges. I have found a connection between you and Ruffulo, and a connection between a Mister Graves and Ruffulo. What I don't have is a connection between you and Graves, but I strongly suspect he works for your *friend*, Ruffulo. Will you help me find out?"

"I don't know a Mister Graves."

That was Conor's cue, so he told her the whole story and everything he knew about Graves. She leaned back, lips frozen, if only for a few seconds, then spoke in a low tone. "I suppose I need to tell you, Mister Dolan."

"Tell me what?"

She leaned forward again in the chair only to be saved by the black-suited waiter. "Our special today, Sir, is the stuffed, boneless Smelts with a mushroom sauce. The soup *de Jour* is tomato rice."

He looked at Viviana and she nodded. Conor said, "We'll have that, please. What do you recommend as a wine pairing?"

"We recommend the Sauterne Cresta Blanca from California, Sir."

"A bottle, please."

With the waiter gone, Conor recovered his train of thought. "You were saying?"

She stared at the empty wine glass, rolling it by the stem. "Let's put it this way. The women your newsboy private eyes saw me with at Lincoln Park were my sister and my mother."

"Ruffulo is your . . . "

"My father. Yes."

"But your name."

"Bensini is my mother's maiden name." It was a mouthful to digest, and he reached for the water glass. His first reaction was relief, vindication, even a touch of excitement. *Perish the thought.* Then confusion. "I take it you're not on good terms."

"You take it correctly, Mr. Dolan."

"Please tell me why you warned me off the investigation on the streetcar that day."

"Simple. People who cross my father tend to suffer from sudden death."

The waiter arrived with the wine and performed the obligatory tasting ceremony. "I have to find Graves," he said, then told her the story of the Wellborn warehouse incident, posing his question at the end of the presentation. "Will you help me?"

"I never heard the name Graves, but I'll tell you what I know. These guys don't use real names."

Conor gave her the complete description, especially the ruby ring. "Have you seen anyone like that?"

"I have not, but you say young Mumbles told you about the man. Were they the only two burglars at the warehouse? Who else mentioned this Mister Graves?"

"As far as I know it was just the two of them. Nobody else mentioned Graves. Only Mumbles."

Her shoulders relaxed and she exhaled, reached for a sip of wine. "I hate my father but force myself to go there on occasion to visit my poor mother. She's trapped in his vile world. The beast has no secrets from my mother. She serves their food at his most intimate and secret meetings. She knows everything. And what she knows, I can find out. I will ask her about this man Graves. It's a description that fits very few people. Will you tell me where all this is going?"

"Among other things, the warehouse held explosive chemicals for export to France. Why would your father care about that?"

"I don't know anything about that, only that my father is a lethal criminal."

"You think Graves is a hit man?"

"Maybe."

"That would mean Mumbles was going to die anyway. He was always meant to die. But tell me, why do you hate your father so much? Wait. I shouldn't have asked." *Remember, this is not personal.*

She answered too quickly, like she'd been hoping for the question. "My father is a cave man, a murderer, and a bully. He never went to school and never had a son. But he insisted I get an education and sent me to the best Catholic schools and on to Northwestern University where I found my life and began in theater. It's the only good thing he ever did for us, but in doing so, he helped make me into everything he hates."

"But you went to Henrici's with your father not long ago."

"My mother's birthday, a surprise party. I'd do anything for her." She paused and Conor filled the silence by refilling their glasses. "Education is freedom, Mister . . . Conor. The more I grew the clearer I saw my father and what he did to my mother. I met someone in my senior year and fell in love."

He sensed Viviana was opening the door to a private place. Had he pushed her into it? "You don't have to tell me this, Viviana." He meant every word of it. He didn't need these intimate details for the case. Yet, he couldn't bear for her to stop.

"I want to . . . unless . . . unless you really don't want to hear it."

"I do. I do want to hear it."

"Alright. His name was David Miller."

"So, he was Jewish?"

"Yes. How did you guess?"

"I'm a quick study— on everything except women."

The waiter suddenly appeared. "Will you be having desert, Sir?"

Conor deferred to his guest. "Viviana?"

"No, thank you."

The man bowed formally. "Of course, Sir. I will return with the check."

Conor nudged her back on track. "So, you said he was Jewish."

"Yes. I was struggling with my own identity issues, but nothing compared to David. His family disowned him because he had rejected Orthodox Judaism in favor of Reform. David was a grad student from Michigan and ten years my senior, a wonderful, sensitive man who filled my life from the time we started seeing each other. He worked at the university full time in the admissions department while studying for his Ph.D."

"Did his family problem have something to do with you being a Gentile?"

"No. They would have, but it never came to that. The break occurred a few years before we met, when David left the Orthodox faith. When we became engaged, he made an effort to mend fences and introduce me to his mother and father. They wouldn't even return his calls or letters."

"How did that affect the engagement?"

"It devastated him. I didn't care. I wanted to get married, move to another state and start our own family from scratch, a brand-new family."

"So, what happened to thwart that plan?"

Viviana took a slow, deliberative sip of the wine, then stared down at the empty glass for a few seconds. "I made a very bad decision."

The waiter appeared with the check before she could explain. The man's timing was becoming annoying. Conor removed six dollars from his wallet and smiled. "Keep the change. Everything was wonderful."

The couple passed the *maître d'* stand near the grand stairway when Conor heard someone calling his name from the main-floor lobby below. It seemed to echo off the marble stairs below and the granite walls of the cavernous space, rendering the descent torturously slow. Knots churned in his stomach. Conor recognized the woman instantly as they reached the base of the stairs. She was waving and still calling his name until the lawyer was certain every eye and ear in the lobby had dropped its business to eavesdrop, even the bellboys'.

Conor gave his best impression of a welcoming smile. "Missus Rowland. How wonderful to see you."

Kate Rowland had been a key ingredient to those turbulent first days when a young, cocky lawyer arrived in

Chicago to learn the secrets of his brother's death and tame this overrated city on the lake. In the course of that first year, the secrets saddened him, and the city humbled him.

"Mister Dolan. What a pleasure. I hope ye are well, Sir." Then, looking directly at Viviana, she added, "And so this is Missus Dolan?"

That was his cue. "Oh sorry, Kate. This is Viviana Bensini, a client. We're just discussing her case. Viviana, meet Kate Rowland, a former client and a good friend."

Kate said, "Pleased to meet ye, Miss."

He felt a crushing need to take control of the conversation. "Are you no longer working at Father Brendan's, Kate?" Conor's friend, Father Brendan White, had befriended the woman after the Nellie Finley affair and provided her work as his assistant housekeeper.

"I am still with the good father, but I work with a restaurant supplier on me days off. I was just checking in with the chef here about his needs for the month."

Kate had never met Maureen, but it was a sure bet she had no secrets from the priest and his busybody housekeeper, Mrs. Fogarty.

When Kate left, Viviana said, "Nice lady. It must have been a memorable case."

"You have no idea."

Conor was relieved when Viviana asked no questions about Kate, but the awkwardness of the conversation was not lost on her. "I hope I didn't get you into trouble."

He'd lied to Kate about their lunch and felt ashamed. "Oh, not at all. It was just a lunch."

He tried to sound cavalier. "I would offer to take you home, but I guess we're already there."

"Yes. I can take the elevator from here." Then she extended her hand, vertically, like a man would. "Goodbye, Conor."

It was a business lunch, he reminded himself, but he couldn't leave it like this. "I'm sorry, Viviana. Truly."

"It's alright. I know you're married. I should never have toyed with you."

"No, it's fine. You've been a great help to us—to me. It couldn't have been easy telling me that and it means a lot." Her smile was the same one he'd seen across the restaurant when he arrived.

He couldn't leave it there. She never finished her story. "I don't get it, Viviana. If it wasn't David's parents, what or who caused the breakup?"

"It was my fault," she said quietly. "I took a big chance and brought him home to meet my parents. David insisted on it. He didn't want to start off our marriage with lies. It was a major event because I had been free of that monster for three years. It didn't go well. My father threw him out of the house after dinner one evening, even threatened to have him killed if he ever contacted me again. I never heard from David again."

"Just because he was Jewish?"

"And because I told my parents I was going to convert to Reform Judaism. You see, my father, in addition to being a ruthless gangster, is the consummate Roman Catholic hypocrite. Murder and robbery and extortion are fine, so long as you go to Mass on Sunday."

"But you must have tried to contact David. You could have been married, gone to live in California or somewhere."

"You don't get it, Conor. Nobody ever heard from David after that night. Nobody."

BACK AT THE OFFICE, HE COULDN'T GET Viviana off his mind. It didn't take much imagination to understand what she was suggesting. Conor's callousness and rush to judgment in branding her a tart only highlighted the triviality of his own selfish concerns. While Viviana was trying to tell him that her father murdered David Miller, all he could think of was Kate Rowland spilling the beans about his rendezvous with a beautiful woman.

The way he'd handled the chance meeting with the housekeeper shamed him and likely diminished him in Viviana's eyes. He had done nothing wrong. The lunch was part of his investigation. Yet he had lied to Kate Rowland to prevent Maureen finding out. Besides, if Viviana had invited him into her apartment, he would never have gone, never in a million years ... never ...

Kate would not tell Maureen about the lunch, but she *would* tell Mrs. Fogarty, Father Brendan's primary housekeeper, and Mrs. Fogarty would surely tell the priest. Father Brendan, in turn, was a confidant of Maureen Dolan. *You reap what you sow, Conor.*

Chapter 17

Monday, September 24, 1917

Conor grabbed a morning Herald at the "L" station on his way downtown. This perfect fall morning would allow him a brisk walk and the opportunity to brief up on the morning news, so he left the new Ford at home.

A Russian general had led a failed coup against the Provisional Government on September 12 and a few days later somebody declared Russia a "Republic," whatever that meant. The attempted coup coincided almost to the hour with the French Prime Minister's resignation.

With summer in the books, his White Sox were 97-50 going into the last week of the season and were a cinch to play in the World Series. It was practically the only nonwar-related news of the morning. The symbols of patriotism appeared in nearly every photograph and patriotic themes drove nearly every story. News of the war, of spies, of sabotage, of women on the home front, of slackers and, of course, features on Chicago boys who died before even seeing action.

The photographs in the papers also reflected the everyday sights of the busy Chicago streets, the parks, the boulevards and even the quiet residential neighborhoods. Flags and posters virtually papered the trees, lamp posts, storefronts, even private homes, to the point where any house or business not overtly advertising support for the war would be instantly labeled as suspect.

Paradoxically, within this patriotic paradise of preparedness, the Dolans had been granted a measure of social redemption, owing to young Patrick's recent enlistment. Of course, Conor and Maureen were proud of the young man's sense of service and responsibility, but in public were careful not to trade or seek benefit on the boy's misguided and not fully developed coattails. They did not advertise, nor did they deny the fact of Patrick's service, but in honor of their son, had decided to hang the new Blue Star Service Flag in their front window. The flag contained a blue star in a white rectangular box on a red flag. Each star on the small flag represented a son in military service.

In an ironic, reverse twist, the service flag acted for the Dolans as the "lamb's blood" of the Israelites, smeared on door frames at the first Passover to spare the first-born son from the Angel of Death. Patrick's service was the very thing that shielded the parents and kept the dreaded American Protective League from returning to the Dolan house, and Conor and Maureen had told Patrick as much in their letters.

Perusing the real estate section, Conor came upon an ad that would surely get Maureen's attention today. They had been talking about buying a small home in the country for summers, likely not for a year or two, but the ad described the exact summer home they were hoping to find: *FOR SALE, 6-ROOM STUCCO BUNGALOW, Elmhurst, 70-ft lot, best residence section, $6,500, $500 cash plus terms.* He tore the ad from the page, careful not to sever any part of the owner's phone number. Maybe Maureen would like to take a ride out there, just to look.

Mrs. Schmidt was already pouring his morning coffee when he walked into the office. Flynn was waiting in his office with a cup of coffee, hand shaking, red eyes swollen. It must have been a long night. With no court cases on the calendar, Conor had arranged for an unannounced field trip with Eammon Flynn to visit the widow, Kelsey Wellborn.

"I'll skip the coffee this morning, Missus Schmidt. Flynn and I need to hit the road." Turning to Flynn, he added, "You'd better finish the coffee. Looks like you need it."

WITH OLD EAMMON FLYNN IN TOW AS HIS prover, Conor set out in a cab for the north lakefront to visit the widow. "How's the boy doing?" Flynn asked.

"Patrick? He's at advanced infantry training, Camp Logan. His Guard regiment has been activated and attached to the 33rd Infantry Division."

"How long will that last?"

"I get your point," Conor replied. "Longer the better. The answer is we don't know. It's my understanding everyone goes through the training so there's still a chance he could be sent for some specialty training that avoids trenches, but we know he won't request it. He can't wait to get to France and kill someone else's children. It's madness."

"Ye mean like cook school?"

"That would be fine with us, but he's a smart boy. I was thinking more like clerk or quartermaster."

"There's a good chance our boys won't even see combat until early next year. Just the threat of two million Doughboys might make the Germans pack it in."

"Thanks, Flynn, but that sounds like wishful thinking." The cab turned onto Lake Shore Drive for the ride north. The driver might have taken another route, but a trip up the lakefront on such a morning was breathtaking.

It wasn't Astor Street, but the Wellborns' beautiful Lincoln Park brownstone nearly made the grade and came complete with the obligatory wrought iron fencing. Surprisingly, Kelsey Wellborn herself opened the door. Conor immediately handed the woman his card. Tipping the Homburg, he said, "Good morning, Ma'am. Are you Mrs. Kelsey Wellborn?"

The door remained only partially open as she sized them up. "Yes."

"My name is Conor Dolan. Let me say initially how sorry we are about the tragic loss of your husband. I'm a lawyer investigating the burglary and shooting at your warehouse some weeks back and wondered if you would spare us a few minutes."

She made no move to open the door further. "I don't see how I can help you. My husband's company is in bankruptcy. It's in the lawyers' hands now. I have nothing to do with the warehouse."

That wasn't true, but Conor wasn't ready to quit. "Mrs. Wellborn, a young boy was shot and killed in that incident and our only interest is in finding whoever shot him."

One lie deserves another. It wasn't his only interest. He wanted to say, "Three years ago your husband was exporting pottery and children's toys from his garage. Now he's a deceased major global arms dealer and supplier to the Allied armies."

The door opened slowly. "Well, alright. My housekeeper is doing the shopping, but I can make us some coffee. Please, come in. We can sit in the parlor." The woman was about fifty, still very much the grieving widow, subdued with noticeable lines under her eyes, hair pulled to the back and balled up.

She returned shortly from the kitchen with the coffee tray and said, "Now then, how may I help you? I didn't know much about my husband's business, you see."

He'd forgotten to introduce Flynn and corrected the omission, then continued. "You have a lovely home, Missus Wellborn. Have you been here long?"

It sounded like a harmless question, but the answer might help explain the extent of the family's sudden financial success. The woman made a polite effort to smile. "Thank you, Mister Dolan. We bought the home . . . Let's see . . . It will be three years ago in November."

The timeline fit perfectly into Wellborn's overnight financial success, but Conor had to tread lightly. "Do you have any idea why someone would break into your warehouse?"

"My husband's warehouse, you mean." She'd already answered one of his most important questions.

"Of course. Sorry."

She leaned back, careful not to spill the coffee. "To steal things. Why else?"

"That's the curious thing, ma'am. The police report indicates they were there for another purpose, a purpose still unknown to us."

"Well, I couldn't imagine what that was."

He needed some goodwill, a distraction. Pointing to some photographs of a young man on the mantle, he asked, "Is that your son? Strikingly good-looking young man."

"Why yes. Thank you. George is in his third year of medical school."

"You're very fortunate, Missus Wellborn, but I'm certain you and your husband were well situated to handle expenses like that."

Her smile seemed to broaden as she gazed at the picture. "Oh, we weren't always this well off. My husband's business was much smaller. Three years ago, he made an acquaintance with experience in the arms and munitions brokerage business. They became friends and the gentleman invested quite a large sum of money in his business. It paid off handsomely for everyone."

"Can you recall that man's name?"

She seemed to hesitate. "I don't recall that my husband ever mentioned it."

It wasn't the answer of a criminal, but he still needed to be tactful. If he asked the obvious question now, the interview would end abruptly, criminal or not. He decided to drive around the block. "But why bankruptcy? Can you tell us what happened to the money?"

The woman's eyebrows closed in around the sockets. More wrinkles appeared and she rose from the sofa. "You would need to ask the lawyers about that." She stood and pointed to the door. "Now, gentlemen, if there are no more questions..."

They were on their way out the door anyway, so no harm in asking the big question. They might as well leave her with something to worry about. People sometimes make mistakes when they get worried. "Do you recall your husband ever doing business with Big Jim Ruffulo?"

"Good heavens. The gangster? No."

A THIN CLOUD COVER HAD TEMPERED THE September heat nicely, so they had lunch and a glass of

Chianti *al fresco* at an Italian place on Fullerton Avenue. "So, what did you think?" Conor asked Flynn.

"I think whatever her old man was into was beyond her salary level, but she knows more than she's letting on, especially about the investor."

"Yeah, I got the same impression. She wasn't packing up her treasures for a move to back of the yards. She seemed comfortable in that big house and still has a maid. I mean how do you go from successful businessman to bankruptcy in a day? Something's not right." If nothing else, they had stirred the pot. Now they'd let it cook awhile and see if they had a stew. "Oh, I got Tommy Rafferty's address. Your protégé tracked it down."

"Titus Freeman, eh?"

"None other."

On the drive out to Oak Park, they dissected their findings to this point. It was possible that the connection between Ruffulo and Wellborn lay inside those barrels of chemicals, but both men may have been barking for bigger dogs. Graves was on a mission that night for Ruffulo, most likely related to the explosive chemicals, with instructions to leave no live witnesses. He shot Mumbles with the intention of killing him. It appeared now that whatever person or entity was pulling Wellborn's strings and bankrolling him had an equal or greater interest in those weapons-making chemicals.

Then there was the lack of interest or involvement from the Chicago Police. Gianelli's "investigation" had been less than thorough. Conor had no evidence of the Bureau of Investigation's involvement in the case, but who else had the power to stop a criminal investigation? Maybe Chicago Police brass themselves. But why?

Flynn had something else on his mind. "The girl warned you to back off, Conor. Was it a threat or advice from a friend?"

"The latter, I'd say."

"Who was she warning ye to watch out for? Her father or someone else?"

"I take your point."

Both Conor and Flynn agreed that APL involvement in the matter was unlikely. Not only had they pumped Conor for the wrong information, but the whole clandestine affair was beyond the APL's level of competence. The obvious conclusion could no longer be avoided. Even before the United States declared war, governments had been engaged in a proxy war on American soil, complete with spies and sabotage agents, a war over arms supplies to the Allied powers beyond the intellectual capacity of thugs.

The key to solving this riddle lay in discovering Graves's precise mission on the night of the burglary. Secondly, they would need to learn whether the police actually stumbled onto the burglary during routine patrol or were tipped off.

The consequences of solving such an intricate geo-sensitive puzzle could do more damage than the affair itself. The truth might have the power to turn ally against ally. The wisest course might be to shut down their investigation altogether. After all, whatever had been going on ended with the insolvency and closing of Riverside Exports, not to mention Wellborn's death. It was all history now. America was at war and the past was done and buried.

But a voice from deep within Conor's soul would never let it die. For him, it was not about geo-politics or war or poison gas or bombs. It was always about a newsboy named Mumbles, a decent kid with no home or family who didn't deserve to die a pawn in some global game of kings and presidents. Nothing would keep Conor from finding the truth and delivering on his promise to a client.

Chapter 18

October 14, 1917

Last night, Conor's White Sox beat the New York Giants 8-5 to take a 3-2 lead in the World Series after ending the season with a record one hundred wins on the regular season. They could end it tomorrow at the Polo Grounds.

The last thing Conor needed on this Monday afternoon was an impromptu visit from Boris, the First Ward "Heeler." A visit from the alderman's bag man these days would generally involve a request to purchase tickets for some campaign event or other and Conor usually obliged, if only to keep the peace at home. The local aldermen and precinct captains didn't send Conor new cases but neither did they try to shake him down for kickbacks or a "ward tax" on his fees anymore. Conor had already fought that fight against O'Sullivan. Those were guidelines agreed to years ago between the two of them, and the arrangement had weathered the test of time. The politicians didn't bother him and *vice versa*. While Conor might on occasion voluntarily drop a dime to some friend or former client to express his appreciation for a referral or hold an axe over a politician's head, he never did it under mandate to enrich one of them. He thought of the practice cynically as "ethical corruption." Blackmailing a crooked alderman was arguably within the Chicago Rules of Ethics.

"Send him in, Missus Schmidt."

The Russian ward heeler preferred the sofa to the client chairs and would remember that Conor always kept a bottle of vodka on hand for such occasions. It was likely the reason Boris timed his visit for late afternoon. "Drink, Boris?"

He shrugged. "Of course. *Spacebo*, Meester Dolan."

The lawyer poured a Jameson for himself and a vodka for Boris, but made Boris get off the sofa to collect it. Just a subtle reminder of whose name was on the door. "*Na zdarovya*," said Conor, raising his glass.

Boris chuckled. "Very good, Meester Dolan. *Na zdarovya*."

"So how may I help you today, Boris?"

The Russian stared down at his empty glass for a few seconds, then said, "My visit is different today. I am here as private citizen."

"That sounds interesting." Conor pushed the vodka across the desk and Boris reached for it. "Can we dispense with the preliminaries and get to the point?"

"I represent third party. He needs great lawyer for case and wants to speak with you."

"Thanks. Tell him to call for an appointment."

"Client is very wealthy. Needs you to come to his house. Of course, we have no interest in case and no interest in lawyer fee."

By "we", he meant the local politicians. "Of course. First, I'd like to know who's paying the fee." It might have been any one of two dozen local politicians that Conor could think of offhand. One alderman would often send another alderman's heeler on a nefarious mission. *The money will always lead to the motive*, Conor had learned over the years. It might simply be someone's nephew or family friend.

Accepting a third-party criminal case financed by an alderman or precinct captain was a no-no, fraught with peril and conflict. The kind that could get you disbarred—even killed. Whoever paid the fee would expect absolute loyalty in return, even if that loyalty conflicted with the client's best interest, or the law itself, so the key was to learn the source without asking too many questions in that direction. It was called managing conflict of interest.

"Client will pay himself."

Conor leaned back in his chair. Boris had his attention. "Really? What's his name? If he is rich, I might have heard of him. Why don't we just stop playing, and you tell me?"

"Big Jimmy Ruffulo."

"Well, I'll be damned."

At first, Conor couldn't believe his luck and wanted to make the appointment then and there. A conversation with the infamous gangster himself could breathe life into his warehouse investigation. The crime boss was up to his ears in First Ward politics, dispensing money and gifts in exchange for favorable zoning and policing and crime-friendly legislation. You scratch mine and I'll scratch yours. Boris could be repaying a debt or a favor.

Ruffulo already knew about his warehouse investigation and the search for Graves, even if Viviana didn't specifically admit it. He might want to buy Conor off, scare him off, or maybe even feed him to the fishes. The last possibility was the least likely if he was inviting Conor into his home and using a third-party contact. Maybe Ruffulo was telling him there was no danger; the gangster only wanted to talk. Despite all the warning signs, Conor knew he could not resist the invitation.

Maybe the invitation was on the up and up. The significance of using a well-known ward heeler as a messenger was not lost on Conor. Ruffulo, if Boris was being truthful, might have just as easily sent one of his own boys, but maybe Big Jimmy wanted Conor to think that highly placed city fathers were watching as well.

The city hosted a multi-layered spectrum of crime and corruption, and shenanigans could be afoot between the crime baron and one of Chicago's prominent politicians. That was the way things worked here—and it was not Conor's concern. It was also remotely possible that Ruffulo might actually need his services. To Conor's knowledge, the mob boss had never been arrested, but there were always reform-minded politicians willing to go for his throat, so it was possible the request was legit. The man was constantly under investigation for something. If that were the case, Conor would only need someone of sound mind with identification to walk in into the office, hand him the fee and sign a receipt. Nothing more and nothing less. "So, you're telling me Big Jimmy will waltz in here and put my fee on the desk?"

Boris shrugged. "Not exactly, but a close associate will bring fee."

"Make sure he brings identification too and I won't take a dime until after I meet with Ruffulo."

"Of course." If asked later by authorities who paid his fee, Conor would simply tell the truth, whatever that turned out to be. Besides, Boris's role as an intermediary meant that Conor could name his own price. He liked that.

"Well now, that certainly wasn't on my list of expected events for today. Tell me, just what kind of case does Mister Ruffulo want to talk about?"

Boris raised his arms and shrugged his shoulders. "This not my business. He invites you to his house tonight after dinner. Do you need address?"

"No, thank you. The house is a Sunday tourist attraction, a pleasant drive out to River Forest on a sunny day."

It might be refreshing dealing with someone who was not pretending to be someone else. The man was known to do regular business with two old criminal lawyers in the Monadnock Building. The crime boss might be looking for young blood to protect his growing enterprise. If Ruffulo really needed his growing criminal defense skills, Conor would happily take his money or anyone else's—with a few conditions attached. But even if he declined representation, Conor might learn something about the warehouse shooting or Graves. He was expecting the worst and hoping for the best.

"I'm happy to do business with Big Jimmy so long as he is the client, the only client. So, if Ruffulo wants me to represent multiple parties or one of his boys, tell him to go elsewhere for a lawyer. I won't sell out one client to save another and I have no intention of waking up one morning with my willy in my back pocket. Put it to him like that. Under those conditions, I'm willing to hear about the case and consider it. Otherwise, no harm done. Everyone stays home and happy."

He wondered how Viviana would take to his representing Big Jimmy. The way she hated her father, it wouldn't be pretty. If Ruffulo was on the level, it wouldn't involve the Department of Justice. The Federal Government was not in the business of prosecuting gangsters, big time or otherwise, so any prosecution was left to the state courts—in this case, the First Judicial District in Cook County. Ruffulo was known to insulate himself in layers of underlings. Flynn had told Conor that the inner circle frequently rotated as one of the confidants would periodically wash up on a riverbank or be plowed up from a corn field.

For Conor, it was a win-win. On the odd chance Ruffulo really needed a criminal lawyer for something unrelated to the investigation, he might think about taking the case. It could get him access to the house, the players, the surroundings. On the other hand, if this was some kind of trap as he suspected, he still might pick up a clue or two from being inside the house and actually speaking with the gangster one-on-one. This was too good an opportunity to pass up.

Chapter 19

The next evening, River Forest

Conor parked the car on the next street west of Ruffulo's house. There was no point in giving the mobster's associates a close look at his vehicle. The neighborhood of big homes and plush lawns was dark and deadly silent save the clickety-clack of overfed crickets. A feeling of walking into the lion's den made Conor momentarily wish he'd chosen a different profession. He'd thought this meeting through carefully, but it could still go south in any one of a hundred ways.

Two muscular men in suits were waiting just inside the iron gates as Conor approached. The mansion was nearly obscured by a line of sculpted fir trees along the fence. The men politely searched him, after which Conor proceeded up the drive, past a massive lawn and around a fountain centered in front. Surprisingly, Ruffulo stood waiting outside the front door. It had to be Ruffulo, but the man in the doorway looked more like a well-dressed dwarf than a gangster, with a silk dinner jacket and a combed-over, nearly bald head. The only thing "big" about him was the ample belly, partially disguised by the expensive jacket. The face was compacted around a wide nose and revealed no trace of emotion.

"Mr. Dolan, welcome," said the gangster, extending both hands in the Italian way. Conor shook the right one. "Won't you come in?"

Ruffulo led him into a magnificent, two-story foyer with a sweeping staircase in the center. They entered the finely appointed library, mahogany finished, complete with a hand-crafted desk and bookcases lined with photographs of Ruffulo with famous people, politicians, even moving picture stars. The only things missing from the reading space were books.

The housekeeper appeared carrying a silver tray with two glasses. "Jameson, isn't it?" Ruffulo asked. The man's voice was scratchy and halting, like something was wrong in his throat.

"Yes, thank you."

"I prefer a brandy in the evening." Conor noticed the man's helpers were gone. They were alone in the room.

"Thank you for coming, Mister Dolan. I have been following your rise up the ranks of the criminal defense bar. I thought we might have a conversation."

The man didn't talk like a stereotypical gangster. His diction was perfect as was his grammar and belied his lack of formal education. "I appreciate that, Mister Ruffulo. Your invitation intrigued me."

Thankfully, the gangster showed no interest in small talk. "I'm sure you know my lawyers, the firm Preston and Jennings in your building."

"I do." *Best to keep outgoing information to a minimum.*

"They're getting up in age, Mister Dolan, and I'll need to find new counsel soon. I have them on a very generous monthly retainer, very generous." *Yes, I heard that.* "Are you interested?"

"I'm always interested in new business, Mister Ruffulo, and I never judge a client by rumor or reputation. My work is pure advocacy. I'll never be a judge. I'm a defendant's lawyer. Are you making me an offer?"

"I'm considering it."

"I have a standard retainer agreement that sets forth mutual conditions and obligations."

The housekeeper appeared with one fresh drink. Conor's first glass was empty; Ruffulo's was not.

"Will you run the primary conditions past me now?"

"Of course. I would be available to you unless otherwise engaged or traveling. My consultation and court services are limited to criminal defense. I suppose the most important condition is that you are my only client within the Ruffulo family or circle of associates. I never accept third party clients. It's bad business that leads to ethical problems, even health problems on occasion."

Ruffulo nodded and finally gave the brandy some attention. "Not unreasonable at all. I will take it under advisement. Why don't you send me over a copy of the agreement? Feel free to fill in the financial details."

"I'll do it this week."

Ruffulo extended his hand. For legal purposes, a handshake was generally not an enforceable contract. But nearly every rule of law was littered with exceptions. If Conor shook the gangster's hand, it amounted to a meeting of the minds, establishment of an attorney-client relationship and a mutual acknowledgement that everything Ruffulo said to Conor privately going forward would be protected by privilege. For Conor's purposes, the handshake would act as a muzzle. It was also an extremely clever trap.

As Ruffulo's attorney, Conor could not disclose the contents of any private communications between the two that would run contrary to Ruffulo's legal interest. The privilege was inviolate, meaning that Conor would face certain disbarment if he disclosed privileged information. As much as he wanted a full confession from this criminal, it was not worth facing a future as a waiter or a mill worker. It would also likely be a crime. Laymen called it accepting a bribe.

Conor did not take the hand but tried to avoid insult. "A handshake would cement our relationship, Mister Ruffulo. I'd be happy to shake your hand if and when we have a signed agreement."

Ruffulo was apparently appeased. "I fully understand. Allow me to digress a moment. I hear through associates that you've been looking into the South Works burglary where the young man was shot. Tragic, of course, but tell me, the boy died. Didn't he?"

Here it comes. "Yes."

"I'm wondering why you would continue working on a case for a dead client."

"It's very simple, Mister Ruffulo. I'm trying to find out who killed him. Do you know something that might help me?" It was a polite way of saying, *None of your business*, but Conor wanted the conversation to continue. Anything the gangster said now was fair game.

"No, of course not, but in my position a man sometimes hears things, little things here and there, things that might help a friend."

"Are we friends?" There was no point in acting like a throw rug.

The wrinkles in the old man's forehead went smooth as a baby's bottom as thick brows squeezed around his eyes and mouth contracted. He spoke slowly. "That's what we're here to find out, Mister Dolan. Best to let it go. The boy is dead. Nothing was stolen. You're an honest man, and I don't meet many of those. We'd work well together."

Conor wanted to get home alive, so he said, "I'll think about it."

He thought the meeting was over, but Ruffulo said, "You are Catholic. Correct?"

"Not fervently, more like an accident of birth. Why?"

Ruffulo leaned forward. "It's a shame, a nice Irish family in Bridgeport. I pity everyone who has never known the Church and its teachings. They are but ignorant victims, condemned by fate. But those who know the truth and turn from it are in eternal jeopardy."

Was he joking? "Not certain I understand, Mister Ruffulo. What does my faith have to do with this?"

"Everything, Mister Dolan. You have a beautiful wife, children."

Easy, Conor. The nature of their conversation had just changed, crossed a line and Conor wasn't about to grovel. "Just what does that mean?"

"It means you were having a very cozy lunch with my daughter at her hotel recently, Mister Dolan. And you, a married man. Perilous business. One can never tell who will learn a secret and what he might do with it."

This was coming out of left field and right for Conor's head. While he was having Ruffulo surveilled, the gangster had obviously been following *him*. Conor's first thoughts were for the safety of his family and young Titus Freeman. The man hadn't said anything about it, but he had to know the newsboys were watching him. Titus could be in real danger. It was careless of Conor to expose the boy to such jeopardy. He should have known better. No matter how smart and savvy the boy was, a fourteen-year-old was no match for a thug like Big Jimmy. Conor rose abruptly. "I think this meeting is concluded."

The gangster stood slowly, methodically for effect. "I agree, Sir. Think about our conversation. The offer of employment was sincere. *Everyone* has conditions, Mister Dolan."

ON THE WAY TO DEARBORN STATION TO collect his wife, Conor tried to analyze the visit but found his hands were shaking on the steering wheel. There was no offer of employment. The gangster had lured him there to threaten his family and back Conor off the investigation with a bribe. Hardly a surprise. But something about Ruffulo was off kilter, unbalanced even. The gangster had been seriously upset about Conor having lunch with Viviana. Was it a protective instinct or paranoia? It was possible that Ruffulo suspected his own daughter of conspiring against him. Could the man really be afraid of Viviana?

Conor was beginning to relax as the Ford turned onto Michigan Avenue and the big takeaway hit him like a hammer in the head. He was right in suspecting the meeting with Ruffulo would bear fruit. He would never represent Ruffulo, but now he had a few elusive answers in his notebook and an idea about who tipped off the cops to the warehouse burglary. For now, he was excited about Maureen's return from Springfield, even as he faced new concerns over his family's safety.

He would discontinue his dialogue with Big Jimmy. The gangster's objective in attempting to bribe Conor was twofold. First, Conor was to drop the warehouse investigation or face unspecified horrors, including possible harm to his family. Secondly, if Conor saw Viviana again, the man would first inform Maureen that her husband was an adulterer. Then, after an appropriate period of mental anguish, he would do something unpleasant, like disembowel the lawyer and deposit his corpse in the Calumet River.

Chapter 20

Wednesday, October 16, 1917

It was the Dolans' fourteenth anniversary, not to mention the morning after his Chicago White Sox defeated the Giants to win The World Series in seven games, and the couple had made special celebration plans for the evening. It hadn't been easy getting Maureen to take young Liam to live temporarily with Conor's aunt in Springfield. She had absolutely refused to leave their home until she realized the threat to Liam was real. In the past four weeks she'd gotten Liam into a Catholic school in Springfield to finish out the term. The whole affair had upended all of their lives and would no doubt cause serious mental stress to their son, but the possible alternatives justified extreme measures. Tonight, they would try to leave all their problems in a drawer.

Maureen had come home from Springfield for the occasion and to pick up some things for Liam. Conor wanted them both to stay in Springfield until this was all sorted, but Maureen would have none of it. She'd made her mind up. She would return to Springfield on Monday, then back home to Bridgeport within a couple of weeks, barring any ominous development. For tonight at least, they would try to regain some sense of normalcy. Conor had two tickets to the most popular play in Chicago.

Under the circumstances, time and distance had been Conor's allies in the whole affair. Not only with Maureen and Liam, but with Viviana as well. He had not heard from or communicated with Viviana since the meeting with Ruffulo. Should he tell Maureen about Viviana? But there was nothing to confess. Nothing happened between him and Viviana. Impure thoughts were only a crime in the Catholic Church. Still, if he told his wife about their lunch now, she might think he'd been hiding something and cause her unnecessary stress. At least that's what he told himself.

He'd considered surprising her with the theater tickets, but she wouldn't appreciate the lack of notice. She'd want to wear the right outfit, fix her hair, all the niceties in which Maureen rarely engaged. The play, *Turn to the Right*, was a wildly popular family comedy/drama at Cohan's Grand Opera House on Clark at Washington. They could forget their problems and celebrate for two or three hours and be thankful for their lives and family. Maureen would be alright at the house this week. Flynn and Lefty Hawk would make certain of it.

Instead, he surprised her with the letter that arrived last Friday from Private Patrick Dolan at Camp Logan, Texas. He thought about not opening it until she arrived but couldn't resist. He was certain she would understand. Patrick was eager for the adventure that lay ahead. He wished them a happy anniversary, sent his love and promised to write soon, hopefully from France. According to the newspapers, American troops were not expected on the front lines until June of next year and the war might be over by then.

With the euphoria of the letter behind her and resettled into their bungalow, Maureen seemed more excited about her investigative research than their coming evening at the theater. The Springfield Library, she explained, contained an exhaustive collection of English language publications from around the world; most notably, *The Paris Herald*, a self-proclaimed "international" newspaper owned by *The New York Herald* and headquartered in Paris, France. Maureen produced a notebook, handwritten, organized with tabs, filled with quotations and other details from various newspapers and magazine articles from the year 1916 and January through March of 1917.

Through an organized presentation of the contents, she explained what the British and French had called the "Shell Scandal" of 1916. Negligent logistical planning and lack of foresight had left the Allied powers desperately low on high explosive artillery munitions. The governments had failed to recognize that the old, shrapnel-based shells would be essentially useless in global trench warfare. In this war, artillery had become a tool for victory, not merely a tool of infantry support. The scandal even toppled a sitting British prime minister. Out of desperation, the Allies turned to the United States to meet the overwhelming demand for weapons of war; specifically, the chemicals to manufacture high explosives.

It was estimated that through 1915 some twenty-five percent of all artillery shells fired had consistently failed to explode. But 1916 revealed a new pattern. Maureen had found a series of articles, almost all based on eyewitness interviews with front line soldiers, that suggested up to forty percent of Allied high explosive shells failed to explode during the November 1916 Somme Offensive. Curiously, there were no official government reports of the increased rate of dud munitions. The figure was not foolproof but fit perfectly into the theory that Wellborn had been a German operative whose mission was to disable as much Allied ammunition as possible.

Conor was transfixed but still skeptical until she produced a mimeograph copy of a photograph from a 1913 issue of *Americana Germanica*, the official publication of the National German-American Alliance (NGAA), an organization dedicated to supporting the Kaiser and promoting friendship between the United States and Germany. They also raised funds for the German war effort. NGAA had come under strict scrutiny since America declared war and was expected to lose its charter in the coming weeks.

The photograph, taken at the organization's Philadelphia headquarters, pictured three executive board members presenting the "Fatherland Service Award" to a man named Bruno Hammerschmidt, known to Conor Dolan as none other than Clifford Wellborn. There was no mistaking the face.

"He was a German agent," Maureen concluded.

"Maybe, but it wasn't illegal then to be on speaking terms with the Kaiser. Maybe two things were true at once."

"What do you mean?"

"I mean he was certainly a Kaiser lover, but it's a good bet now that the Germans pumped big bucks into his business. He owed them. If his German friends pulled the pin on Wellborn, he might have ended up in Alcatraz. So maybe they were putting the squeeze on him. With all the legitimate money Wellborn was making, he didn't need to become a saboteur."

Maureen was a quick study. "So, Wellborn might have been the owner in name only."

"Right, but our friend Wellborn was reaping the profits. Given the chance, I'd say he would have dumped the old Kaiser. I remember about a year and a half ago when the attaché from the German Embassy was expelled for running a spy ring. His name was Franz von Papen, and he was found to be the head of a major German spy ring that was trying to buy up American chemicals and explosive manufacturing companies. Their aim was to slow the flow of reliable arms to the Allies. I'm betting they were into warehouses as well as manufacturers."

"You mean they were also buying up brokers?"

"At least one broker—Riverside—and the government investigation missed it. They planted Wellborn and helped him move up in the explosive export business. He was sabotaging the chemicals for the Germans so the Allies would be firing harmless shells. Even the time frame lines up. The sabotage was an element in the spring offensive coming from the Germans next year. This was all part of the German defense plan."

They sat on the front porch chairs with a whiskey while waiting for the cab. He said, "I fully expected you would do a good job, Maureen, but not this good. You filled in the spaces. I admit to having my doubts because there was a fair chance this might all end up helping the English and I know how you feel about that."

"I'll learn to live with it, even if it helps the bloody king. With a son on the way to a trench in Europe, I'm beginning to see the world differently. If one shell explodes that might otherwise have fizzled out, we might be saving Patrick's life."

After all these years, Maureen could still surprise him with some profound comment or insightful observation. It only meant that Conor continued to underestimate his wife. Maureen was a survivor. She didn't expect life to be fair. Like a boxer who refuses to stay on the canvas, Maureen could be put down but would never stay down. Yet she was capable of evolving, growing. "I never thought of it like that. Now we have to decide what to do with the information. Flynn might have an idea. The sabotage operation is shut down for now with Riverside out of business, but this could mean our own government knows about the German involvement now. I don't know where this will lead, but at least Liam won't be here."

"I'd rather carry a fecking pistol in my underskirt than leave here. Liam will stay in Springfield to end of semester. Sure I'll go down for a visit every week until this is over, but no one is chasing me from my home again." There was no arguing with her. She'd made up her mind and that was that.

The big picture was becoming clearer. Someone discovered Wellborn was working for the Germans and moved to eliminate him from the cast. Graves's assignment might have been to confirm that the chemicals were tampered with, sabotaged. But if that were the case, Graves was working for one of the Allied governments. With Wellborn gone, the sabotage would end now, like cutting off the head of the snake. As difficult as it was to believe, it now appeared possible that the U.S. Government or people working for it, had hired a gangster to commit murder on American soil. *Talk about high explosives.*

THE GRAND OPERA HOUSE, MANAGED by and now named after George M. Cohan, was a sight to behold, a palace of gold and bronze, of polished brass rails and velvet chairs. From the interior entryway, Conor imagined himself looking into the floral-patterned bud of an elegant crimson rose, framed by arched rows of soft lighting along the ceiling, all funneling down to its core, the stage where so much theatrical history had been made.

Their first-row mezzanine seats, although a level up from the main floor, were close to and intimately situated just above the stage. This performance, like every one before it for thirty-four weeks running, was sold out, even in the high balcony and along the walls of tiered private boxes. The entire cast and crew would finally pack up next week and take the play on the road.

Maureen had even purchased a new gown for the evening and drew stares from seated gentlemen, and even some ladies, on their escorted walk to the seats. The ankle-length dress was a rich midnight blue with delicate strapped shoulders and accessorized with long pale-blue gloves. Around her waist, a thin blue lace wraparound fell to just below the calves. Her Crimson hair was done up with a single curl falling to each ear and turned forward. She had never been more beautiful.

The play itself told an endearingly funny and sometimes heart-wrenching story about the trials and travails of a widowed mother and a young couple's determination to find a life together in the face of loss, tragedy and injustice. Well into the final act, two reformed villains—friends of the male protagonist—met two young local girls, whom Conor expected they would shortly marry on the way to a happy ending. As the two ladies made their entry from stage left, time stopped for Conor Dolan. Fate was conspiring to ruin his life, one way or the other, but not before an extended period of mental anguish. As the taller of the two women turned toward the audience to deliver a line, he swore that her eyes looked past and through the hundreds of attentive playgoers, like a spotlight, to focus directly on his face. Conor almost felt like she'd been expecting to see him.

This was a pure coincidence that Conor had not considered. He had not spoken to Viviana since their lunch at the College Inn and had even managed not to think of her all day. He knew the woman was an actress, but Chicago was home to at least fifty theaters. He told himself he was overacting. She could not possibly have recognized him in the crowd, not with the theater lights focused on the stage. As an actress, she would be concentrating on her performance. He'd known a few actresses and actors in his time. It seemed all of them suffered from brief, sporadic attacks of narcissism, always and only occurring during a performance and hardly worth criticizing. Conor Dolan was the last thing on her mind tonight.

As the play ended, the crowd went wild. On the second ovation, the crowd rose to their feet. Cheers, clapping, whistles and hoots. As the cast returned for what would be its fourth curtain call, an elderly usher tapped Conor on the shoulder. "Excuse me, Sir. Are you Mister Dolan?"

"I am." He wasn't a surgeon. Nobody called lawyers out of the theater.

Holding out his hand, the man said, "I have a note for you, Sir. If you and your lady would care to follow me . . ."

There was enough light now to read the brief note. *"Wonderful to see you. Please bring your wife for a backstage tour."*

He wanted to decline politely and quietly, but it was too late. "What is it, Conor? Who's sending you a note in the theater?"

"Seems one of the actors recognized me. She's offered us a backstage tour."

"Oh, sure that'll be a great craic." She was already up and holding her shawl. "Let's be off then."

VIVIANA WAS WAITING, STILL IN COSTUME, as the usher guided them through the door marked, "Cast and Crew Only." The actress addressed Maureen first, "You must be Mrs. Dolan. Wonderful to meet you. I'm Viviana Bensini."

Was it possible the two women had gotten together and planned some humiliating revenge against him? Had old Mrs. Fogarty spilled the beans to his wife? Did she tell that blabber-mouthed Father Brendan? It was Brendan who'd given him the tickets. Or maybe Brendan and

Maureen arranged everything except the backstage tour to teach him a lesson. Viviana recognizing him would be frosting on their cake. Maureen was certainly clever enough.

If his wife was acting, she was immersed in the role and commanding the stage. "How do you do, Miss Bensini? I don't recall my husband mentioning you. A client?"

Conor could hear the rumblings from his stomach and felt short of breath. The air became stuffy—he needed fresh air. Then Viviana replied, "I would know your husband anywhere, Mrs. Dolan. He saved my life."

It was not a trap. It was not Maureen's revenge. Viviana had thought this out. Her purpose was not to embarrass him but to toy with him and satisfy her curiosity about Maureen. She knew he would be fumbling for a plausible explanation, so she assumed the initiative and let him off the hook, in effect limiting the damage. He said, "I wouldn't go that far, Miss Bensini."

Viviana waved him off. "Your husband is trying to be humble, but he rescued me from attackers at the last peace march several months back."

"I recall the march," Maureen replied. "I had my own trouble at the same march. Come to think of it, he saved both of us."

Viviana gave them the grand tour, the makeup department, costume room, even a few empty dressing rooms periodically occupied by great stars of the theater. But the highlight of the tour was a private audience with the star of the show, Maybel Bert, the beloved star of *Daddy Long-Legs*, which played in Chicago to sold-out crowds and rave reviews only a few years ago. Miss Bert even signed a photograph and playbill for Maureen.

On the short walk to the car, Conor decided he'd have to risk another meeting with Viviana. The woman was now in a place from which she could never return. She'd likely tipped off the cops to the warehouse burglary, made an anonymous telephone call to the general police number, thus avoiding detectives and higher ups likely warned to steer clear. If Graves had been captured at the warehouse, he might well have implicated Ruffulo, thus potentially exposing the persons or entity behind this, not to mention sending her father to jail.

Had Ruffulo figured out his daughter betrayed him? Or was his objection to their association purely possessiveness? Viviana would know because her mother would have told her. If she knew more about the whole affair, she might be ready to confide in Conor now.

Chapter 21

Monday, October 21, 1917

It had been a brutal week on the 3200 block of South Normal. On the night of October 17, a German submarine attacked and destroyed the U.S. Army troopship Antilles in the Bay of Biscay. The loss of sixty-seven American lives, included the twenty-year-old son and only child of the Dolans' good friends down the block, Olaf and Greta Larsen. Maureen had spent most of her days at home trying to console poor Missus Larsen. The two were now life members of that most dreaded of sororities, The Mothers of Fallen Sons.

Conor dropped Maureen at Dearborn Station to catch the Springfield train and was ten minutes late for his meeting with Eammon Flynn. He'd thought about telephoning Viviana's hotel but she didn't have a private telephone and Ruffulo's reach might easily extend to the hotel staff. With Titus Freeman out of the game and reduced to clerical tasks and court filings, he decided to send Flynn to arrange a meet with Viviana.

Conor knew the thirty-four-week run of *Turn to the Right* was coming to an end soon. The entire production would be hitting the road for a multi-city, one year run. It shouldn't matter to Conor Dolan if Viviana stayed in Chicago or left forever, but the question was constantly in the back of his mind now. She would be safer away from the city, but some part of him wanted her to stay. He couldn't deny it any longer.

He spotted Flynn at a quiet booth in Dick's Diner on Randolph. Things were moving too quickly. If he didn't get control of himself soon, he'd have no family or friends to worry about. His life would simply leap from one lie to another until he lost track. It would be a straight drop from there.

Conor ordered poached eggs and coffee and had to watch Flynn slurp through a disgusting menagerie of fried sausage, runny eggs and some kind of smashed up, yellow potatoes. "So, what did she say? Will she meet with me?"

"Oh, yes, indeed. Ye have a dinner reservation on Wednesday evening at a little place in Garfield Park called Tuto Italia."

"I didn't ask you to arrange a dinner date. A park bench would have been fine."

Flynn shrugged and wiped the egg from his lips, probably to be certain Conor could see the smirk. "Sorry, Counselor. Those were her conditions."

He told Flynn about Maureen's library discoveries and the photograph of Wellborn/Hammerschmidt. Flynn quickly came to the same conclusion as Conor had. The detective said, "With Wellborn dead the Allies' problem is fixed, so whoever is working so hard to shut ye down is trying to prevent a major scandal."

"Or worse," Conor added. "It could even cause a rift between The U.S. and Britain, depending on who was behind it. So, what have *you* found out, Flynn?"

"I found out I would be able to go to the moving pictures once in a while if ye would pay me. The police pension doesn't create millionaires."

"Alright. Don't worry about that. Tell me what I'm paying for."

Flynn pulled out his notebook and began flipping through pages. "The warehouse is still operating as of last Tuesday. Interestingly, the employees were kept on, except for one who was fired not long after the burglary."

"Let me guess. Tommy Rafferty."

"One and the same. I managed to get his address for ye. He may have some interesting things to say if they fired him because of yeer visit."

Conor took the note from Flynn. It was a Pullman address. "It's possible. Nice work, Flynn. Let's pay him a visit after breakfast." The waitress came to refill their coffee cups. Thankfully, she left with the disgusting residue of Flynn's breakfast.

"I think I should come with ye Wednesday night when ye meet the Bensini woman. You know I don't trust her. I could lie back in the weeds and keep an eye on ye."

"I appreciate that, but I'll be okay."

Flynn shrugged. "Your call."

"I still think Viviana blew the whistle on her father the night of the warehouse burglary. She thought if Graves were caught, he would expose Ruffulo's connection. The state courts would finally have a case on him, something to put him away. She had something special with that boyfriend Ruffulo scared off."

"How does she get all this information?"

"Her mother hears everything. Viviana really hates him. Apparently, Ruffulo mistreats the mother."

Flynn started cleaning his teeth with a fork. "Maybe so," said the wily old detective. "Maybe not."

"Okay. What does that mean?"

"It means she might be playing ye, Conor."

Conor signaled the waitress for more coffee. "Explain."

"So, she warns ye off the investigation on the streetcar one day. But ye keep right on digging. A few weeks later, her father does the same exact thing, but in stronger terms. That sounds to me like they're working together. I think he sent her t' visit ye on the bus that day."

"No, no, you're wrong, Flynn. I saved her life at the peace march."

Flynn laughed. It was annoying because the old coot was laughing *at* him, not *with* him. "That's what the girl tells ye, Conor. I think she was at the rally that day for the purpose of meeting ye. Ye're a smart lawyer, but still an easy mark for women, especially a smart beauty like that."

The lawyer shook his head while fumbling in his wallet for breakfast money. "Oh no. I don't think so." Conor knew he had a track record of misunderstanding women, but he wasn't as inept as his friend believed. It wasn't possible Viviana was deceiving him. It simply wasn't possible. As they rose from the table, he handed Flynn some folded bills. "Here's your money. It's seven dollars for the week. I was going to give you ten before you said that about Viviana."

THEY TOOK THE FORD DOWN TO PULLMAN

on the chance that Tommy Rafferty might still be unemployed and at home. The man was not only at home but was ready to sing like a bird. Tommy was holding a baby, and Conor could hear another one crying in the background.

"Oh sure, Conor, come in, please. Me wife is working as a maid these days t' make ends meet until I start me new job. I'll be tending bar at a local saloon."

He led them into a tiny kitchen. With only two chairs and a baby seat, Conor decided to stand, letting old Flynn rest his legs. After introducing the retired detective, Conor said, "The saloon wouldn't by chance be Bell's, would it?"

"It is and do ye know Bell?"

"I do. Nice lady. Have you met her son?"

"Not yet. Something I should be aware of, is there?"

"Let's just say keep an eye on him and don't let him get to you. Bell needs someone she can trust right now. Let's leave it at that. Tell her we're friends."

Tommy poured them all a whiskey while holding the baby with one arm. "*Sláinte,* lads. So how can I help?"

"Too early for me, Tommy," said Conor. Flynn had suggested Conor take the lead as he knew the man from previous encounters. "When we last spoke, you were very helpful, but I could tell you were worried about your job at the time."

Tommy nodded. "I was indeed, but sure it doesn't matter now. They fired me the day after ye left the warehouse. I heard they went bankrupt, the miserable fecks. Fair play t' them."

"So, I take it someone reported our conversation?"

"They did that."

Having downed his own shot, Flynn reached for Conor's glass. Conor asked, "Can you tell us anything more, Tommy? Anything you might have been reluctant to tell me before?"

"I can, Conor, and I will. About a year ago, a group of three men came to the warehouse one afternoon. They were from Riverside corporate office with instructions to inspect a large chemical shipment we'd recently received. 'Twas headed for France and was the first of its kind that I'd seen. I thought nothing of it. Strange thing was that they had gas masks and cases and my crew had to vacate the warehouse while they worked. Usually took about an hour."

"Did you ever question the men?" Flynn asked.

"I did now. Straight away I asked if my workers had anything to worry about. One of them told me not to worry, said they were only doing the inspections for our safety. Sounded reasonable enough then."

"How often did they come?" Conor asked.

"Roughly every month, whenever a shipment would arrive."

If they needed confirmation for Conor's theory, they'd found it. Graves's primary mission was to gather samples from the barrels for analysis. Once sabotage was confirmed, the next step in the plan was to eliminate Clifford Wellborn.

On the drive back from the South Side, they considered how the plan went wrong. Flynn said, "Sure Graves was always going to murder that poor newsboy, but if ye're right, Viviana forced him to adapt on the spot by tipping off the cops. Graves tried to kill Mumbles on the scene, but his shot was forced, hurried, and he only wounded the boy. I'd say Graves would have come back and killed him in the hospital, had the Good Lord not called the lad home."

Flynn's analysis raised another possibility. "What if Graves did come back to the hospital? What if he or someone working for him got into the room and smothered the kid? Maybe the lad didn't die of an infection."

Was it possible? Could someone have gotten past the cop at the door? The old patrolman had seemed more interested in snoozing than security. Someone might have easily donned a hospital gown and walked right by him. "I agree, Flynn, and I have a candidate in mind."

"Graves, either on his own or under Ruffulo's direction."

The German operation might include other ports and involve other export companies. At this point, there was no way of guessing how big an international sabotage operation they had stumbled into. With the pieces of the puzzle finally coming together to form a partial picture, Conor said, "I think we have enough now to confront Gianelli."

Flynn had a way of scolding him when the lawyer was becoming too aggressive, a certain way of slowly shaking his head as he rolled his eyes. "Wrong word, Conor me boy. Confrontation is precisely what ye don't want. The lid is clamped tight on this thing, and I doubt Gianelli would risk his career t' pry it open."

"Why don't we find out?"

"Well, he's still on a day watch. I'd say this is the best time t' catch him at Harrison Street. He'll be sorting paperwork."

"Let's give it a try."

"But, Conor, perhaps let me do the talking. He won't reopen this, but he might give us something—if we don't piss him off."

GIANELLI WAS AT HIS DESK IN THE COMMON detective room on the second floor when the two men appeared unannounced from the staircase. The detective seemed to deflate upon seeing Conor, his eyes and head dropping toward the desktop. Flynn's status gave him *carte blanche* access to every area of the Harrison Street Station. Conor hung back a step or two as Flynn approached the desk. Gianelli spoke without raising his eyes. "My day was going so well, Flynn. Twenty minutes and I'd have been out of here." Then the detective pointed to the sitting area at the front of the room.

With all of them seated at a long table, Gianelli opened the impromptu meeting. "I'm here for *you*, Flynn, you only, and you have fifteen minutes. The detective made an obvious effort to avoid eye contact with Conor. *Fine with me.*

Flynn laid out the whole case for him. Viviana, her father, her mother; Graves, and his relationship with Ruffulo; the missing bankruptcy file; Rafferty; Conor's meeting with Ruffulo and the threats; Wellborn and his connections with the Germans; even Maureen's research.

With everything on the table, Gianelli spoke directly to Flynn in a low voice. "Do you realize that the minute you leave here, I'll be grilled by my commander about what I told you? Worse is that they'll ask about what you told me."

"Sorry about that," Flynn replied. "I should have approached you at the saloon or somewhere else."

"No, that's not true. If we were seen at a saloon or at my house, it would be worse. Here I can lie believably." He was going to tell them something important. Gianelli fidgeted in his chair and glanced across the room to account for all the ears. "I don't like what's going on, but there's nothing I can do. I already know everything you told me. But I know one more thing as well, one thing you don't know. If I tell you, I want your word this will remain confidential."

"Of course," Flynn said.

Looking directly at Conor, Gianelli added. "Him too."

"I swear it."

"Let me confirm what you already suspect. We have verbal orders from above to take no further action on the deaths of Kazmirski and Wellborn."

Conor let Flynn handle the closing. "And what exactly does 'above' mean?"

Gianelli smiled. "If you learn the answer to that question, be sure not to tell me."

Chapter 22

Wednesday evening, October 23

Coming home to an empty house was a lonely feeling. He still had Dillon, of course, but the hound couldn't warm his bed or saturate the house with those peculiar and sometimes annoying sights and sounds that make the place a home. With an hour to kill before dinner, he stopped at Scanlon's while walking the dog.

Despite the diversion, he arrived at the restaurant fifteen minutes early to avoid Viviana having to sit alone. He took a circuitous route, keeping a careful lookout for unwanted followers. She had chosen the place well. Tuto Italia was a neighborhood joint on Lake Street under the "L" train structure and near the Garfield Park

Conservatory, the real deal with checkered tablecloths and soft lighting along the walls to emphasize the hand-painted murals of Italian street and dining scenes. The clatter of the trains above seemed only to enhance the quaintness and urban charm of the place. It was a sure bet her father never made the trek to Garfield Park from River Forest.

Viviana's outfits were becoming increasingly *avant-garde* with each encounter. This dress was rose-colored and plain over a burnt orange, long-sleeve top with a wide, lay-down collar. The skirt section dropped free of petticoats, defined only by a simple belt of the same fabric and color. The net effect was to highlight the hair, again done up with the familiar twin curls around the ears. He held the chair as Viviana promenaded toward the corner table. "You look beautiful," he said. It was a clumsy start to a serious meeting.

He ordered a bottle of Chianti as Viviana perused the menu. "Does Maureen know we're meeting tonight?" She had this need to see him squirm.

"Maureen is out of town visiting relatives with our son for a while—out of a sense of precaution."

Her face softened; the glint in her blue eyes disappeared. "Sorry about my father."

"Oh, that."

"I heard about the meeting from my mother. Of course, she didn't talk about the content of your visit, but I can guess. I'm so sorry." And the eyes told him it was true.

Despite the real and compelling reason for seeing her, he didn't begin with the warehouse affair. "I know the show closed. The papers said the entire cast will be touring. Is that right?"

She was going to make him own up and ask a direct question. "You mean am I leaving town?"

He sipped the Chianti for what little support it might offer. "You know I do. Why toy with me?"

"I only want you to be honest, not just to me but to yourself. You're an accomplished fence walker, Conor."

"So, I've been told."

Viviana ordered the entrees, some pasta *speciale* or other. He didn't much care and decided to change the subject to an equally grim topic. "You know he's been following you. Don't you?"

"I do now, but don't worry. I was careful."

"Good. I think he'll have me neutered if he finds us together again. The crazy part is that we haven't done anything wrong. Nothing."

It was Viviana who reached for the glass this time. "Who's toying with whom? The fact is that both of us are exactly where we want to be tonight. Can we get the business part out of the way? Tell me, why is it you think you invited me here tonight?"

She was right. He'd been giddy as a puppet on a string since she agreed to meet him tonight and knew down deep, she would pick a quiet restaurant. He'd even donned evening dress for the occasion. He was only kidding *himself*. "Alright. Your father issued a vague threat against me and my family if I don't back off this investigation. He's also very unhappy about us having lunch at your hotel. I'd rather not think of what he'd do if he finds about tonight."

With her lips to the wine glass, she captured his stare from just over the rim and the corners of her mouth turned up ever so slightly. "Tonight's not over." She was having fun with this. Rather than sound like an eejit, he said nothing, and she picked up the conversation. "In any case, I can handle my father's lap dog, Mickey Lucchesi. I'm aware he's keeping an eye on me."

The salad arrived. He poured them more wine. The music was gentle, accordions and violins, old country Italian. He couldn't understand the words, except for *amore* in every second lyric. The wine was mellowing. He signaled Giuseppi for another bottle and said, "**You tipped off the cops to the warehouse burglary.**" He stopped to wait for a reaction that didn't come. "Didn't you?"

"That's the second time you asked me that. The answer is still no."

Her left palm was on the table. Instinctively, he covered it with his right hand. It felt good, too good, and she didn't flinch. "If you did, it was a big step that could have had consequences for you."

"I doubt it. You see, I hate my father, but he doesn't hate me. Maybe it's just his vanity, but he would never harm me. My mother is a different story."

"Do you think your father might be working for a greater power here?"

She laughed. "He's a gangster, not a spy. My father only cares about himself. He's a pig."

Conor hardly tasted the ravioli, or whatever it was, but the excitement of being alone with her boosted the wine's effect. For dessert, she ordered tiramisu and cappuccino. He needed to call her a cab and get home before this went any further. But he'd already betrayed his wife. He wanted this woman, so what did it matter? *It matters. Whatever you do, stop pretending you're being coerced, victimized. At least be a man about it. You're not a naïve youngster anymore.*

She said, "Well, under the circumstances, I think it's best I order a cab home. We don't need to take chances."

"You don't have to go home," he said. "I could get us a room at the Graemere Hotel across the park. We could walk there."

This time Viviana took *his* hand. "Are you certain, Conor? I don't want to . . ."

He'd had enough of excuses, rationalizations, and logical explanations. Tonight, he would surrender to his dark angels. He would find a way to live with himself tomorrow.

Part III

Chapter 23

Monday evening, April 16, 1918

With Easter in the books and Conor's investigation having hit a brick wall, the slaughter in Europe had only intensified. Last November, the British finally reached Passchendaele, but not before suffering horrendous casualties over the course of the senseless, six-month campaign. In December, Bolshevik Russia opened peace negotiations with Germany and in March of 1918, signed a humiliating peace treaty that effectively freed up fifty German divisions from the Eastern Front. Only last week, Germany launched a dreaded spring offensive, her final push to end the war before the Americans could enter the fray and turn the tide. The papers were calling it The

Battle of Lys in the British sector or Armentieres. They had captured the supply ports of Calais, Dunkirk, and Boulogne.

On the home front, the local papers had been raising red flags about a local outbreak of Influenza. The first Conor had heard of it was through a front page, non-headline story a couple of weeks ago. For whatever reason, he'd stowed the article in his wallet and had added two or three more to his collection since then, including one from yesterday reporting an unusual outbreak at the Great Lakes Naval Station. He knew there was a problem with the Influenza in Spain, but Spain was long way from Lake Michigan and folks just seemed to go about their business without concern. On the "L" ride south that evening, he pulled out the original story to track the details best he could. The caption read:

ODD EPIDEMIC STRIKES 34 IN SINGLE OFFICE:
Thirty-four out of one hundred and twenty-five employees in the Freight Office of the Chicago, Milwaukee and St. Paul Railroad were taken ill yesterday and a number of them, including girl stenographers, were so sick that they had to be removed from their homes . . . The acting head of the health department said the outbreak showed symptoms of Influenza . . . Though the outbreak is not considered

serious, according to Dr. Kohler, health officers visited a number of people in their homes last night and took throat cultures in an effort to diagnose the disease.

The outbreak was something to keep an eye on, especially with a boy in a military camp. Meanwhile, the Dolans' lives had returned to some sense of normalcy. Young Liam had returned to Bridgeport and re-enrolled in Saint Bridget's school. The boy was adjusting well and the temperature from the warehouse investigation had cooled considerably. The Espionage Act had effectively killed all anti-war activities and public discussions. Americans who refused to be silenced were marking time in jail cells or camps across the country for raising a voice in support of peace.

Such was the state of affairs when Conor arrived home that evening from a long day of lawyering. He hadn't spoken to Viviana Bensini in months and had made no further progress on identifying the mysterious Mister Graves. Big Jimmy Ruffulo had likely covered his tracks. Still, Flynn maintained close contact with Detective Gianelli in hopes of a break and Titus Freeman was back keeping an eye on Mrs. Kelsey Wellborn with instructions to avoid Big Jim.

The Chicago winter had been brutal. The city endured one of its worst storms ever during the first week of January, and the Arctic blow lingered into early spring. Chicagoans, especially its Irish and German immigrants, were weary of winter, weary of war, and weary of weighing every word before speaking in public. And American boys had still not begun to fill the cemeteries.

Conor saw the letter from Patrick on the dining room table before Maureen said a word. True to his promise, their young private had written often since arriving at Camp Logan. Grabbing the letter with one hand and his eyeglasses with the other, he skipped his usual stop at the liquor cabinet before settling into his chair.

Dear Ma and Pa,

Well, I can finally tell you that the 33rd Infantry Division will soon embark for France. I must be sparing with details, as our letters are all reviewed and security protocols must be observed. Of course, we will undergo more training on the continent before joining the fight, possibly for months. Have you heard that British soldiers are calling us "Doughboys?" I think the name is meant to be sarcastic, if good-natured, but our boys here all like it very much. I hope you are all doing well. Tell Liam I'm sorry to have not sent a birthday gift, but I will make it up to him. I don't know when I will be able to write *again, but in any event, I will certainly write promptly upon reaching French shore. Stay well and write to me at the same address.*

Love

Patrick

Maureen and Conor had just sat down to dinner when their telephone rang. "I have a call from Mrs. Gertrude Schmidt," came the operator's voice.

"Put her through, Operator. Thank you."

"Hello, Mister Dolan? I'm sorry to call your home, but I thought it might be important."

"That's fine, Mrs. Schmidt. Go ahead."

"Well, just after you left the office this evening, I was finishing the last correspondence when a woman came in and asked to see you."

"A woman?"

"Said she's a nurse. You met her some months back in connection with the Jan Kazmirski matter."

"From Cook County Hospital?"

"Yes. Her name is Gina Poletti."

The secretary had his undivided attention. Conor sat down in the chair beside the telephone nook and grabbed the notepad. "What did she say?"

"Something has been bothering her for the last few months. She thinks it's probably nothing but . . ."

"But what?"

"She will only tell you. I took her address, of course. The woman said she is off tonight and tomorrow. If you think it's important, she prefers you not come to the hospital."

Conor wasn't in the habit of leaving dinner on the plate and nearly forgot to wear his coat on the way out the door. He could hear Maureen as he left. "I'll warm it up for ye when ye get home."

Gina Poletti's home was a three-story, brick rowhouse beside a storefront shop called "Rotunno's Cheeses and Olive Oil." There was a staircase down to a fourth apartment at basement level and the nurse's first-floor flat was raised from ground level and accessible from a staircase. The three brass doorbells were unmarked, telling Conor that unsolicited visitors were uncommon at best and unwanted at worst. He chose the one on the left and recognized the nurse immediately as the door opened, even without the trademark nurse's kit. Her hair was parted down the middle and pulled back into a bun behind each ear. She was holding a toddler, and he could see two older children playing a card game in the front parlor.

"Thank you for coming, Mister Dolan. As I told your secretary, my husband thinks it's nothing but that's for you to decide."

"Is he here?"

"No. He works two jobs. We'll all be in bed when he gets home. My mother lives with us and helps with the kids."

They sat on the sofa after he moved a stack of folded clothing and towels. "I'm grateful, Missus Poletti. I'll try not to take up too much of your time. Mrs. Schmidt said you remembered something."

She put the toddler on the floor, lowered her head and took a deep breath. "The truth is I never forgot it. I was afraid to say anything."

He leaned forward. "Go on."

"I've been a nurse for a long time. Infection is a common cause of death, even now with drugs that help fight it. When someone dies inexplicably after surgery or a wound, doctors have a tendency to call it an infection and move on. It's a convenient diagnosis that often covers up a doctor's mistake."

"Do you have reason to believe that Jan Kazmirski did not die from an infection?"

"Possibly."

The two bigger kids began arguing, and one of them threw a baseball that missed its target, narrowly avoiding Conor's nose. After she calmed the kids down, Conor said, "What is it?"

"If I questioned a doctor's diagnosis, I'd be out on my ear. The resident made the call. He's young and brash. If you ask me, he's not much of a doctor. Jan Kazmirski did not have a fever on the day he died, and no one dies of an infection without a fever."

"Missus Poletti. If someone got into the room and smothered Jan Kazmirski, would it be apparent to the medical staff? I mean would there be evidence?"

She shook her head. "I'm not a doctor, but I can't imagine how anyone would know. Oh, Mister Dolan, will you keep my name out of it? If I gave evidence in court or to the police, that would be the end of my career."

"You have my word. But tell me, do you recall seeing any unfamiliar faces on the ward the night Jan died? Even a doctor or nurse you didn't recognize."

"As a matter of fact, I do, but I didn't make the connection. There was a man I didn't recognize. I thought he was a doctor. It's not unusual."

"Anything else? Did you see him near Jan's room? Was he holding anything?"

"I'm sorry, Mister Dolan. I just can't remember, other than I didn't know him."

"Can you give me any kind of description?"

"Sorry. He was just average."

Keeping the woman's confidence could be a fatal blow to a case against Graves and Ruffulo, but Conor's hands were tied. At least he had a lead on how Jan Kazmirski died.

MAUREEN WAS WAITING UP FOR HIM AND eager to hear about his visit with Gina Poletti. She agreed that Ruffulo had no call for worry so long as Graves's identity remained a secret. But did Ruffulo order Mumbles's murder? Did Graves act on his own? Worse yet, did the government order it? Nothing they had uncovered to date pointed directly to a government intelligence operation, despite the logical inferences from the totality of circumstances. So, who was Graves's puppet master? It was possible the gangster, Ruffulo, was the real puppet here. In any case, if they could identify and locate Graves, the whole house of cards might collapse, thus exposing all the naked secrets inside. "Find Graves," Conor said, "and we find our answers."

Conor might truly be opening Pandora's Box. If the Department of Justice was in any way involved, its people would stop at nothing to cover up the operation. For the first time, it occurred to Conor that he might be playing way out of his league. Even if he found all the evidence he needed, what could he do? He couldn't force local authorities to prosecute, especially in defiance of a DOJ mandate, and he was powerless to act against the government. He couldn't even go to the newspapers because nearly all of them were pushing official government propaganda. *Nearly all, but there might be one or two* . . . The lawyer knew he could never let this go, and hoped he wasn't painting himself—and his family— into a corner.

Chapter 24

Tuesday, July 9, 1918

With American troops finally being deployed along the Western Front, the Russians were out of the war, and the German spring offensive was making territorial gains. The papers were calling it the Ludendorf Offensive. There was no expectation of peace into the near future and the Allies had suffered a number of battlefield setbacks. On the bright side, the effect of fresh American troops provided a distinct air of optimism, as the Americans had not yet deployed in sufficient numbers to turn the tide. General Pershing had insisted on both intensive training and direct American command before sending his men into battle.

For their part, the Germans were going all out to achieve a strategically significant breakthrough before having to face the Doughboys in action. For the moment, the British were holding the line, if only barely.

Independence Day celebrations were especially loud and visible in 1918, with parades, bands, fireworks, and speeches to be seen and heard virtually everywhere coast to coast. The Wilson Administration had worked diligently this year to use the holiday as a means of solidifying support for the war. On its face, at least, America had never been closer to real solidarity.

Despite Flynn's best efforts and Titus Freeman's surveillance of the major hotels, Conor's team had failed to identify Mister Graves. Since mid-June, Conor had even made a systematic re-canvas of all bellboys and hotel clerks in an expanded list of fourteen hotels, all without result. Maybe The Congress Plaza wasn't his exclusive spot. It looked very much like the investigation had hit a dead end.

He and Maureen walked Dillon late that night and stopped at Scanlon's for a nightcap. They were discussing Patrick's impending deployment to Europe, when Maureen said, "Sure why don't ye send me back to the library?"

Conor lifted the shot glass carefully to his lips to prevent spillage and sipped. Sipping was permissible in the evening, especially to clear the rim of the glass. "To do what this time? Study law? Truthfully, you'd make a successful lawyer. Most of them fear the bulldog type."

"Actually, I was thinking about yeer investigation."

She had his attention. "Go on."

"So ye have a good description of Graves. What else do ye know?"

He shrugged. "Nothing."

Her chin lowered, lips curled. "Not true. Ye know for a fact that he was in town t' perform some nefarious deed. If we could discover his prior sins, we'd know exactly who the man works for."

He thought for a minute. "Yeah. It just might help, and we won't confine the search to gang murders. I'm thinking you look for anything involving the war, sabotage, political assignation. We'll keep open minds."

"Brilliant idea, Conor. So, I'll start tomorrow. Yeah?"

His wife was having him on, as usual. He smiled. "Off to the library with you then. Maybe we can get this ball rolling again."

LEFTY HAWK WAS PACING AROUND ON their front porch when the couple arrived home with Dillon after ten that evening. It looked ominous. Lefty hurried to meet them on the front walk. "Toad came to see me. Gimpy's gone missing."

Conor had feared just this scenario. It was the reason he'd called Gimpy off any surveillance of Big Jimmy Ruffulo. "Where's Toad?"

"Out looking for Gimpy, along with every newsboy I could muster."

"Did you make a formal report?"

"Not yet."

"Alright. Come on in. Tell me what you know."

Lefty explained that Gimpy appeared as usual for the morning rush at his Jackson Street corner and left around ten o'clock for a ride down south to check on his other location. According to Toad, he never showed up. Nobody had seen him since then and he didn't tell anyone he'd be away. Besides, he would never ignore his business during the evening rush.

"So, what about the cops?" Conor asked.

"Are you joking? We're talking about a newsboy. You and me got a better shot at finding him ourselves. You know that. So, I got my own damn police department working on it. First thing is we gotta find him alive. Either way, I'm gonna personally kill whoever done this."

Conor sat the cop on the sofa and gave Lefty a drink to calm him down a bit. "Let's think this through. If they wanted to kill him, they would have done it straight off.

Shoot him and get away. Why take a chance hiding a body or killing him somewhere else? Twice the chance of getting caught."

"What're you getting at?" Lefty asked.

Maureen interrupted. "He's saying that Gimpy might have found out something, something ye're not supposed to know. Either that or he's getting too close."

Lefty was recovering his wits. "Yeah. That or they want to pump him for information."

Conor said, "Okay, his South Side corner is near here. Right?"

"Yeah. It's actually a bunch of corners around Thirty-Third and Giles, near the Illinois Guard Armory. He never made it there."

"How does he get there? Does he take the same route every day?"

"It depends where he is. Usually, he'll take the State Street streetcar all the way or he'll hop on the 'L'."

"So, let's get busy covering all the routes during the relevant time periods. Talk to everyone, especially passengers who travel the same route at the same time regularly."

"I'll have them work the stations at street levels and the newsstands as well."

Maureen had been taking it in from the sofa, facing the two men. She said, "I think we all know who the prime suspects are. Conor and I have firsthand experience at being kidnapped off the street."

Both men nodded. The conversation simply hadn't progressed that far. "Lefty, will you come with me tomorrow to visit our friend at the American Protective League Headquarters?"

"Try n' stop me."

"I think if they have Gimpy, he'll show up tonight unharmed. They might have grabbed him to ask the same questions they asked me. I still think they're operating in the dark, but we'll know soon enough."

THE NEXT MORNING CONOR FOUND TOAD on the Jackson Street corner hawking papers with another kid. Gimpy was noticeably absent. "No word, Toad?"

"Nuttin', Mista Dolan. I saw Lefty early this morning and we got kids out retracing his steps t' see what they can find out."

"Good. I'm on my way over to the alley now to get Lefty. We'll pay our friend at the APL a visit and find out what he knows."

The APL was the most obvious suspect in Gimpy's disappearance. If they took the kid, they'd have no reason to deny it, but simply make up some excuse or other related to the war effort and *patriotic* duty. After all, the thugs worked under the umbrella of the government and the local cops had been warned to stay out of their way. It was pure insanity on a national scale.

On the five-minute walk to Newsboy Alley, Conor reviewed the script for his interview. Despite the evidence, he would have to be convinced that this was the work of the APL. During his own kidnapping ordeal, their questions had revealed only a rudimentary understanding of the dynamics and the players in this grand conspiratorial scheme. Conor had come to believe that the APL were operating only on information published in the daily papers. A "murdered arms broker in the service of the Allies," a "German Luger casing recovered at the scene of Allied arms burglary" and the salacious assumption splashed across page one of more than one daily: "Did German Agents assassinate Chicago arms broker?" The totality of the APL questions to Conor that night supported nothing more than this simplistic understanding of the reported facts. Conor believed they were acting on their own because the Bureau of Investigation had purposely excluded them. He and Lefty would soon find out if he was off base.

DESPITE THE LACK OF AN APPOINTMENT, Joseph Norton consented to see the men immediately.

Conor remembered Norton had introduced himself as the local APL Director, a retired U.S. Army Captain, and an advertising executive. Anyone following the local news stories would have known as much. In a few short months, Norton had become a feared and powerful arbiter on questions of "loyalty" and "patriotism." The inner offices were less than palatial, with a dozen or so flimsy chairs and a few reclaimed desks in the outer area. A cork board dominated the north wall, filled with newspaper articles, photographs, and myriad documents in no obvious order.

Norton's inner office was equally spartan, although impeccably orderly; with file cabinets, stacks of neatly organized files, notebooks, and a telephone atop the only impressive piece of furniture in the building, a mahogany desk situated in front of a window facing Halsted Street.

Norton was seated at the desk, eyes down, and did not rise as Conor entered. After a few seconds, he looked up, pointed to one of the two chairs and said, "Welcome, gentlemen. Won't you have a seat?"

"Thank you, Mister Norton, and thank you for seeing me on such short notice. This is a friend of mine, Officer Hawk."

"How do you do. Delighted to see you. I feel we acted hastily with you and your wife. How is your son? I imagine he will be headed to face the Hun soon."

"You mean Patrick. Yes. In fact, he's probably on the troop ship as we speak."

"Never met the boy, but he's obviously a fine lad to be among the first volunteers."

Conor felt uneasy. He wanted to shift in the chair but held steady. It wasn't the first time he'd been forced to lick boots but found the aftertaste repulsive. "Mister Norton, we're here asking about a friend who disappeared a couple of days ago, and it occurred to me the lad may have run afoul of your . . . department."

"Here? In Chicago?"

"Yes. He boarded a southbound streetcar in the Loop and hasn't been seen since."

Norton leaned forward, elbows on the desk, then reached for a pen. At least he hadn't thrown Conor out of the office. "Have you checked with the police?"

"Yes. He's not in custody."

"Alright. Give me his information. I will make some calls."

Conor gave the man both of Gimpy's names and a rundown of the boy's newspaper business. Then he added, "The lad also works for me as a private investigator."

"Does he now? Well, he must be a clever young man."

"Not as clever as he thinks sometimes."

"I will put someone on this immediately, Mister Dolan. Can you stop back tomorrow morning? I should have an answer for you. In the meantime, if the boy shows up, please let us know right away."

"Of course. Thank you."

Conor took the cue. He and Lefty rose, and Norton escorted them to the door. As they shook hands, the APL man said, "I'm actually glad you stopped in. I do feel badly about what happened. If there is anything else we can do for you, don't hesitate to ask."

As they headed for the Ford, Conor said to Lefty, "I'd rather have slept with a rattler. What do you think?"

"I think they're just what they seem to be, a pack of animals pretending to be cops."

Chapter 25

Friday, July 19, 1918

Even Haiti had declared war on Germany as of last week, but the real news provided a bolt of reality. The Bolsheviks had murdered Czar Nicholas II and his entire family for fear they might be released by White Russian soldiers.

Conor was having coffee in the kitchen as Maureen fried eggs. "I didn't want to wake you when I got home last night. It was before nine, but you were in bed." He and Lefty had gone looking for Gimpy.

"I had a splitting headache, but all good now. What about Gimpy?"

"Nothing. We went everywhere. What did you find at the library?"

"Nothing at all that would raise an eyebrow. No gang murders, nothing connected to the war or the government, just three unsolved murders that don't fit into any box. I looked for anything, not only murders and sabotage. But I have some ideas. I found out more about your man Franz von Papen from the German Embassy. He was expelled from the country after the scandal involving explosive chemical manufacturers. Their objective was to gain control of as many arms and chemical manufacturers as possible. Then they would send the chemicals to the wrong places, blow them up or add a neutralizing chemical into the barrels. It might have worked, but the newspaper articles claim British intelligence broke the German code and intercepted their messages."

"So maybe when the Bureau of Investigation pulled the weeds, they didn't get all the roots. This could be an offshoot of that group. After all, Riverside is an exporter, not a manufacturer. They might have missed it."

He told her about the meeting with Mister Norton of the APL and of his offer to help. As he was about to ask her a question, he heard a knock at the front door. Dillon went nuts, then Maureen asked, "Who could that be?"

"I have no clue, but you'd better stay in the kitchen. If anything happens go out the back door and get to the neighbors."

Conor slowly opened the door to find the smiling face of young Titus Freeman, complete with bowler hat, and apparently unharmed. "Come in here! So, where the hell have you been for the last two days?"

The boy smelled like a horse barn but looked to be unharmed. "I don't know. In a basement someplace. A couple guys was tryin' t' squeeze me."

Conor escorted Titus into the living room, where Maureen was already waiting with a glass of water. "Sit down," she ordered.

Conor said, "I met with that vigilante chief earlier. He swore he doesn't know anything about you being picked up."

Titus shook his head. "It wasn't them. It was Big Jimmy Ruffulo."

"What? Did you see Ruffulo? Talk with him?"

"I was blindfolded. He never said his name, but I ain't stupid."

"What did the voice sound like?"

"Like gravel."

Pointing to his own chair, Conor said, "Sit down and rest a bit. Maureen will get you something to eat. First thing you have to do is let Lefty and Toad know you're okay. They're turning the city upside down looking for you."

Maureen said, "Will Lefty still make the report?"

"I'm sure he won't," Conor replied. "It would only make more trouble. Gimpy's back safe. That's enough."

"Yeah, I ain't going to no cops. Lefty's the one who sent me over here. I saw Toad too."

"So, what was Ruffulo after?"

"He wanted to know everything we found out about Graves."

"Strange question to ask if Graves was his own guy. Why wouldn't he ask me directly?"

"He said he can't ever meet with you again. If you see him again, his face will be the last thing you see."

"Lovely. What else?"

"I think it was more he was sending you a message. They didn't hurt me and fed me okay. I slept a bit, too, so it could have been worse. My future income is a different story."

Maureen interrupted. "Come sit down at the table and get some food in ye."

"What message?" Conor prodded.

The fried eggs didn't slow down his reporting. "Ruffulo said he's a patriot helping out his country and you need to back off."

"Fat chance. Ruffulo had Mumbles killed to keep his mouth shut," Conor said.

Maureen had reached her own conclusion. "Sounds like the gangster is afraid the whole thing is getting out of his control."

"Or maybe realizing he was never in control. Is it possible our own government could be involved with organized crime?"

Titus momentarily interrupted his love affair with the eggs to chime in. "That's the way I see it, Boss. Hey, can you slide them potatoes over this way? I hate to see them wasted."

No matter how smart or resourceful Titus Freeman might be, he was still a kid accustomed to arduous life and sudden death. Even with his friend, Mumbles, in the ground, this was all still a game to him. "I have a busy day ahead, Gimpy. You stay here and rest awhile. Let Toad handle the morning editions. You can come downtown later." He did not mention that his day included a meeting with Viviana Bensini.

Getting Viviana to talk to her father was a hard sell for Conor and possibly a dangerous step for Viviana. There was no telling how Ruffulo might react if he thought his daughter had blown the whistle on the warehouse burglary. It might go badly for her mother as well. She'd phoned the office and left a message for Conor to meet her inside the new Central Park Moving Picture Theater in Lawndale. The silent movie was

"Closin' In with William Desmond, but Conor had no interest in being entertained. The theater was dark and roughly half full, but Viviana had spotted him from a back row as he walked in. "Conor," she whispered, and he took the seat beside her on the aisle, back and away from the crowd.

They both kept to a whisper. "So how did it go?"

"My father is worried and thinks he's in a pickle. It seems British agents hired him to help Graves navigate the city and get into the warehouse. One of the two men who contacted him claimed to be from the Bureau of Investigation. My father liked the idea of becoming an overnight patriot. He thought helping the British might give him leverage later with the Department of Justice. It was my father's idea to use one of the newsboys. I get the impression the tough gangster is feeling vulnerable."

"Why is that?"

Then a loud voice from three rows up. "Hey, will ya please shut up and watch the picture?"

They went silent for a minute as the movie ended. When the orchestra struck up for the musical finale, Viviana whispered, "He contacted the Bureau of Investigation and asked to speak with the agent who had introduced himself. They never heard of him. There is no agent by that name."

"And they only have two hundred agents for the whole country. Let me guess. Now he thinks the British hoodwinked him into thinking he was working for his own government."

"Exactly."

"So, it looks like the British were running an operation on American soil without authority, an operation that ended with the murder of a seventeen-year-old kid. That puts your father in a tight spot with our government, not to mention the ruckus it would cause if the newspapers got ahold of this. There are still one or two that would run the story. What about Graves? Can your father contact him?"

"No. He doesn't know the man's real name. Graves would contact him, or my father would run a coded newspaper ad."

"That explains Gimpy's interrogation. I can't sit through this movie again and your father likely has a tail on you. Does he suspect you put the cops onto the warehouse burglary?"

"Absolutely not and, for the tenth time, I didn't."

"Good. You leave now and go straight home. I'll stay through the credits."

CONOR ARRIVED HOME BEFORE EIGHT o'clock to a house strangely dark and silent. He switched on the light to find Maureen lying face down on the sofa, perfectly still. He figured her headache had returned. He sat down beside her, a gentle hand on her back. "Maureen, what's wrong? Where's Liam?"

"At the Reilly's."

"What's going on?"

Her head hadn't moved, her voice muffled by the cushion. "There's a telegram on the dining room table."

He settled into the chair, his chair, the one from which he had presided over so many joyous and a few not so joyous family gatherings and occasions. Then he looked down at the telegram. He didn't want this thing in their home and his first thought was to burn it in the fireplace, burn it until the thing became ashes, until the ashes became smoke and the smoke rose over the great lake until it became pure, like it never existed. So, he looked away. But to destroy the thing he must touch it, and if the paper moved in his hand, if he felt its texture, the thing would exist forever. He looked again and the paper was still there, sloppy, careless and wrinkled with typeover corrections.

Washington DC 2:25 PM July 13, 1918
Mr & Mrs Conor Dolan
3230 South Normal Avenue

Chicago Illinois

Deeply regret to inform you that your son, Pvt Patrick Dolan, died in the line of duty May 19 at Saint Nazaire France. Cause of death bacterial pneumonia as complication of flu. G.S.R. Form 120 will arv by mail with details relevant to return of body to U.S. for burial. Please accept my heartfelt sympathy. Letter to follow.

Harris Adjt. Genl.

Conor had still not put his hand to the vile thing. "Does Liam know?"

"No. I wanted to wait for you."

The man who rose from the table was a different man from the one who sat down only minutes ago. "I'll go get him."

Chapter 26

October 15, 1918

The Influenza that descended upon the Dolan household three months ago from across the ocean was now ravaging the East Coast. Talk of a pandemic had started back in March as a low rumble, hardly noticeable, and spawned into a typhoon of death. After ravaging the troops in Europe and the Continent generally, it had erupted into global disaster. Now it had infected Chicago.

Until recently, North America had been largely spared, but a new, more dangerous strain had now begun blanketing the continent. Still, Chicago had fared better than most major urban centers due to a quicker response than most. Near the end of September, placards were distributed on all "L" trains and streetcars warning against sneezing and coughing in public. By the beginning of October, hundreds of new cases were being reported every day, whereupon the Health Commissioner ordered the closing of virtually all places where people gathered, including restaurants, theaters, and organized sports. Public funerals were banned the week after Patrick was laid to rest in Mount Carmel Cemetery. Even Parick's funeral was scaled down in the spirit of common good. There would be time later for a proper memorial. It seemed only churches and saloons managed to escape closure. Because the Influenza had largely not manifested in children, the Health Commissioner determined that children were safer in school than on the streets and for that reason, schools remained open. As of last week, citizens were being arrested for sneezing in public without a face covering.

If there was any good news, it was that the vaunted German offensive of 1918 had fizzled in the mud and ash of the French and Belgian countryside. American troops had joined the fight at the Second Battle of the Marne in mid-July and effectively broken the German spring offensive, then sealed the deal at the Battle of Amiens in August. Although the Americans had begun to feel the weight of heavy casualties, the German morale was believed to be plummeting badly. Still, more American troops were dying from the dreaded Influenza than from German munitions.

With his court calendar open the entire day, Conor decided to stop by Newsboy Alley to check in with Lefty and their youthful spy network. Fighting his way through the disorganized hustle and bustle of the alley, he found the cop sitting outside his "office" on a crude chair and reading The Herald. With his feet up on an empty crate, Lefty conveyed the image of a Dodge City Marshal overseeing his fiefdom. Only the awkward police helmet belied the image.

"Just in time for coffee, Counselor," said the copper, swinging his legs from the crate. "Here, pull up a box and I'll grab you a cup."

"Sounds like just the ticket. It's a fine morning."

With steam from his cup rising into the brisk morning air, Conor said, "So anything new on the warehouse front?"

"Not a thing. Sorry Conor. Oh, I hear your . . . ah, friend, Viviana, left town with the cast." Conor had no intention of engaging on the subject. Lefty liked to keep up on everyone's personal business. Maybe it was the cop in him, but more likely the busybody. Lefty seemed to catch the silent message and changed the subject. "How is Maureen coping with the loss?"

He didn't want to talk about Patrick's death either, but the subject seemed to ambush him every day. He'd learn to deal with it because folks like Lefty genuinely sympathized with the Dolans and were well-intentioned. "She has her good days and her bad days, Lefty. The mornings are the worst. The only time either of us can put it aside is when we're asleep, if we're lucky enough to get there. In the mornings, I think she wakes up to a new day expecting to hear him fiddling around in his bedroom. Doing the library work helps her. I hope to Christ it helps her, but who knows?"

Conor spotted Gimpy and Toad heading up the alley with leftover morning editions. Despite the limp, Gimpy never had trouble keeping up with his friend. Conor hadn't realized it was after nine-thirty. They stopped in front of the office to exchange greetings.

"Tell the Missus we're thinking about her," said Gimpy as Toad nodded.

"I will, boys. I should tell all of you that when this damn plague, or whatever it is, leaves us, we're going to have a proper funeral for Patrick. Will we see you at the memorial tomorrow at Scanlon's?"

"Of course, Mister Dolan. We'll be there," Titus replied.

THERE WAS NO COMFORT TO BE HAD AT a memorial lunch for an eighteen-year-old boy any more than there was at a funeral. Endless speeches and alcohol fueled tears, peppered with periodic prayers and blessings from their friend, the well-meaning Father Brendan White.

The ordeal began at noon with a prayer, of course, when the crowd of about fifty friends milled into the seating area for the catered buffet. Conor's aunt had even made the trip up from Springfield and fell in immediately with the large contingent from the parish. Six or seven newsboys, including Gimpy and Toad, sat together at a table with Eammon Flynn. Viviana did not appear, although Conor knew that her absence was a signal of sincere condolence.

Maureen carried a brave, if periodically tear-streaked face, throughout the event and into the after-rounds of alcohol, when Father Brendan finally gave his personal eulogy. "Sure I knew young Patrick before he could walk or chew or have a thought of his own and I cared for the boy as much as I care for his dear mother, Maureen. I remember..."

Maureen had sensed Conor's discomfort and made sure there was a double Jameson and two beers at his place. As the well-intentioned speech turned to afterlife and Jesus and celebration, Conor's mind began to drift. Whether by force of will or influence of spirits, the lawyer found himself back in County Clare, Ireland, the day before he and Kevin left home bound for America. Their poor Pa was less than a year in the grave when his wife and children were evicted.

After watching the British Constabulary set their cottage ablaze and turn the three surviving Dolans into the road, the boys spent days building their Ma a crude mud hut to protect her from the rain and cold. Ma and Kevin tried to convince seven-year-old Conor that the shelter was a palace by the sea where Ma could spend her days relaxing in comfort until the day the angels came to reunite her with Pa in heaven. He could picture Ma standing in the entranceway waving as the boys set out on their epic journey. In his heart, the young boy did not buy the story, but was only too happy to cast doubts aside and rely on the assurances of his beloved older brother. The little boy had conveniently suppressed those memories and the doubts until his fateful move to Chicago and the life-altering events of 1903.

If that child did not truly understand the boys were leaving their mother to die a lonely death of starvation and cold, it was thanks to Kevin. Conor had been giving great thought to these questions since Patrick's death and honestly could not reach a conclusion. Maybe he just found Kevin's carefully crafted excuse easier to live with.

It had always been convenient to tell himself he didn't know. He was too young to understand, couldn't tell the difference between a real cottage and a large mud coffin with a chimney. But the truth was that Kevin, and surely his mother as well, had offered him a convenient escape from guilt and the little boy had grabbed onto it like a lifeline.

The conspiracy had worked. The little boy was now a respected and successful lawyer with a beautiful, strong wife. He missed Kevin today, more than he had ever missed anyone in his life, except for Patrick, and for the first time, began to resent his mother for burdening Kevin with all that guilt. Kevin should have been here today. He wanted this day to end and to wipe it from his memory.

He found Gimpy and Toad, still eating and drinking the free goodies at four o'clock. It was a good chance to talk to them, if they weren't too drunk. "Did you boys get enough to eat yet?"

"Had our fill, Mister Dolan," Gimpy replied for both of them.

They were young boys but had long ago shed the compulsion for normal juvenile eccentricities and excesses. They were, by any standard save age, mature adults. They had come here today with a spirit of mourning and respect and maintained obligatory decorum. "Thank you, boys. It means a lot having you here today." Turning to Gimpy, he added, "Titus . . . or

Gimpy, why don't you just pick one name or the other? I don't care which. Eventually everyone will catch on."

"I'll think about it, Boss."

"Okay. Well, do you have any idea if Detective Flynn knew Mumbles? I mean did they have some kind of relationship or friendship before the burglary?"

They looked at one another and laughed. Gimpy said, "'Course they did. Mumbles was a real smart kid. Adults thought he was stupid 'cause he stuttered. He knew how to play the game, think shit out."

"What does that mean?"

"Mumbles could get over on anybody," Gimpy said.

"Yup."

"Explain, please."

After swallowing another shovel full, Gimpy said, "He did jobs for Ruffulo. Newsboys say Mumbles could climb walls like a spider and crawl through a water pipe. That was his side job. He was an artist who could find a way into any building. He only took a few jobs a year for Ruffulo's crew, but he made a load of dough. He would treat us all to meals and buy drinks for weeks. Then he would lose it on poker."

"I know about Ruffulo. Did he do jobs for Flynn?"

"Hell yes. He was always doing some investigator work for Flynn, even when Flynn was still a cop. I was too young to know myself, but all the guys say he started working with Flynn when he was eleven."

"Yup."

Conor's friend, Eammon Flynn, had apparently forgotten to mention that fact. So, Flynn and Mumbles had at least a working relationship and were the only two people with information about this man named Mister Graves. Was it possible Flynn and Mumbles concocted this story in advance? Why? This new disclosure also meant that Flynn might have known about the burglary in advance. The stew was, indeed, thickening.

Chapter 27

Thursday morning, October 17, 1918

Conor could tell something was up. All along Halsted Street on the drive to the office, crowds were swarming the newsstands. Parking his Ford on Clark Street, he walked east on Jackson, as had become his habit lately, and spotted Gimpy and a helper on his prime corner in front of the Monadnock. Handing Conor a morning edition, he said, "Mornin', Mister Dolan. You heard the news yet?"

Opening the folded Tribune, Conor gasped. "Well, I'll be damned." *Big Jimmy Ruffulo shot dead on Randolph Street.* It was big news, even in a city weaned on violence, brutality, and corruption. The underworld boss had apparently been assassinated while walking out of a restaurant. "A single bullet to the back of the head" was how the Tribune described it.

The implications of Ruffulo's murder were wide-ranging, terrifying even. Immediate suspicion, of course, fell on the rival criminal organizations, of which Chicago had no shortage. The murder might easily trigger wholesale killing and gunplay city-wide. The saloons and brothels of the city's levee districts along with the enormously profitable backdoor casinos could become forums of open warfare as rival gangs fought for control or pursued retaliation. Chaos loomed over the city by the lake.

Conor went straight to his office only to find the outer door. Mrs. Schmidt had failed to appear for work without notice for the first time since 1903. The woman lived alone in a flat up near Division Street. Naturally, she had no telephone, but the grocer at street-level was a kind man who would give her access to the telephone as needed.

Before Conor could leave the office for his secretary's flat, a middle-aged woman appeared in the open doorway of his private office. She appeared frazzled, slightly unkempt but fashionably dressed. "Mister Dolan?" The woman asked meekly.

"Yes. How can I help you? Sorry but my secretary didn't appear for work today."

"I know, sir. That's why I'm here. I'm her daughter, Greta."

Conor reached out to her. "Here, let me take your coat. Won't you please sit down? I would offer you coffee but..."

She took a chair opposite his desk and said, "It's alright." He waited patiently until the woman was ready to continue. "I received a call this morning from the grocer downstairs from my mother. The lady in the next flat heard my mother crying for help early this morning and found she had fallen in her apartment,"

"Oh, my goodness. How awful! Is she alright?"

"We think she will be . . . but it appears she broke her leg, the tibia, I believe the doctor said. She's at Cook County Hospital now."

"I'm so sorry, Greta. Is there anything I can do?"

"Not now, but . . ."

"Anything at all."

"Well, my mother is worried about her job. As you know, she's seventy-one but sharp and active. She's afraid of losing her job."

"I'll go see her now. Hopefully she's out of surgery. I'll talk to her myself about her job. I'm certain it will be a long healing process and she needn't worry. Her job will be here when she's ready and I will continue to pay her salary."

"Oh, thank you, Mister Dolan! I would go with you, but I have little ones to care for."

"Of course. No worry. I'll put her mind at ease."

CONOR LEFT THE HOSPITAL IN TIME TO make his two-thirty arraignment over at Hubbard Street. It appeared Mrs. Schmidt would recover, barring complications from surgery, and for the first time, it occurred to him that his law practice was without administrative assistance. On the drive to Bridgeport, he considered that his long-serving secretary would be a difficult person to replace, and a busy law practice could simply not function without a typist and someone to administer day-to-day operations and scheduling. Toad was an asset in the streets but a liability in the office. By the time he parked the Ford on Normal Avenue, the obvious answer had revealed itself.

Maureen had tried to put on a brave face since Patrick's death, but a sense of morbidity had faded the emerald gleam in those *Leitrim* eyes. She routinely lingered quietly in bed before rising, had dropped her participation in parish charitable events, and declined nearly every opportunity to leave the house. Conor felt completely helpless in the face of her overwhelming grief, a destructive force beyond his power to touch or vanquish.

Maybe, just maybe, Mrs. Schmidt's misfortune might prove a path to Maureen's recovery. It was worth a try.

"DON'T BE DAFT, CONOR. I CAN'T EVEN TYPE. Besides, I have the child to look after."

Young Liam generally did not inject himself into parental conversations at the dining room table, but apparently couldn't resist. "Ma, I ain't a child anymore. I'm fourteen."

"Ye're 'not' a child anymore and no one asked ye in any case."

Conor saw his opening. "The boy is right. You could come into the office when he leaves for school and come home when school ends. As for the typing, nobody can type until they learn. I could get someone to teach you. You could practice at night. It won't take more than a couple of weeks."

Her cheeks turned the color of ripe apples, and she squeezed on the serving fork. "Ye forget, dear husband, that I've never been in the workforce, and I don't know the first thing about mixing with all those posh people. I don't even have the proper clothes."

He would have to fight her with logic. "Do you think just anyone could do that library research? You're bright, intuitive, and personable." Then he smiled maliciously. "Not to mention attractive. A pretty secretary is never bad for business."

She shook her head. "Absolutely not."

Young Liam had injected his two cents and was apparently content to let his parents sort it out from here. "Ma, would you pass the sweet potatoes?"

Conor decided to play his hole card. "Well, I promised Mrs. Schmidt I'd pay her salary until she returns. If I'm forced to hire another woman at the going rate, it will hurt us financially. What I'm saying is that I need you, Maureen."

He hadn't seen her impromptu smile in a fair bit. It felt comforting, if only for a second. She was quiet for a moment while filling his coffee cup. Then the smile began to slide to one side until it became a smirk. "Ye're a sly one, Conor Dolan, a sly devil indeed. So, we'll give it a go then and that's the way of it."

"Perfect. I'll go in tomorrow at the usual time and you can join the team whenever you're ready. Later in the week or next week will be fine."

"No. If I'm going to do it, tomorrow is the day. I'll go in with ye; Liam can get himself to school. On the weekend I'll pick up some proper office attire."

CONOR'S LAST COURT CASE WAS A HEARING on his motion to suppress evidence for a man accused of assaulting a streetcar driver. It was a straightforward case on the issue of whether the detective had coerced the man's confession, with the burden of proof having shifted to the State. The prosecutor's only witness was Detective Gianelli. His direct testimony refuted the allegations of physical abuse in the defendant's motion. Following Conor's cross-examination, the State rested and Conor put his client on the stand to contradict the officer's version. The Court then took the matter under advisement for decision.

COURT RECESSED JUST AFTER THREE IN THE afternoon and Conor hurried to catch Gianelli in the hallway. "Detective, can I speak with you for a minute? It's about Big Jim's murder."

"Sure. I have a few minutes. Seems you never quit."

They sat down on a bench in the hallway, and Conor got right to the point. "Have you considered that Big Jimmy Ruffulo's murder might be connected to the Wellborn killing and the warehouse burglary?"

"If I wanted to, I could give you a list of a hundred guys who'd stand in line for a shot at Ruffulo, if they thought they could get away with it."

Go easy, Boyo. "Well, can you tell me if you've made any progress on Wellborn's murder?"

"I can tell you it's still technically an open investigation, and no one has been arrested. No more questions."

Gianelli tried to walk away, but Conor followed. "Let me put it another way. Would you like to hear *my* evidence connecting all three events?"

The detective kept walking toward the staircase like he hadn't heard the question. Conor pitched one last fastball. "Will you just tell me who warned your department off the case?"

"Don't contact me again about this. You know the answer to that question as well as I do. Just like you, I figured it out for myself."

Gianelli's withholding of information on the condition of the 9mm casing from the warehouse burglary had already told Conor that the detective was not being forthcoming, but now the deception was blatant and obvious. Conor still might have more information than the police, but the detective had apparently shed his sympathetic attitude.

With pressure to keep a lid on the Wellborn murder case and suppress a connection to the burglary, someone high up might be trying to protect this Graves character. *Did they connect Ruffulo's murder as well?* Conor would have to pursue the leads on his own. There would be no help from the cops.

Only three people had come forward with information on Mister Graves: Mumbles, Viviana, and Flynn. Of those three, only Mumbles's information was based on firsthand contact. Flynn's account was hearsay based on observations made by a security guard at Ruffulo's casino. The third was Viviana's account, double-hearsay based on conversations between her mother and Ruffulo. He couldn't cross-examine the deceased newsboy, and Flynn's account was leaking like a sieve. He had questions about Viviana.

Investigating a murder case was like following a trail with many forks; one wrong turn could lead you into an endless wasteland. The detective may or may not know the connection that bound all three incidents, but it was now clear he would go no further. Gianelli was not prepared to put his career at risk, whatever his personal feelings. In a way, Conor didn't blame him. Anyone could be trapped in this cesspool of deceit and corruption. There was simply nowhere to escape it. The cops were muzzled and that was that. Until the German war machine was vanquished and the Influenza banished to history, Chicago would remain a city oblivious to social ills, forbearing of evolving criminal sophistication, and blind to institutional trampling of individual civil rights.

Chapter 28

Friday, October 21, 1918

The gangster's funeral mass filled Saint Bernadine's Church to the rafters. The Forest Park parish was located near the Ruffulo family home and an easy commute from the Forest Park train station down the street and the end of the Aurora, Elgin & Chicago service in Bellwood.

The obituary noted that the A&E single-track trolley shuttle would be adding additional cars on the Mount Carmel Branch from Bellwood out to the cemetery in Hillside, a courtesy traditionally reserved for high-ranking politicians and titans of industry. Even in death, Ruffulo reaped special treatment. Technically, it wasn't a funeral, as there would be no public service at the cemetery and "mourners" were asked to go directly from the church to the restaurant. No doubt the actual plan was to simply ignore the Influenza restrictions.

It was a High Mass, of course, a ritual all too familiar to the Irishman Conor Dolan, and marked by three lit candles on each side of the altar. It meant the mass would be torturously long with the celebrant priest obliged to sing every word of the service, off key—in Latin—and accompanied by a dreadfully bad organist.

Despite the crowd, Conor spotted her immediately. Viviana had returned for the funeral and sat dutifully, tear-free, beside her grieving mother in the front row. From the choreography, it appeared Viviana had only one sibling, a sister. Finding her on the road was never an option, as the troop had been performing in Midwest venues when Big Jim met his fate. Now, if he could find a way to speak with her alone.

There was no point in suffering through the mass. No one had noticed him, nor would anyone have cared. The pews overflowed with mourners of most ethnicities and all social classes, including the political variety. It was no surprise. Big Jim was, after all, a Chicago legend and a widely admired philanthropist. He was also a sadistic murderer.

Conor snoozed in the Ford until a sturdy altar boy appeared in the doorway struggling with a five-foot gold-plated cross; the priest, the family and the coffin in tow. Conor managed to reach the front archway before the pallbearers loaded Ruffulo's corpse onto the cart for the short walk to the funeral train. He placed himself in direct line of Viviana's sight as she emerged, mother on her arm. In contrast to the mother, Viviana walked stone-faced—until she caught Conor's stare. She smiled broadly, if only for a split second, before returning to character. The woman was, after all, an actress. With contact made, he headed for the restaurant.

Conor parked in the lot at the Venetian Garden Restaurant on Twelfth Street, where according to the obituary, mourners were invited to join the family for a memorial lunch. The lawyer figured a Jameson at the bar would be a better use of his time than sitting through another religious service. Besides, his stomach couldn't tolerate any more idolatry for a man who became rich enslaving immigrant girls, bribing politicians, and killing people.

It was nearly one in the afternoon when the funeral crowd began to trickle into the restaurant. Most had arrived by rail, making the short walk up Wolf Road to the restaurant. MoMo Storino, One-Ear Raimondi, even the recently paroled Irish thug, Lucky O'Leary, like the Litany of the Saints performed live on stage. The politicians in attendance were largely retired and immune to bad publicity. Conor spotted reporters and cops, lots of cops, with no way to distinguish among dirty cops, curious cops, and on-duty cops. A few might have attended only to be certain the gangster was dead.

The drinks were free after one-thirty, and around two o'clock the crowd began to mill upstairs for the luncheon. The meal officially began with Father Militello's rendition of the Grace, an obligatory act of the Catholic mourners. The old priest's manufactured tears and fond recollections of "a great and generous" man warranted a Jameson, but Conor decided against it. He was here for a reason. No doubt this cleric would miss his regular cut of the ill-gotten proceeds from the "great man."

The disgustingly effusive speeches and stories carried beyond the antipasto, the minestrone, three types of pasta, and clear into the tiramisu until, at last, the gathering began to dissipate, and the mourners left or gathered in small groups at the bar. The drinks were still free, but Conor held it at three. He wasn't here to drink any more than he was here to mourn.

Viviana came to him at the bar as he'd hoped, where they stood shoulder to shoulder without acknowledging one another. "Water," she said to the bartender.

Conor didn't turn to face her. "I need to talk with you."

"I know," she replied. "Let's go outside. They have a few tables. It's cold so we'll be alone."

Conor knew only too well how much she detested her father, at least he thought he did. He struggled to find the appropriate words. *Keep it simple, nothing religious or hypocritical.* "I'm sorry, Viviana. He *was* your father."

"I keep telling myself that."

"I saw in the papers you were performing in St. Louis when he died."

She laughed gently. "Are you still stalking me?"

He shrugged. "I like to think I'm not but. . ."

Once outside, she said, "It's time we talked." Then she leaned back in the chair. "How would you like to do this? Would you like to ask me questions or should I give it to you all at once?"

"First let me take a guess. You have a three-month-old baby and I'm the father?"

She laughed as a waitress came out the back door. The woman seemed surprised to see them. "Oh, sorry, I didn't know anyone was out here. Too chilly. I just came out for some air. Can I get you folks something? Open bar closes in fifteen minutes."

Conor waved her off. "No, thanks. We're fine."

Viviana turned back to Conor. "I wish that were the case. It would be simpler. Go ahead. Fire away."

"This means you know more than you're telling me."

"Much more."

He was afraid to go further down this road. Was he about to learn all the answers? How much did she know? Was she going to say she lied to him? He wondered how ugly this could get and that fact terrified him to his core. *Alright, get to the heart of it and find out.* "First off, I'd like to know who killed Mumbles."

"It was my father's dog, Lucchesi. It had to be. Lucchesi didn't know my father was helping the Allies. It's still possible the boy was meant to die from the beginning. But it doesn't matter and it's all my fault."

"I don't know about that. Remember, your father called the Bureau of Investigation to verify the identity of the agent who approached him with the British. He didn't exist. Your father might have thought he was in trouble running a rogue operation for the British."

"I still think Lucchesi was acting alone, as much as I believe my father capable."

How would Viviana know that? She only knew what her mother told her. And why was it her fault? He tried to prepare himself to be shocked. "Why your fault? And what plan?"

"That's complicated, but I was telling the truth when I said I didn't alert the cops."

She was fumbling. Why? It didn't matter whether her father ordered the hit or not. He thought briefly about telling her to stop. Did he really need to know more?

Mumbles was dead and Ruffulo was involved up to his ears. Now Ruffulo was dead. Game over. But it wasn't over, not for Conor and not for Mumbles. He had to know for sure, and he had to know everything. Did this woman know the whole story? If so, *what is she? Who is she?* "I have time. How do you know all this? Does that mean everything else you told me was a lie? Even the personal . . . things?"

"Of course not. I was as honest with you as I could be. It's a long story."

"I have time. I could even buy us a drink."

Viviana's mother chose that moment to walk out onto the patio. "Oh, there you are, my dear. The waitress said I might find you here. Our motor car is here for us. Come say your goodbyes." She stood at the table and added. "I'm so exhausted. I need to sit a minute. I don't believe I know your friend."

"Mother, this is Mister Conor Dolan. He's a lawyer and did some business with father."

Conor stood politely. "How do you do, Ma'am? Sorry for your loss."

The mother rose. "Thank you for coming, Mister Dolan. Now dear, let's be off."

As the two women headed for the door, Conor said, "I simply loved your performance, Miss Bensini. Will you be in town long?"

"I'm not certain, Mister Dolan. I shall stay until my mother is well and until things are settled. I hope to see you again."

ON THE DRIVE BACK TO THE MONADNOCK Building, Conor considered the current state of affairs. Most importantly, where was she staying? He presumed with her mother, but he could hardly show up and ring the doorbell. The place would be swarming with cops and gangsters for a few days. No. His only choice was to wait until Viviana contacted him. *The Lord knows she can find you when it suits her.*

Questions besieged him. *As honest with you as I could be?* What the hell did that mean? She told him Lucchesi killed Mumbles to shut the kid up. But that's it. She didn't retract one specific lie. So Lucchesi killed Mumbles and Viviana didn't tip the cops? She told him nothing beyond the fact that she lied. What were the lies? How could he believe anything from her mouth now after she admitted deceiving him? Only one thing was certain: if Ruffulo had Mumbles killed, he did it to protect his own ass. He had to talk to Viviana again—and soon.

CONOR WAS SURPRISED TO FIND MAUREEN still at the office past five o'clock. He needed a secretary but wasn't willing to trade a wife for one. She was practicing typing when he arrived. He hung up his coat and kissed her on the cheek. "I see you're taking this seriously. You have a habit of that."

She stopped and looked at the clock. "Oh, Lord I didn't realize the time. Poor Liam will be starving."

He laughed. "He'll live. This works out. We can ride home together. How was the typing lesson?"

"Good. The woman is very patient, but I don't think I need her anymore. It's not difficult, really. A matter of practice and I rather like it, to be sure. How did the funeral go?"

He motioned for her to follow him into the private office. "I have to grab a few files to take home. Viviana was there. I expected she would be. It was a pompous affair, of course, but I managed to have a private chat with her while the free booze was flowing at the restaurant."

"I can't wait to hear about it."

He wasn't certain if his wife was being sarcastic. "Basically, she admitted lying to me."

"About what?"

He relayed the entire conversation to Maureen, almost. "So, what do you think?"

They grabbed their coats, locked up the office and headed for the staircase. Maureen didn't like elevators. "I'm not certain what I think. 'Tis suspicious alright, but I can't imagine what part Viviana could play in all this. Why would she say it's all her fault?"

"I don't know. Do you think it's possible she killed her own father?"

"Don't be daft, Conor. Sure I have a sense for people. She's not without vices, to be sure, but ye can be certain she didn't kill her own father, no matter how much she hated him. I think ye should be focusing more on yeer friend, Eammon Flynn."

They reached the Ford parked on Clark Street where Conor opened the door for her. "Oh, I intend to, but you know that if Flynn is involved in this, he's doing it to aid the rebellion in Ireland. That would mean he's working for the Germans."

She glared at him across the seat. "And?"

"You hate everything British. Remember? If Flynn is involved and we go after him, you'll be aiding the British war effort. The library research was borderline, but this . . ."

"Shut your yap about it, Conor Dolan. An intelligent person can change opinions if the facts dictate. The fire that burns in Flynn doesn't usually burn itself out, Conor, no more in Flynn that in yeer own departed brother, the

Lord rest his soul. But I have no more energy left for hate. What happened in Ireland is in the past, and we must live in the present. We have another son and I nearly forgot that in my grief. Besides, our son died as an American soldier. He was proud of that uniform, and I'm proud of him. I know ye bloody well are too,"

Chapter 29

Monday, October 29, 1918

With nearly all of occupied France and Belgium back in Allied hands, the war in Europe was winding down. Only last week, Germany had terminated its policy of unrestricted submarine warfare as the Allied Powers considered it request for an armistice. In Chicago, the Influenza outbreak had finally peaked in mid-month and the number of recorded new cases were finally dropping dramatically. There was even talk in the papers of lifting some of the most repressive restrictions—like dancing in public.

"Good morning," said the operator, "I have a call from the Cook County jail for anyone from a man who identifies himself as Neil Kaplan. Will you take the call?"

Neil Kaplan was a young deputy at the jail who often worked in jail intake and had been a regular recipient of Conor's Christmas envelopes over the years. He had a young family, as Conor recalled, and would often refer neighborhood miscreants to Conor's office with a kind word. "Yes, Operator. Put him through."

"Mister Dolan?"

"Yes. Go ahead, Neil. How are you?"

"I have a couple of your newsboys down in intake here. They say you're their lawyer and I wanted to give you a heads up."

"Thanks, Neil. What are their names?"

"We don't have family names. They call themselves Gimpy and Toad."

"Yeah, they're mine, Lefty's really. I was on my way up there in a few minutes anyway. Can you tell me what it's about?"

"They were in a fight with some other boys. They're not hurt badly, just some bruises, but they both had knives. That's what supports the felony complaint. Bond hearing is set for eleven o'clock."

"I appreciate the heads up, Neil. I'll see them back in the bullpen before the hearing. Anyone else arrested?"

"Yeah, three or four bigger boys, but they were cut loose. I don't know the details."

It was unusual but not unprecedented to have Gimpy and Toad locked up. They could take care of themselves pretty well, especially together, and were generally successful in avoiding trouble. Productive newsboys tended toward that mindset, but sometimes this city wouldn't let a boy turn his back. Whatever had caused the mayhem, it was likely unavoidable. He would stop at the alley on his way and let Lefty know about the hearing.

As a policeman, Lefty was allowed to enter the bullpen interview area with the lawyer. Conor saw roughly a dozen overnighters of all ages in the holding cell behind the courtroom, a normal weeknight's haul. A few were still drunk; one was nearly naked, and another was masturbating on a bench, as if he were alone in his bedroom. All but three were still in civilian clothing. Bullpens all carried the same pungent odor of the unwashed criminal horde. Conor didn't want to linger. Gimpy and Toad spotted him immediately through the bars and came forward. They were filthy and bruised but seemed uninjured.

Gimpy said, "Thanks for coming Mister Dolan, Lefty."

Conor said, "You know the drill, boys. We won't talk about the case until you're out of here. I'll do the talking, and I'll put Lefty on the stand if we need him. In any case, the judge will see Lefty standing just behind the rail. What names did you give them? Christ, even I don't know your real names."

"I told them I'm Hans Christian Anderson and Toad's Abraham Lincoln."

"The judge will love that. Are either of you hurt? Need medical treatment? Should I use Lefty as next of kin?"

Both boys shook their heads. Titus said, "We okay. Yeah. Use Lefty."

Both kids were released on signature bonds under Lefty's supervision with instructions from Conor to report to his office after they cleared out-processing. Maureen would have orders not to admit them without first showering at the common facility in Newsboy Alley. The boys were waiting for Conor in the outer office when he returned from lunch.

"Alright, one at a time. What was it about?"

"We was working our investigator jobs," Titus began. "A few of them West Side thugs didn't like the questions we was asking. They tried to rob us."

"Yup."

"Toad, tell him about your cousin."

"My cousin Rolo is a newsboy out west around the Forest Park Station. We ain't really cousins but we look alike. He's strong like me, about the same age. We first met up at one of them Christmas parties the city throws for the newsboys. Me n' Gimpy had some dealings with him too. I was telling him about this, and Detective Flynn's name came up."

"Okay, tell me about Flynn."

Gimpy turned to his friend and held up his palm. "I'll help you out, Toad. Toad was asking about Flynn and got a tip from Rolo. Flynn lives out there near Forest Park. Well, he hired three or four of them boys some months back, maybe a year ago, to keep an eye on some warehouses and factories for him. He wanted to know if they were raided, damaged, anything that might be suspicious."

The young investigators had his attention. "Did you get the locations?"

A big grin on Toad's face gave Conor his answer. Toad ripped a page from his little notebook and handed it to Conor. "There's the list, Boss."

Conor turned to Gimpy. "Can you handle things without your partner for a couple of hours? I need a witness for an interview out in Forest Park. It may prove to be enlightening."

"No problem, Boss."

THEY TRIED THE FOREST PARK CASINO first, but Flynn had not made an appearance yet, so Conor parked down the street from the detective's Oak Park hotel, The Plaza, and the two entered the lobby. It was a far cry from The Sheridan House, but solidly middle-class: contemporary, dark-colored décor and a comfortable sitting area around a fireplace. The hotel bar was just beyond the clerk's desk. The man was completing check-in for a new guest. The "guest" was a middle-aged man, balding and plump with an expensive suit. The girl with him was no more than fourteen. Conor said to Toad, "Sit down and make yourself comfortable. I'll check the bar. If he's not there, I'll go to his room."

As the boy walked away, Conor approached the clerk. Handing the man a business card, he announced, "I'm here to find Eammon Flynn. Don't say a word about the boy. He'll sit there quietly, and we'll be out of here in thirty minutes."

The man shook his head vociferously. "I'm sorry, sir. The management doesn't allow Negroes in the hotel."

"Let's put it this way. Flynn is a friend of mine. He's also retired detective, as you may know." Then Conor leaned over to get a quick look at the guestbook. Even upside down, it was easy to read the most recent entry: *Mr. and Mrs. John Smith*. Conor glanced quickly at the clerk's name tag. "I don't want to make trouble for you . . . Charles . . . but . . . "

"I understand, sir. Take your time. The boy is welcome."

Flynn was standing at the bar, alone and nursing a beer. "Ah, Counselor, what brings ye out to the hinterland this afternoon?"

"You, Flynn. I wanted to run a few things by you. Can we talk in the lobby? Toad is out there, and I didn't want to cause a scene."

"Of course, me boy. Can I buy ye a beer? They'll bring it to the lobby."

"No thanks. Wait for me in the lobby. There's a pharmacy next door. I have to pick up something for Maureen."

Returning to the lobby a few minutes later, Conor saw no need for small talk. "I have one big question, then a few small ones. Alright?"

Flynn shrugged his shoulders and took a long pull on the beer. "Shoot."

"Please don't play with me, Flynn. Have you been telling me the whole truth about this Wellborn murder and the warehouse burglary?"

The old man's head drooped; his shoulders slumped. He inhaled a deep breath and sat still as a stone for a full minute before lifting his head. "What tipped ye off?"

"No, Flynn, we're not doing that. You want to know what I know first. Either be truthful with me now or we will work through this case without you and get to the bottom of it. Either way, I'll find the truth."

"Alright. I'll tell you. Graves is a British agent sent to kill Wellborn."

"How do you know that?"

"Unlike ye, I never assimilated. I hate the feckin' word. I remember Ireland and I carry my old baggage as a responsibility. Also, unlike ye, I will carry my Clan-na-Gael oath to the grave. What hurts England serves the cause of Irish independence. It should be no secret to ye that men like me don't quit on the Clan-na-Gael in a storm. The Clan still exists in New York. There are a few of us who will fight the British to our last breath. It's not that I blame ye for it, Conor. Ye're a different man with a different story and responsibilities."

"That doesn't answer my question."

"The boys in New York keep close contact with the German Consulate. No names. They gave me a list last year, a small list of a few factories and one arms broker with a warehouse working very hard for the German cause."

Conor had the list and saw no point in dwelling on it. "The arms broker being Wellborn."

"Yes. To us, the German cause is Ireland's cause, Conor. I was to keep an eye on these places and an ear to the ground in the event they were discovered or raided. The more British arms they can neutralize, the greater the chance Germany wins. That means Ireland wins."

At that moment, two carloads of uniformed cops pulled up at the front door and two cops burst through the double brass doors. They ran past Conor's group and half swarmed up the main staircase.

Conor was up in a flash. "Come on. Let's get out of here. We'll finish this outside."

Toad fell in line without a word spoken, and Flynn made the wise decision to follow. "What's all that about?" Flynn asked, struggling to keep up.

"Keep moving. I'll buy you a sandwich at the pharmacy lunch counter and tell you all about it. When's the last time you had ice cream?"

The store was a one-man operation, and the druggist donned his white apron to help the strange trio at the counter. "Any problem with us sitting here?" Conor asked.

"None whatsoever," the man replied. "What can I get you boys?" Then he looked at Conor again. "Hey, weren't you just in here using the telephone twenty minutes ago?"

"I suppose I was."

Flynn said, "I thought you had to pick up something for Maureen."

"Oh, I forgot. I'll do it before we leave."

After they ordered, Conor picked up the questioning. "So, you knew Wellborn before he was murdered?"

"Absolutely not. I had no names until I learned about Graves from Mumbles. That was before the burglary. But when Mumbles told me Ruffulo was going to burglarize the warehouse, I investigated Riverside on my own. That's how I found out about Wellborn. I thought about contacting him but decided it would be too risky and not necessary. When Wellborn turned up dead, it wasn't a stretch to conclude that Graves was sent to kill him. Then I decided to foil the Allied plan. I was acting alone."

For fourteen years, Conor had considered Flynn a true and loyal friend. He wanted to believe the man now but knew he could never see the old detective through yesterday's lens. "What do you mean by foil the plot?"

"I tipped off the cops to the burglary. I was waiting in the weeds that night, watching, and saw the whole thing happen."

"So, you saw Graves?"

"Yes. He was dressed in black and masked, but it had to be him. A slender fellow, he was."

"Who shot Mumbles?"

"Graves."

So, Gianelli's report was correct. Mumbles told Flynn about Graves and the burglary in advance, and Flynn dropped a dime. "Why did you not tell us about your prior relationship with Mumbles?"

"It didn't seem important. Besides, Mumbles was already dead, and it didn't matter."

"And you didn't tell Mumbles you were going to tip off the cops. Flynn, that decision killed him."

Tears began to bead around both eyes, one breaking free to trek slowly down old, wrinkled cheeks. "I know that, and there isn't a waking minute it doesn't torture me. I didn't think it would come to shooting. At worst, he'd pick up a simple burglary, and I would bail him out. The kid was never caught before. He was an artist."

"Well, your first act of penance will be to keep the hotel from evicting you."

"Why is that?"

"Because the hotel management won't appreciate you bringing the cops down on them for child sex offenses."

"What?"

"I just made a police report in your name." Conor should have taken a small measure of satisfaction for uprooting the old man's life, but he didn't. Flynn's blind devotion to the Clan-na-Gael was true to the man's character and beliefs, even if it had obscured his sense of decency and loyalty. A boy was dead, and a friendship ruined forever.

On the drive back downtown, Toad pressed him. "Mista Dolan, you think Flynn killed Mumbles?"

"No, but we can't rely on anything Flynn says now. Maybe he's telling the truth, maybe not, but we can't break ties with him now. We may need him, so we'll play along and keep sniffing around."

Flynn was a dedicated Irish Republican by any definition, but a far cry from the radical, undisciplined crowd that had tried to assassinate the Prince of Wales back in 1903. The leader of that breakaway faction had been Conor's own brother, Kevin. The older brother had rejected the fierce discipline and tactical limits imposed on the Clan by New York's legendary Irish Republican, John DeVoy. Kevin had embraced the concept of unrestrained violence, in virtually any form, to impose maximum damage on anything or anyone in step with the Crown.

In the end, it was Flynn who helped put an end to Kevin's insane assassination plot. The old detective could have killed Conor himself after the lawyer discovered Flynn's Clan-na-Gael leadership led all the way into the office of the chief of police. Instead, Flynn had extended the hand of trust to Conor Dolan and Conor had never betrayed that trust.

At the moment, there was no telling the depth of Flynn's involvement. Until there was clarity, Conor would not face the question of what to do about Eammon Flynn. But of one thing Conor was certain; the man he had left only minutes ago was the same Flynn who had pointed a pistol at him over a kitchen table in near darkness years ago and decided to let him live. The old man was a bad liar, and Conor had come away with the feeling that Flynn was still holding back. He would put Lefty on the trail to review and verify every aspect of Flynn's story.

Chapter 30

Thursday, November 1, 1918

The great Allied offensive across the Forest of the Argonne was into its sixth week and poised to break the German lines for the final and decisive time. According to the papers, the three-pronged attack was a massive pincer movement on the verge of isolating the poorly provisioned German forces. Hopes were rising that this Battle of the Meuse Argonne would finally break the Germans' backs and end the war.

Maureen's only acknowledgement of the war in Europe since Patrick's death was the new flag in their front window. Like the last one, a white box on a red background, but this flag hosted a gold star where a blue one once lay. The Dolans no longer discussed the war at home, but Chicago rubbed it in their faces with each trip to the moving pictures, the post office, even the church where they had to endure a litany of the fresh American corpses each Sunday from the ongoing battle.

Over twenty thousand American boys lay dead along the Meuse River with another hundred thousand suffering missing limbs, disfigured faces, or shattered minds. Still the battle had raged continuously since September twenty-sixth.

If there was good news to be gleaned in this *annus horribilis,* it was that the deadly Spanish Flu pandemic was finally beginning to recede since Chicagoans endured the deadliest day of the epidemic on October 18, when over five hundred people died. The lethal scourge finally led the city fathers to impose a complete lockdown on the city—almost. The saloons remained open.

CONOR MET LEFTY AT THE HUBBARD Street Courthouse that morning, where Gimpy and Toad were scheduled for a preliminary hearing in their criminal case. The hearing was in lieu of a direct grand jury indictment at the prosecutor's discretion. The procedure was employed widely in less serious cases like this. It was less costly than the grand jury process and afforded a way for lawyers to negotiate quick plea deals or have weak cases tossed out of court. Lefty always liked to appear at court *in loco parentis* for any boy who wanted and needed his help. Lefty's presence was a strong signal to the Court directed toward a boy's character.

Conor and Lefty exchanged pleasantries and pulled up two chairs at one of the small side tables. Then Lefty said, "You know, I've followed up a few leads on my own the past couple of weeks. Didn't want to bother you with you and the wife grieving and all."

"And what did you come up with?"

Lefty scratched at the coarse skin beside his nose and considered the question. "Well, it ain't what I came up with, more like what I didn't come up with."

"Such as?"

"I been thinking about that security guard fella at Ruffulo's South Side casino, the one who talked to Eammon Flynn. Seemed he was the only person who saw this Graves at the casino or anywhere else. I mean other than Mumbles. Viviana didn't lay eyes on him."

"That's right. Go on."

"So, I've been going down there out of uniform getting friendly with the security guards. It's true most of them are ex-coppers or even current ones."

"And what did you find out?"

"There are only five guards. Ain't nobody quit or got fired lately. It's a pretty good side job. Not one of 'em knew Eammon Flynn and not one of 'em ever saw a guy what fit Graves's description, not even the ring."

"Hmm . . ." The information took Conor off guard. "Maybe you missed one."

"I don't think so. I'm getting pretty good at this detective stuff. Had to track one of them down at his flat."

"Are you trying to tell me Graves doesn't exist?"

"I woulda come right out and said it, Conor, except for Viviana's story that her mother seen him."

"What do you mean *her story?*"

"I don't trust her like you do. You already know that."

In the back of his mind, Conor had begun to question Graves's existence himself, but it conflicted directly with Viviana's information. He had tried to dismiss the suspicion because, if there was never a Mister Graves, then Viviana was a fraud, and he didn't want to believe that. He said, "It doesn't make sense. Why would Flynn make up the story about Graves? We've both known him forever. He lied to us, sure, but that would take this to another level."

Lefty pushed back in the chair until it looked ready to spill him out backwards and replied, "I ain't got no answers; I'm just telling you what I found out. I think the question we need to ask is why Viviana would pick up the story of an imaginary Graves and run with it."

"But mumbles himself told me about Graves and the casino before he died. He was very specific. Then Flynn told us the security guard saw Graves approach Mumbles at the blackjack tables. That's our connection between Ruffulo and Graves."

Lefty's chair slammed back onto all four legs. "What?"

"Graves approached him at the blackjack tables over a couple of weeks, got friendly, and offered Mumbles a way to pay his debt to the casino."

"Holy shit, Conor. Flynn was lying to you again. Did Mumbles mention anything about blackjack? Or was it just Flynn?"

"Come to think of it, only Flynn."

"Impossible. Mumbles would quit gambling before playing blackjack. He hated it. Said it was a house game. The only way to win was to start the game with a wagon load of cash and keep doubling up until you got lucky or broke. He was a poker player. Nothing else."

"Well, I'll be damned. What was Flynn's game? Why would he lie about that? I'll talk to Gimpy . . . Titus. He might be able to fill in some blanks."

"Good idea. In the meantime, I'll get word to you if I find something else."

The preliminary hearing came off on script. The arresting officer testified to his own observations and the hearsay statements of two witness. Under cross-examination he admitted that both complaining witnesses had felony convictions. The court concluded that it was a simple fist fight. Gimpy didn't help their cause by mouthing off to the cop, the judge added, but addressing the cops with vulgarities was not a crime. Accordingly, the Court entered a finding of no probable cause and that was that. Gimpy and Toad were well acquainted with courtroom etiquette and respectfully delayed any show of emotion until hitting the street as free men . . . well, free *boys* anyway.

Conor might have joined in their impromptu celebration, but before he reached the exit, a familiar voice summoned him by name. "Good, work, Conor. Another notch in your belt."

He knew the voice well and hearing it today would not result in good news or laughter. He hadn't seen the priest since the memorial and his appearance in the courthouse could only mean one thing: Kate Rowland had shot her mouth off about Viviana. "Thank you, Brendan. Must be something important on your mind to bring you down here." Brendan's parish was on the North Side, but the man was liable to show up anywhere if the cause warranted. "I'm heading back downtown. I could drop you somewhere first. I assume you want to talk."

"I do, but why don't we find a quiet saloon and have a bite first?"

They stopped in a little place across the street where the lawyers liked to hang out and ordered a beer and a sandwich. Conor had no clue how Brendan would approach the subject. The priest knew better than to hit him with threats of fire and brimstone. Father Brendan was a man in a glass house, having sworn an oath to be faithful to God while living a blissful life of carnal knowledge.

In all these years, Conor had never met the woman in Chinatown, but had no doubt she existed. A couple of years ago, their mutual friend, Murph, had told Conor the couple even had a child back in 1912. Conor wasn't about to be bullied by a hypocrite, no matter how much he liked the man.

Like Conor, Brendan was born in Ireland, but the priest had never carried the baggage of hatred and bitterness toward the Crown and had always avoided the Clan-na-Gael like the plague. Brendan had never fit the standard model of a proselytizing cleric either, preferring instead to rely on his personal style, redemption of individual souls, one at a time with an emphasis on extra-spiritual necessities like food, shelter and a caring friend.

"Are you going to tell her, Conor?"

"None of your fucking business, and if you try to preach to me, I'll vomit on this table. And remind me to thank Kate Rowland and Missus Fogarty for their discretion."

Brendan was quiet for a minute as the barman produced two pints of beer. Then he said, "What about Mrs. Fogarty?"

Conor had no intention of playing this game. It was beneath Brendan's dignity to even try. "Please, I know very well it's Missus Fogarty who told you. And I'll tell you something else. The only thing Kate Rowland saw was me having lunch with an attractive woman. So, unless God has a problem with that, fuck off."

The priest was about to take a big draw on the beer but slowly returned it to the bar, foam head intact. "It wasn't Missus Fogarty who told me."

"What? Kate Rowland then."

"No."

Conor thought briefly about walking out then and there. He would never speak to this fornicator of a priest again and would not have to hear the answer to the pending question. He would have given his right arm to turn back time just five minutes and go on from here, try to put his life back together and forget this conversation that ever took place.

"Did you think I came here to preach to you, Conor? I think you know better. I'm here because Maureen asked me to speak with you. She's afraid you're going to leave her."

This isn't happening. "What? Leave her? Never." He thought about asking, *why would I leave her?* But that would play right into his trap. Then he thought about lying. There was no evidence, only a lunch. But if he went down that road, this would never end. Now, especially in this moment, the very thought of Viviana Bensini should repulse him, but it didn't. That was the worst of it. He loved Maureen and would never leave her, but he loved Viviana as well and that love just might ruin four lives. He should have ended the conversation then and there, but he couldn't. He had to know. "How did she find out?"

"Your wife only had to see you with the woman once to know. Maureen loves you; she knows you and is afraid she's going to lose you. She doesn't know what to do. Maureen has been an immigrant woman alone in this city before. It's not a comforting option, but you know all about that. A woman can vote, but she can't walk into a hotel alone through the front door, can't even open a bank account."

Conor pushed the beer to the side, burying his face in both palms on the table. "Oh my God. With her son still warm in the grave."

"So, what shall I tell her, Conor?"

"Tell her the truth because I don't know if I can do that."

The priest spoke slowly in a quiet voice, the words carrying a fatalistic tone. "Honestly, Conor, I need to know what the truth is first." Brendan's disappointment was an arrow in Conor's heart, but losing the cleric's respect would be an incomparable tragedy. His friend wasn't preaching, only trying to understand what evil would drive a man who had everything to risk it in a self-indulgent act of hedonism.

"Jesus, Brendan, you know I'm not leaving my wife. I love her, and I love our son."

"And what about this Viviana? Was it a moment of weakness or something else?"

"What is this? Am I making a confession? Are you going to give me absolution and some Hail Marys? Why don't you get the fuck off my back?"

Brendan got up to leave. "I'm not here as a priest, Conor, but as your friend. You'll need to walk your own road. You know where I am if you want to talk."

Conor moved over to the bar and ordered another beer. Maureen was at his office at this very moment. He wanted to crawl under a rock and stay there until Christ returned to earth. He'd have to face her, admit his sin and find a road forward for the three of them. Trust was a tenet of Maureen's character. She had a temper, sure. She could be cantankerous and irascible, but jealousy, pettiness, or deceit had never lined her quiver. He would take his medicine and win back her trust, if that were possible.

Viviana deserved an equal measure of honesty. He wouldn't ignore her and disappear from her life like a slithering eel. He knew Viviana had no expectations of him. She had never once hinted at a long-term relationship. Still, he couldn't dismiss or ignore her effect on him. The lawyer couldn't hire or assign anyone to extricate him from this mess. He dug the hole and would have to find his own way out.

Chapter 31

Friday, November 2, 1918

Maureen rode to the office with her husband on Friday morning. He had detected no change in her behavior since Father Brendan's ambush yesterday. He wished she would have let it all go, start throwing lamps and plates at him, throw his clothes out the window. But she wasn't afraid for herself; she was afraid for young Liam. Conor tried to imagine her thoughts, the fear and disappointment she must be feeling. He could still deny sleeping with Viviana but couldn't continue running from the conversation. Maureen deserved so much better. Yet he couldn't bring himself to cause more pain to Maureen by telling her now.

To make a bad situation worse, he could not avoid another conversation with Viviana on the elusive subject of Mister Graves. He knew the actress was still looking after her mother in the Ruffulo family home and had dismissed the idea of telephoning her to arrange a meeting, deciding instead on a surprise visit to the River Forest home.

The Ruffulo home was the perfect place to meet as Viviana's mother would almost certainly be home, giving Conor an opportunity to test the reliability of her daughter's hearsay account of Mister Graves.

He picked up Titus Freeman in Newsboy Alley after lunch and headed out to River Forest. Curiously, there was no guard at the Ruffulos' iron gate and he pulled the Ford around the circular drive, parking virtually at the front door. He saw Viviana in the doorway before they reached the front steps. He whispered to Gimpy. "Don't say a word."

"Conor, what a nice surprise. Won't you come in? Give me your coats."

"Thank you, Viviana," Conor replied. "I won't stay long."

Then he heard a voice coming from one of the rooms beyond. "Who is it, dear?"

"Just a friend, Mother. I won't be long." She led them into the front parlor, a richly appointed sitting area with dark, flowered wallpaper, oriental rugs, and hand-carved furniture. "Please, sit. Can I get you coffee? A drink?"

"No thank you, Viviana. I'm sorry to come by unannounced, but there have been some new developments, and we think you might be able to help us complete this puzzle."

"Of course., but I've told you everything I know."

"Well, we now have reason to believe that Eammon Flynn might have invented Mister Graves."

It was a powerful suspicion to drop onto Viviana because Conor's stated belief amounted to a direct attack on her truthfulness. One would expect an angry response to such a challenge, but her expression did not change even slightly. Her voice even maintained its normal conversational tone. "I doubt that, Conor. Unless I'm mistaken, Mumbles himself told you about Graves before he died."

Her reaction was a dagger in his gut and amounted to a *de facto* confirmation that she had lied about Graves. He had to know why. He said, "True, and that's a problem, but we also know that Mumbles and Flynn had a prior relationship. Mumbles told Flynn about the warehouse burglary before it happened. It was Flynn who tipped off the cops."

Her eyes seemed to grow cold. "What is it you need from me, Conor?"

It was time to finish this, time to learn the truth. "We'd like to speak with your mother, I mean both of you, together right here. It will only take a few minutes. It would help a great deal to hear the exact scenario from her about this Graves."

Viviana seemed to deflate before his eyes like a ruptured tire. She sat there staring out the front window at the fountain and the leafless trees beyond. "I understand. You are checking to see if I made up the story about Graves."

"I have to do this, Viviana."

She rose from the sofa, walked over to the picture window. Still looking out on the grounds, she said, "I never liked fall here, even when I was a little girl. It's a dead place. No flowers, no colored leaves, no neighbors, just grass. There's a reason for that. My father's associates needed a clear field of fire in the event a rival gang might try to surprise them in the night. Let me make you some coffee, and I'll tell you a story, Conor."

"I'd like that."

She returned in short order with three whiskeys and a bottle on a tray. Each of the three lifted a glass and Conor said, "*Sláinte*." They sipped. Throwing down the shot was considered unsociable. Conor would let her weave the tale in her own way.

"You are quite correct," she announced. "There is no Mister Graves. I was Mumbles's accomplice in the warehouse burglary."

"What?" Instinctively, Conor threw back the rest of the whiskey and slapped the empty glass on the tray. Titus quickly mimicked the move.

"We better have another one, ma'am." Titus said. He'd grabbed the words straight from Conor's mouth.

Viviana poured as she spoke. "Most of what I told you is true, but . . . not everything. I work for a new government department called simply Military Intelligence. I was recruited from Northwestern University in late 1916 as one of the inaugural class. We were trained by a highly skilled team of British Intelligence officers for the war effort."

"To do what?" Conor asked.

"To fight the war on the home front, at least in my case. I can't say too much, but part of our job has been to root out German spies and saboteurs, through infiltration mostly."

"That would explain your presence at the peace rally the day we met. But your father . . ."

"By that time, I was already estranged from my father. My fiancé had left the university. It was common knowledge among those who would care to know. Every hypocritical detail of my father's life revolted me. Do you know he once brought venereal disease home to my mother?"

"I'm sorry about all that, but why would they recruit you knowing that your father was a gangster?"

She chuckled. "That's what made me most attractive to them, Conor. Intelligence can be a very nasty business. Last year, they gave me an assignment. I was to recruit my father and his apparatus to confirm the existence of a sabotage ring."

"Wellborn."

"Precisely. The job required breaking into a Chicago warehouse and nobody was better at committing crimes in Chicago than my father. He was elated and jumped at the chance to become an overnight patriot. His people arranged the whole thing, even got me the best covert entry man in the city."

"Mumbles. So, you had no idea Lucchesi would shoot Mumbles?"

"Of course not, but it quickly became apparent to me afterwards that Mumbles was meant to die whatever happened. Lucchesi couldn't risk Mumbles exposing him and neither could my father. Whether my father ordered it is something we'll never know. That's what my father and his crowd consider insurance."

"Lucchesi? He's a bad one. What about the day we first met? The peace rally. Was that all scripted? Were you acting?"

"Of course not. It was pure coincidence. I was there keeping an eye out for the department, mixing with demonstrators, trying to identify the leaders. Then I took those boys to lunch and, well, I got to really like them. I never saw Mumbles again until the night of the burglary. Obviously, I was shocked. I had no idea he had a relationship with my father's criminal activities."

"And what about the Mister Graves story you told us?"

"I'm truly sorry about that, but it was the perfect cover for our operation. I didn't know in advance that Mumbles was also working with Flynn, but later, I assumed the two of them concocted the Graves story in advance should Mumbles get arrested."

"What about the Luger?"

"I don't know, but I think that was my father's idea."

"Did you have anything to do with the cops' investigations being shut down?"

She shook her head. "No. That was always above my level."

"One more question. If Flynn's aim was to make this all go away, why would he invent a story that linked your father to the burglary?"

"That's the one question I can't answer, Conor."

As Viviana escorted them to the door, Conor said, "This may not be over. Why are your father's people not watching the house?"

"My mother won't have it. She's finished with all that. We're looking at places she might move."

As Conor started to enter the vehicle, she called out. "Conor, one more thing. Come back for just a moment."

This was what he had dreaded. "Why did you bring Titus with you today? Don't tell me you needed a witness for my statement."

"Fair enough. It was a cowardly thing to do. Maureen knows we slept together, Viviana, and she hasn't said a word to me. She goes about her life pretending she's fine, we're fine, and I have to face up to this at some point."

Big tears began to form around the corners of her eyes and trail slowly down her face. "It's my fault. I pushed you to it."

He held her by the arms. "Look at me." When she could not lift her head, he helped her, gently, with one finger under her chin. "It's nobody's fault but mine. I wanted you since the first moment I saw you all beat up at the peace rally. But . . ."

"It's alright, Conor. I understand. I'll be going back to the show in a few weeks, if Uncle Sam doesn't come calling first."

"You don't understand. We can never see each other like that again, but it's not because I don't want to. Words are so easy to throw around. Losing you will be one of the great losses of my life. You see, I love Maureen too, and I've mistreated her badly. She knows what it's like to be abandoned and alone. Women can vote, but how many abandoned women do you see thriving in this city? She's afraid I'm leaving her. Can you imagine how frightening that must be? Everyone who looks at her, especially the people in the parish, would wonder what she did to lose her husband. That's what she thinks and, frankly, it's not far from the truth. She's strong, like you, but never had the same opportunities."

"Go," she said, "before I shoot you myself. But thank you for that, Conor."

"Listen to me, Viviana. You and your mother should go somewhere safer for a while. Unless you know something I don't, we still have no clue who killed your father."

Conor was clutching the "list" of Chicago saboteur operations inside his front pocket and wanted desperately to hand it to her. The list could still be of great value in identifying and prosecuting traitors. Strange how a dead son could alter a man's geo-political perspective. He decided to hold back the list. It might prove a valued commodity in the near future.

TITUS HAD ALREADY PROVED A QUICK study, so the kid would not have missed the sentimental front door scene. He thought briefly about letting the boy in on his carnal dilemma but thought better of it. How could he explain it to a fourteen-year-old when he didn't understand it himself? Titus would keep his mouth shut. Besides, the kid couldn't make any dough peddling the information anyway.

That's all Mumbles was trying to do. In the newsboy world special skills and secrets were a prized commodity to be traded and sold like manufactured goods. Mumbles never bore Viviana any ill will. For a Chicago Newsboy, it was all one big business, built and nurtured around hawking newspapers.

"So, who do you like for Ruffulo's murder, Titus?"

"Hard to say, but I don't see no connection. I heard Ruffulo's been bumping heads with Lucky O'Leary up on the North Side."

"That would be a big move for an upstart like O'Leary. Let's wait and see if the cops come up with anything, but it wouldn't surprise me if Ruffulo's murder is hooked up with our case. Should I drop you on Jackson Street or are you going somewhere else?"

"Drop me at the alley. Toad will be looking for me. Afternoon edition time."

Chapter 32

With dinner in the books and Liam in bed, it was time to walk Dillon and call it a day. Maureen was fiddling in the kitchen, probably hoping to avoid the inevitable, just as Conor was. He could put it off no longer, grabbed both of their coats from the rack and found her at the little kitchen table writing out some list or other. He held the coat out for her. "Come on. It's a nice, mild evening. Let's walk this mutt down to Scanlon's for a nightcap."

"Not tonight, Conor. I must finish the shopping list. Tomorrow perhaps."

He held the coat steady. "We can do it here in the kitchen or we can walk, Maureen, but it won't wait another day."

She looked up at him, directly, for the first time in days, then eased into the coat. "That's it then. We'll be off."

He opened the back door for them to leave. It led to the alley and the most direct route to Scanlon's. "Conor, are you forgetting something?"

"Dillon. Right. Let's go out the front door then."

It was still before nine o'clock, but only a watch could tell. With a sliver of a moon high in a clear sky, electric streetlamps alone marked the path to Scanlon's Saloon. It was a fifteen-minute, often-traveled stroll for the lawyer, but tonight was fraught with anxiety, regret, and the most toxic enemy of all—guilt.

"Father Brendan came to see me yesterday."

"Did he now? And?"

"I don't know any other way to say this, Maureen. . ."

"Aye, well, move yeer lips up and down and let the words tumble out."

"I did sleep with Viviana Bensini, once and only once."

They had to stop at Halsted Street for a passing streetcar and a few motor cars while Dillon lifted a leg at one of his favorite fire hydrants.

Maureen did not turn to face him. "Once, is it? And do ye love her?"

She might have wanted to know initially if he had been unfaithful with other women as well. *How many women? For how long?* But Father Brendan had been on the mark. Maureen knew he was no womanizer. She had a way of seeing through the nonsense and fakery, of seeing the truth and focusing like an arrow flying straight to the bullseye. How would he answer the question? Telling the truth might destroy their marriage and lying would destroy her trust forever. Why could she not allow him the preliminary excuses, the mitigation that comes before sentencing? *I never so much as desired another woman before Viviana.* Maureen had denied him the option of pseudo-virtue and self serving platitudes. He was a lawyer; he looked for a lawyerly answer. Finding none, he stopped and turned to her in front of Scanlon's front door and spoke the words that could likely become his undoing. "I think so."

Maureen didn't cry. He waited for her to break into a run back toward home. Then he waited for her to scream and carry on, call him names, vile names, he hoped. She did none of that. Instead, she said, "Tie him up then. Let's go in and talk."

Scanlon seemed to sense the solemnity of the moment, bringing them each a Jameson and a beer at one of the small tables along the wall. "Enjoy, folks," said the proprietor and disappeared behind his bar.

Conor expected her to down the shot, but she sipped. "And do ye love *me*, Conor?"

"With all my heart."

"Not quite *all*, I'd say. And is it yeer intention to stay with me and Liam?"

"Until I die, Maureen."

"And Viviana?"

She still hadn't shed a single tear. This was not what he had suspected. This was . . . a cross-examination. "What I feel for Viviana will pass. What I feel for you and Liam is forever."

"Let's leave Liam out of it for the moment. Shall we?" She signaled Scanlon for two more Jamesons, then downed the rest of her whiskey. "Alright then. Now I have a story for ye as well, Conor."

It wasn't supposed to go like this. "You do?"

"Indeed, I do, if ye're ready to hear it."

"Of course."

"Father Brendan has no girlfriend in Chinatown, Conor. He never did . . . well, not the one people think he had."

He didn't much care about Father Brendan in that moment. "I don't understand."

"It's saloon talk, Conor, fifteen years of it and it's not true, well, not much, in any case."

Scanlon arrived with the whiskeys and started to linger at the next table, ear pointing in their direction until Conor gave him an annoyed glance and he scurried off. Maureen was just starting. "I'm not finished. Contrary to everything Father Brendan and I told ye, I never had intimate relations with yeer brother, Kevin."

This was too much. She had blindsided him, his own wife. "But . . . everything you told me . . . "

She held up a palm at his face. "I agree, I misled ye, but I never said we had relations. What I told ye was true. I lived with Kevin. Without him, Patrick and I might have ended up in a brothel. He was mean a drunkard, but he saved us, Conor."

"What was the point of making me believe you were his mistress?"

"Because the truth will be harder for ye, Conor."

She was wrong. Nothing could be harder than this. He could forgive her for surrendering to his brother as a survival mechanism, but lying to him like this? And for years. Kevin was a murderer, of course, and a violent fanatic, but now she was describing his brother only as her savior. It was all too much. "And what is this truth that will be harder, Maureen?"

"Ye know that I lived in Father Brendan's church basement with other homeless immigrant women before I met Kevin."

"Of course. I know all about that."

"Well, Conor, before, that I had an apartment in Chinatown, paid for by . . ."

"No."

"Father Brendan. I was his girlfriend for a brief period in Chinatown. We cared for each other deeply, Conor, but he worried for my safety. If people found out, they might . . ."

"Why that . . ."

"'Twas my fault, Conor. He nearly left the priesthood over it. It only lasted a few months before I moved into the parish shelter."

"So how did Kevin get involved?"

"Father Brendan asked Kevin to take me in and tell people I was his wife. Kevin agreed. It was a pure act of kindness by a troubled and broken, but decent, man. Brendan and I have never seen each other in that way since and never will."

The evening had taken an unexpected turn, to say the least. It was too much to process. He needed time to think this all through. He couldn't seem to get his thoughts straight, the implications of all this, the future. "We should start back," he managed to say.

"Not yet, Conor. First, I want ye to know something else. My sins are far worse than yeer own. Still and all, when ye get up from this table, know that I love ye with all my heart. I believe a person can love two people at once, but not as a way of life. It's one of the few things that separate us from old Dillon and his crowd. If ye can find it in yeer heart to forgive me, then I will do the same. But ye must forgive Brendan as well, for, if he is a sinner, it's because he's a slave to his own selfless nature and loving heart, just as yourself, dear Conor."

They didn't speak on the walk home, but she reached for his hand, and he responded in kind as Dillon pulled on the leash. For whatever reason, Conor's mind began to replay one of the most tragic, although formative events from his early life in Ireland. Maureen knew the story well enough, as did Father Brendan and Conor's loving but complicated brother, Kevin.

Their old Pa presented six-year-old Conor with a wee border collie pup from a recent litter. He and the pup, whom he aptly named Boy, became the best of friends for the better part of a year. But in Ireland, dogs were farm animals; although loved and valued as contributing members of the harsh peasant society.

At some point near the end of a pup's first year, the farmer would cart him off to the fields for sheep tender training with the lead collie. Some pups pass muster and become reliable sheep herders. A precious few can do the work of ten men. Sadly, a fair percentage of the puppies would be born to love and play, to fetch and run endlessly with the children.

There was at that time in Ireland, no food to spare for such *lazy* dogs and old Pa would often complain that "Boy" would not make the grade. That pleased young Conor because it meant he and Boy would grow old playing together.

Then one day, old Pa announced he was taking Boy for a walk. It was a strange thing because Pa only walked to farm and to reach the pub in town. So, Conor followed out of sight as Pa played fetch with young Boy all the way to the Cliffs of Moher. As they neared the cliff's edge, Pa launched the stick high and far out over the cliff. Boy, trusting pup that he was, leapt high and far over the cliff and to his instant death in pursuit of the falling stick.

Pa and Conor never spoke of the incident, but it tormented Conor, and Kevin did his best to make the little boy believe that his dog might have landed on one of the many ledges and scampered his way down to the beach to find a new life.

Even as a little boy of six, Conor was no eejit, but would often walk to the very scene of the crime and peer over the cliff, plotting the route that his little Boy might have taken to safety. An hour ago, Conor Dolan's own journey seemed destined to end in a straight drop to the rocky beach below. But Maureen had thrown him a rope, and he would grab onto it with all his strength and scamper his way to a new life.

Chapter 33

November 5, 1918, 7:00 p.m.

The Battle of the Meuse-Argonne still raged and had crowded out virtually every other news story, both local and national. After over a month of bitter and bloody fighting, the Allied offensive had broken through on multiple fronts and the Germans were on the cusp of defeat. It was said that one and a half million Allied soldiers participated in this final push toward victory, the Americans alone suffering twenty-six thousand deaths and over a hundred and twenty thousand wounded. Like The Great War itself, Conor's puzzle seemed close to a just resolution, or as just as a solution can be without bringing back the dead and undoing the destructive work of God's most vicious species.

Conor was sitting quietly with Lefty that afternoon in the lobby of Flynn's Plaza Hotel when Flynn came through the brass doors. The old detective stopped abruptly upon spotting the reception committee, even took a step back. He flashed something that vaguely resembled a smile, the kind a child would make when caught in the cookie jar. "Well, hello boys. Are we having a shindig then? Oak Park is a long way to come for a drink. Shall we go into the bar and get comfortable?"

Conor said, "We're comfortable, Flynn, and we didn't come here to drink." He pointed to the last available chair in the circle, facing the others and back to the fireplace. "I'm surprised they haven't evicted you yet."

"No thanks to ye, Conor." Flynn settled into the chair without resistance. "Ah, a trial, is it then? And what is the crime of which I stand accused?"

Conor wasn't about to let the cagey old detective take control of the confrontation. "We know Graves only exists in your imagination. I need to hear you admit it and tell us why."

"Why would ye think that?"

"Please, Flynn, don't fuck with us. Viviana already told us she was the second burglar that night, dressed in black and masked. She ran with your Graves story because it deflected suspicion from her role—and her father's part in all this. My big question is simple. If you and Mumbles arranged in advance for a cover story, why would you make up a yarn that included Ruffulo's casino? Mumbles's account gave us the connection we needed between Ruffulo and the burglary."

Flynn let out a muffled laugh. "Yeah, Mumbles was a smart kid, too smart. He just had to add something to the story to make it better. That's what made everything go south. I could never get that lightning back in the bottle. If the lad had listened to me, this all would have worked out."

"So, the British were never involved in this. Right?"

"As far as I'm concerned, they were, but I have no evidence. The British? The Department of Justice? Allied spies? I don't care. Neither does the Clan-na-Gael. They're all on the side of the English."

Lefty had enough. He had his own question. "Did you see who shot Mumbles?"

"No, Lefty, of course not. But it's my fault."

That wasn't good enough for Lefty. He leapt from the chair, lifting the old man literally into the air. "Convince me."

"Alright! Put me down."

Lefty slammed him back into the chair. "Do it fast."

The startled clerk suddenly appeared from behind the desk. "Mister Flynn, I'll have to ask you and your associates to maintain decorum in this hotel. The management is well aware of the unfounded allegations you have made against the hotel, and they will certainly not tolerate any disorderly conduct from you."

"I'm sorry, Charles. My friends and I are simply having a business discussion."

With the clerk gone, Flynn lowered his voice. "I didn't see who actually fired the shot, but Ruffulo had to be behind it, so I killed him. It should have been slower and more painful."

It was a revelation that seemed to tie this entire cesspool of events into a neatly finished package. Or did it? Conor had nearly lost focus in this avalanche of new admissions. Then it came to Conor. "You killed Wellborn too."

Flynn nodded. "So I did."

"Why kill *him*?"

"The man was no ideologue. Sure, he had connections with German nationalist organizations, but the German Embassy didn't consider him a patriot. John DeVoy made that clear. Wellborn did it all out of greed. It was about money. The Germans fed hundreds of thousands into his business and made him rich. He was ready to sell them out for a deal. I killed Wellborn to keep him from exposing the German spy network. He knew he was finished. Conor, would ye mind if I asked just one question?"

"Go ahead."

"How did ye know about Graves? Ye had it from three sources."

It all came down to one word. "Blackjack."

Flynn nodded. "Ah, so that was it? Well, it hardly matters now. The lid will be off these cases, with the war ended and all. It won't take the cops long to come looking for me. Sure I'm too old to spend me last days in a cell, but if the good Lord pleases. "

"Tell us what you saw in the moments just before the warehouse shooting. You must have seen something."

Flynn sighed. "There was a third person with the burglars. I never saw him because he never came out in the open, but I saw the flash of his pistol. It was an assassination."

"If you want sympathy, you're looking in the wrong direction. Do me one favor, Flynn. Stay in the hotel until I contact you."

"Right."

Conor turned to leave but stopped near the door. "Oh, for what it's worth, Flynn, Ruffulo's goon, Mickey Lucchesi, was the third man at the warehouse. He shot Mumbles. It's a good bet Ruffulo ordered it. So at least you shot the right guy."

Flynn snarled. "One of them anyway. Lucchesi is still out there and will skate free as of now. Gimpy's in grave danger. So let me ask you one question, Counselor. How far will you go to protect Gimpy?"

Conor did not answer. He and Lefty headed directly for The Berghoff Saloon on Adams to meet with Detective Gianelli. Surprisingly, it was Gianelli who had asked for the nine o'clock meeting earlier in the day. Conor spotted the detective at the bar. "Thanks for meeting me, boys," said the detective.

Conor couldn't resist. "This is a switch."

They ordered beers. Conor paid. "So, tell us what you got, Detective."

"I have an eyewitness in Ruffulo's murder."

"Somehow I expected that," Conor replied.

"My witness saw one of your newsboys hanging around outside the restaurant while Ruffulo was having dinner. He was there for over an hour. If the kid didn't do the job, he might have seen who did. Maybe it was a rival gangster, maybe not. I was coming to see you tomorrow as a courtesy before we start picking the boys up for lineups. I have a few in mind already. We'd rather do this the easy way."

Conor couldn't keep his mouth shut. "So, you want to question this kid as a witness or a suspect?'

Ignoring Conor's question, the detective turned back to Lefty. "I'll stop by the alley tomorrow morning. Would you put together a list of the boys for me? It was a youngster, maybe fourteen, typical newsboy clothing with a slight build. But I want a list of every male newsboy, including age. We can narrow the list down from there and pull in the most logical suspects for questioning and identification."

"Sure, I have lists that I update as often as possible. Did your witness get a good look at the boy's face?"

"Nice try, Lefty, but no dice. I know how you feel about those boys, but we'll do this my way—officially and by the book. Okay? Oh, and I have no problem telling you we have a few questions for our mutual friend Eammon Flynn as well."

"Like what?" Conor asked.

"All in due course, gentlemen. Can I stop for the list tomorrow, Lefty?"

"Sure. I'll have it in the morning."

Lefty and Conor didn't speak until they were outside the saloon. Conor said, "So it looks like the Federal Government lifted the lid off Gianelli's cases. He's on the loose."

"Yep. Do you think his witness is Mickey Lucchesi?"

"Not a chance in hell, Lefty. You know that. He'd never go to the cops. This is a civilian witness, and it only makes things worse for Titus or Gimpy or whatever his damn name is."

"What do you think he has on Flynn?"

"No way to know, but my bet is it's about the Ruffulo murder. Gianelli might have been sitting on a tip, something that ties the Ruffulo and Wellborn murders. He was probably working this case all along quietly. Flynn is seventy years old, Conor. He left a trail everywhere, his relationship with Mumbles, the Forest Park newsboys. That was a huge mistake. Them guys probably sold that list of factories to the cops and told the whole story about Flynn. The man ain't no professional killer. He made mistakes. Even the best criminals do. Could be more, a cabbie, a neighbor of Wellborn's, something that ties Flynn and Gimpy to one, or both, of the crime scenes. I mean we found out about the history between Flynn and Gimpy. Why couldn't Gianelli find that?"

"I agree, but Flynn is clearly trying to shield Gimpy. Is it possible they were involved in both murders as a team?"

Lefty said, "That's a scary thought."

On the way to the Ford, a troublesome thought popped into Conor's mind "Lefty, why do you suppose Gianelli would tell us he's coming to question Flynn?"

"Good question. I'd say it's confirmation they already got something on Flynn. Hell, why not? We do, so why shouldn't the cops?"

"So, he was telling us to warn Flynn?"

"I suppose he was, and he wouldn't have done it unless Flynn was in a real bad spot."

"Like murder?"

"Yeah, Counselor, like murder. He was telling us that the lid's off this case. They're coming for Flynn. He was saying lawyer up."

TITUS FREEMAN, AKA GIMPY, WASN'T difficult to find. He and Toad were sitting around a barrel fire, halfway up the alley drinking beer and playing dice. As the two men drew closer toward the fire's glow, Titus spotted them and displayed no reaction, instead returning to the dice game. It was as if the lad was expecting them.

"Gimpy," Lefty called out, "come on over here for a minute."

The three made the short walk to Lefty's makeshift office, where Titus spoke first. "I figured at least one of you would be coming around to scoop me up."

"Ain't nobody scooping you up. Sit down."

"What for?"

"What do you know about Ruffulo's murder?" Lefty asked. "Tell us now, boy, because they're coming for you, and you'll need our help."

Gimpy began to cry, not audibly, but definitely. Until that moment, Conor had not seen him as a child, not in the way he did Liam. Experience, pain, and deprivation can harden a child, force him into adult habits and behaviors, even responsibilities. But the child remains until the process of maturity equips him physically and mentally to face the inevitable consequences of adult life. It all came too quickly to these boys. It wasn't real.

Then the child appeared to shed his emotions as quickly as they had engulfed him. "Yeah, I killed Ruffulo. I'd kill him again too. Had to follow the fat pig for three nights before I could get a good chance. I couldn't get him when he walked in, had to wait until he came out. I knew he'd be full of wine. I had a great hiding spot tucked into the awning behind the front door. It was pitch black outside. Ruffulo's bodyguard went to pull up the car for him, and the pig passed by me not two feet away when I blasted him. Nobody saw me do it. I was gone almost before it happened."

It was time for the lawyer to intervene. "Maybe nobody saw you do it, but somebody saw you hanging around there. Or maybe Mickey Lucchesi saw you do it and he's decided to handle this himself."

The boy stiffened, his facial features compressing into a defensive wall. "I don't care. I'll go in there myself with you and turn myself in. I ain't saying a fucking word to them cops. I know how to play it, Mister Dolan."

"Save the tough guy stuff," Conor said. "This isn't a burglary, Gimpy. It's a double murder. We're here to help you, but explain one thing. Why would Flynn cop to Ruffulo's murder? He swears he did it alone."

"He's covering for me. Flynn knew all about it, tried to stop me from doing it. Afterward, he said he was going down for Wellborn's murder anyway so he would confess to both. He told me to keep my mouth shut, that he would take the rap. He said you might beat both cases for him."

"Oh, he said that, did he? Well, don't be in such a hurry. I might have a better idea."

Conor turned to Lefty, pointing to the telephone. "Can I make an outside call with this thing?"

"With that one? Sure. Go ahead."

"Gimpy, get out of here and stay away from trouble until you hear from me. If they grab you first, be nice and lawyer up."

"Right, Mister Dolan."

When Gimpy had left, Conor picked up the receiver. "Hello, operator? Please give number River Forest 327 for anyone. This is Conor Dolan calling."

Chapter 34

November 10, 2018

Viviana was waiting outside the gate when Conor pulled up to the Ruffulo estate just before ten o'clock that night. His hands were shaking badly enough to make the car weave, and he took a deep breath as Viviana boarded on the passenger side. Whatever he might say in such a bizarre situation would sound ridiculous, so he kept his mouth shut. She was dressed like a man in trousers, boots, a black Navy coat, and wool cap. He decided not to ask if it was the same kit she'd worn for the burglary.

"It's all set," she said. "He'll be on the shore of Wolf Lake at an inlet a quarter mile south of the old boathouse, alone."

"How do you know?"

"Because he thinks this meeting will make him rich beyond his wildest dreams. He also thinks my sister is coming, so he won't have his guard up. I had her make the telephone call. Also, because it's an open spot with a full moon, completely isolated and exposed at night. No trees, no people, nothing and no one except for that crazy old man who lives across the lake and thinks he owns it. If anyone is with him or tries to sneak up on us, we'll know. What did you tell Maureen?"

They were about to commit a capital crime in the middle of the night, and Viviana wanted to know about his marriage. "I asked her to trust me. I said I had something important to do and the first thing she asked was, 'Will Viviana be there?'"

He turned the car around and headed south for the ninety-minute drive to Wolf Lake down on the Illinois/Indiana border in a remote area not far from Hammond. "Did you lie to her?"

He was terrified down to his toes and Viviana was annoying the hell out of him. "That's none of your business." But the question was on his mind and this woman knew it. He could hardly have told his wife they were going to kill someone. He had to lie to Maureen about that, so what's the difference between one lie and two? At the most, a couple of Hail Marys. "Tell me about the phone call."

"Went just like we planned. My sister told him she found two suitcases full of cash when she was cleaning out the house, too much to count, but over a million dollars. She said with no experience in washing money, the cash was no good to her and she needed help, someone she could trust who knew the ropes. He smells a huge payday, most likely figured out how he's going to steal it."

Lake Shore Drive looked like a ghost road as they crossed Seventy-Ninth Street heading toward the recently completed Dunes Highway, a concrete road superior to the dirt and gravel roads of Indiana. Without a word spoken, Viviana reached into her coat pocket, producing a .38 caliber revolver. Holding it out in his direction, she said, "This one's for you, just in case you need it. But don't worry. You won't."

Conor took no comfort in the assurance. "I don't want a gun. I'm only an accessory. Right? Besides, I haven't fired a gun in years, and it was a rifle."

This was far from the playful Viviana from the College Inn. "Put it in your pocket. If you need to, just point and pull the trigger."

He thought of asking if she'd killed people before but decided against it. If she said yes, he might think her a deranged murderer. If she said no, it would dial up his level of terror. Who wants to go on a hit job with a novice killer? He took the pistol as instructed and stowed it gently in his coat pocket. "I think we should have brought Flynn with us. I don't know about murder, but he's been in plenty of gun fights."

"I explained to you; this is not murder, well, not legally anyway. The DOJ and Military Intelligence have covertly sanctioned it, as you know. Flynn may have already killed two people so we can't be with him. Lucchesi knows enough to present a security threat to the country. Can I help it if killing him saves Gimpy's life?"

"How did you get them to agree to it?"

"I just made the case. It wasn't difficult. Besides, I'm considered a rising star since my success in the Wellborn affair."

"You're awfully relaxed. I'm not sure what to make of that."

"Do what I asked you. No more and no less. Okay?"

"Okay."

A thick November fog settled into the darkness as they crossed into rural Indiana, forcing the vehicle to a near crawl. The head lamps became virtually useless soon after they left the concrete road. Small farms dotted the landscape. If he missed the turnoff, they might end up in Lake Michigan, or worse.

"Conor, stop. There's a deer in the road ahead." Their reduced speed allowed him to bypass the animal and continue on. The fog soon lifted enough to enable the lights. He said, "How close should we get before turning off the lights?"

"It doesn't matter. If he's there, he'll expect them. We'll take the car right to the beach if we can. My sister told him she had to hire a driver. That will give us a chance to scout the area."

Conor had never suffered from the urge to be a spy or a war hero, never mind a hit man. He preferred law and languages to lethal, lakeside lawlessness. They turned onto the narrow, dirt, lake road and could see Wolf Lake ahead beyond the flat, dead grass. "Alright, follow this road around to the left away from the boathouse. Keep the lights on."

As the road wound back toward the lake, Conor could see a car not far from the water. The driver's door opened, and a man emerged. He wore a long coat and a newsboy type hat pulled low. They were fifty yards from the car when Viviana said, "Stop here." Then she turned to him and added, "Remember, don't get out of the car for anything. If it goes badly, get out of here fast. You understand?"

His throat was so dry he could barely form the word. "Yes."

She walked slowly toward the car. The man remained still, hands deep in the coat pockets. They stood face to face. Even with the window rolled down, Conor could hear only the crickets. Then he saw Viviana wave. She was beckoning him to approach. This wasn't a part of the plan. What was happening?

Carefully holding the pistol inside his pocket, he stepped out of the car, left the motor running, and walked slowly toward Viviana and Lucchesi. As their faces became clearer, Conor heard Viviana say, "Looks like someone beat us here." Under the newsboy cap was the face of the old detective, Eammon Flynn. Just beside Flynn, stretched out cold on the ground, lay the corpse of what could only be Mickey Lucchesi. "I'll be damned."

"I figured one or both of ye would be here."

Viviana said, "How did you know I was meeting him?"

Flynn shrugged. "I didn't. I borrowed a car and followed him all day until he led me out here. It was a perfect place to end his miserable life. I think I misjudged you, Miss Bensini. I'm guessing ye're a spy of some sort, but neither of ye have the requisite experience for a job like this. Besides, I killed two people already. Why not three? The three of them together wouldn't make a boil on Mumbles's arse."

The full moon shone a soft, white light upon the dead gangster's face, a bullet hole marking the place where his hairline had once started. Conor was shivering, from fear or the wet cold, he wasn't sure. This wasn't over. "What happens now?"

Flynn waved them both off. "Not to worry. Conor, help me get him into the back of his car. Then the two of ye disappear. I guarantee the body will never be found."

"What about the car?" Viviana asked.

Flynn chuckled. "It's going with him. Gimpy will be alright now, but never breathe a word of this to the lad. Ye both promise?"

They did.

ON THE DRIVE BACK TO THE CITY, NEITHER of them spoke for a long while. Then Viviana said, "How do you feel?"

"Like a murderer, I guess."

"Well, you're not, thanks to Flynn. He's a cool customer."

"Yeah, he is. But, Viviana, tell me, have you . . ."

"No. This would have been my first. If it makes any difference, I threw up when I saw the body on the ground. My stomach was in knots all day."

The fog had lifted on the Dunes Highway, improving the visibility considerably. Still, he wouldn't make it home until after two o'clock. It was as if the woman could read his mind. She said, "What will you tell Maureen?"

"I honestly don't know. But what happens to you now?"

"Time will tell. With the war over, there will be massive cutbacks on military spending. I'd like to keep doing this work, but I love acting. I'll be okay. We would have matched up well, Conor Dolan."

"I think we would have."

She reached into her coat pocket and produced an envelope. "I almost forgot. Flynn handed me an envelope before you got out of the car."

"Open it. Do you have enough light to read?"

"I think so. It's a letter addressed 'To Whom it May Concern.' It's dated tomorrow. Wait. It's two letters. The first is a short note to you, undated. The other looks like a confession. It's longer and signed. Hold on, it's the confession that is dated tomorrow."

"Read the note first."

"It says,

Robert W. Smith

Dear Conor,

Enclosed ye will find my written and signed confession to the murders of Wellborn, Ruffulo, and Lucchesi. You know what to do with it in the event Gimpy gets charged. In the meantime, I plan to enjoy life for a week or two until Gianelli and the boys come for me. We may not have seen the last of each other, my friend. I will need a good lawyer in the coming days.
Eammon."

Chapter 35

Thursday, November 7, 1918

One of the most destructive wars in the recorded history of mankind was within hours of coming to an end. The Germans were offering to surrender, and an Armistice would be signed by the warring parties within days. The conflagration had claimed over twenty million dead, military and civilian, and another twenty million wounded. Across the European Continent, the war had obliterated an entire generation of young men in a noxious haze of poison gas, a volcanic horror of artillery shells and the raging terror of a global pandemic. Among the unfortunate millions this Thanksgiving was an eighteen-year-old soldier named Patrick Dolan.

What kind of world might this peace produce? Wilson's proposal for a League of Nations offered hope that men might at last put aside their differences in favor of a more just and peaceful world. In the space of only two short weeks, optimistic historians were already calling it *The War to End All Wars*. The fighting was ended, Germany ground into defeat, but would the terms of the peace eventually mitigate the massive sacrifice and slaughter or at least give some meaning to each individual death? To Patrick Dolan's death? Conor Dolan could not speak for his wife, but for him this Thanksgiving would be less about thanks and more about hope.

Conor and his wife were getting to know each other again, each trying to become more involved in the other's daily routine and frustrations. She enjoyed going out to lunch during the week and was adjusting well to the eclectic hordes of thieves, prostitutes, perverts, and swindlers that packed his office during the week, so they had decided to make her position permanent. She would be Mrs. Schmidt's assistant when and if the secretary returned to work.

The Dolans were still eating dinner when the telephone rang. It was the night watchman from the Monadnock Building. "Mister Dolan? There's a soldier here was hoping to find you in the office. I told him you left just after five o'clock. He's from out of town. Says he's on his way back home and knew your boy. Should I give him the address?"

"Of course. Wait. He doesn't know the city. Ask him to stay there and I'll pick him up in twenty minutes."

The young man was waiting just inside the row of brass-framed doors when Conor pulled up. The lad came out to the car wearing the brown dress uniform with overcoat. The left sleeve was limp, empty. Conor noticed the sergeant stripes adorning the coat as the soldier threw his duffle into the back and settled into the seat. "Conor Dolan, Sergeant. Welcome home. Have you had dinner?"

The boy looked gaunt and thin, obviously exhausted, and not a day over twenty. He took Conor's outstretched hand. "Billy Campbell, sir. No, I haven't eaten."

"We'll fix that in short order, Billy Cambell."

Maureen had the dinner place set as they came in the door. Conor took the duffle into the boys' room as Maureen tended to the soldier's needs, and Liam took the situation in.

The soldier devoured enough food for three lawyers, topping the feast with two slices of pie. "So where are you headed, Billy?" Conor asked.

"Home. Crown Point, Indiana, sir. Got my separation papers in New York a few days ago. I have a train ticket home tomorrow."

"Sure ye'll stay here tonight, Billy. We've an extra bed in the boys' room. Conor will drive ye to the train tomorrow."

"I sure appreciate that, ma'am."

They moved into the living room in the warmth of the fire. "Can I get you a drink?" Conor asked.

"No, sir. I don't drink. I mean, I drank a little in France when I could, but I don't really fancy it. Another glass of milk would be fine."

The soldier was in Conor's chair, closest to the fire, and Maureen settled on the sofa end just beside the chair. They both took care to ensure Liam was there and a part of the conversation. Maureen couldn't hold back any longer. Resting her palm on the young soldier's knee, she asked, "Where were ye wounded, Billy?"

"Second Battle of the Somme, ma'am, in September, artillery shell. I was one of the lucky ones. It's all over for me now . . . well . . . " Then he looked down the empty sleeve and added, "except for this. But I wanted to come here to talk about Patrick. He was my friend and one of the kindest people I ever knew. He didn't die in battle, but he would have done his duty had it come to that. Everyone respected him for his leadership. I was with him a few hours before he died from that damned Influenza. He got it on the ship over to France. I did too, but I recovered. The division lost hundreds of men to that scourge. Patrick asked me to come see you."

They all cried, openly and without reservation. It was the right time to cry. This was the closest they would ever come to seeing and talking with their dear Patrick. Even the one-armed, battle-hardened soldier cried. But Billy Cambell was just getting started. "I'm supposed to tell Liam to keep studying hard." Looking directly at Liam, he added, "He said you were always a better student. He wanted to be more like you and never told you that.

"Mister Dolan, he asked me to tell you how much he appreciated your patience. Whenever he goofed up, you were there willing to hear his side. He couldn't recall you ever raising your voice. You were his real father, the father he would have chosen.

"And Mrs. Dolan, he knew you traveled a long, difficult road and protected him all the way. He loved you with all his heart. Oh, he also hopes Mister Dolan is wrong about the Catholic Church. That way he'll see you again in heaven. I'm not sure if he was joking. Patrick also had a great sense of humor."

WITH THE WOUNDED SOLDIER SOUND asleep in Patrick's bed, Conor and Maureen decided to walk Dillon to Scanlon's. The night brought with it a taste of the looming Chicago winter. A frigid lake wind could not deter the pair from bundling up for their walk. They'd been making a habit of the nightly walk to Scanlon's before bedtime. It gave them a chance to talk as the neighbors tucked in warm and cozy for the night. They would chat about clients, cases, Liam's high school plans, or anything that happened in the world that day. Today had been special. They would never forget Billy Campbell's visit. Maureen suggested they both drive Billy home to Crown Point on Saturday.

Conor thought they were getting past Viviana and that deceitful, fornicator of a priest who had called Conor friend. At least the unholy business occurred before Conor and Maureen ever met. Conor would never raise the subject of Father Brendan White again in his life.

"Thanksgiving is coming up in a couple of weeks, Conor. Sure I've been considering who to invite to dinner. A month ago, I'd have wiped Thanksgiving and Christmas from my memory, had I the power. It won't be easy, but I think we should do it for Liam."

"I haven't given it much thought, but it's a good idea, I suppose. Who are you thinking of? The Kellys across the street? They have no family at home."

"Actually, I was thinking of inviting a specific group of friends, the folks who helped us get through this past year."

"You don't mean Eammon Flynn?"

She nodded. "And others. Gimpy, Toad . . ."

"Fine with me, assuming Flynn and Gimpy are not in jail for murder. There's a good chance of that."

They got stuck in the wind at Halsted Street again as Dillon tended to business on the hydrant. "So, what really happened then? Were they involved together in both murders or did one kill Wellborn and the other Ruffulo?"

"We may never know, Maureen, and it might be better that way. I don't want to remember Gimpy as a boy who put a bullet in someone's brain, even if he had it coming."

"Things are better now in the city, better than back in 1903, but there are still very few happy endings for the wandering, penniless souls. How will this all play out?"

"Honestly, I don't know. I'm working on it, but we have to take it day by day."

It was too cold to leave Dillon tied up outside, so they brought him into the saloon and the dog sat quietly beside them at a table. Women were still not allowed to stand at the bar. As Scanlon placed Dillon's water bowl on the floor, a small wave of beer spilled from a glass onto the floor. Ignoring the water, Dillon slopped up the spilt beer and assumed a begging position beside the table with his tongue doing the talking. "Well, I'll be damned,"

Conor declared. "Take the water back and give the dog a beer. After all these years, Dillon has acquired the taste."

It was a good craic. Maureen and Conor laughed and told stories until well past midnight when there was no telling who was drunkest among the three of them. They had to walk home against the lake wind. The Chicago protocol for such a walk called for walking backwards, face shielded from the wind, a dance not easily performed under the influence in the dark. They reached Halsted Street without falling and, by that time, were being shocked into sobriety. That's when Maureen said, "So will I invite Father Brendan to Thanksgiving?"

Conor was certain he misunderstood her through the fog of alcohol. He laughed "Sorry, I thought you asked if you could invite Brendan to Thanksgiving dinner."

"I did."

He thought briefly about turning around and heading back to Scanlon's. Maybe he'd passed out and was having a nightmare, but the sight of his big, black dog staggering down the sidewalk reinforced his grasp of reality. His wife's former boyfriend, the priest, would be at his table on the holiday.

All evening, he had wanted to tell Maureen about his telephone conversation with Viviana Bensini but hesitated. Maybe Maureen had just presented him with the solution. If he could handle it, why couldn't she? "So," he said, "I am mature enough, and I trust you enough, to sit across the table from that miserable, predatory charlatan of a priest and be polite to him for an entire evening."

While they were still walking backwards, Maureen smiled, leaned over and kissed him on the cheek, whereupon they both tumbled to the sidewalk and Dillon went trotting off toward home. "Thank you, Conor."

As she began to rise, he pulled her back down. "Wait. I now have a request of you." He recited to her in detail his telephone conversation that day with Viviana Bensini. With his cards all on the table and his ass still planted firmly on the icy sidewalk, he added. "May I then invite Viviana for Thanksgiving dinner? Perhaps we could seat them side-by-side and call it a blind date."

EPILOGUE

Monday, November 28, 1918, Thanksgiving

In the spirit of Thanksgiving, the Dolans had indeed carefully chosen their guest list this year to include, exclusively, a tight circle of friends bound by a single series of tragic events and two disturbing episodes of carnal shenanigans. Over the past eighteen months, their friendships had been tested, loyalties strained, and trust shattered. Yet here they sat at the Dolan table, together, each with his or her personal story, biases, loyalties, loves, flaws, and heartbreaks, to celebrate what? Conor couldn't put his finger on it but was eager to let the show play out.

Father Brendan White, Conor's close friend since the early days in Chicago, the man who had guided him through the minefield of Chicago politics years ago, had an affair with Maureen that the two had hidden for nearly fifteen years, sat at Conor's left. Only Conor's own infidelity had unlocked the secret and enabled the married couple to assess and reset their relationship going forward. The lawyer was trying very hard that afternoon to be thankful for Brendan's friendship.

At the other end of the table sat the hostess, Maureen Dolan, the woman who had invited her former lover to celebrate the holiday. Young Liam took the chair beside her. Along the side chairs sat Lefty Hawk, the one human being in Conor's life, aside from Liam, who had not lied to him during the last eighteen months. Beside Lefty sat Conor's dear and trusted friend, Eammon Flynn, the man who had once spared Conor from a bullet and had evolved into a German agent, a liar, and a cold-blooded murderer. Across from him sat the man of the hour, Gimpy, aka Titus Flynn, a humble newsboy with his nose in ten rackets and possibly the slayer of Chicago's feared gangster, Big Jimmy Ruffulo. Toad, Gimpy's faithful business associate, friend, and partner in crime, rounded out the guest list--almost.

The *de facto* guest of honor for the celebration was none other than Viviana Bensini, Conor's . . . friend. Viviana, who was performing with her theater company somewhere on the East Coast, had arranged a sabbatical to attend the Dolans' affair, there being no current demand for her espionage services.

Viviana graciously offered to help Maureen with the service. Conor made certain everyone consumed several drinks in the parlor before gathering at the table for what he hoped would end up The Last Supper. He even allowed Liam a full glass of wine.

The dinner was an unqualified success: American style with turkey, salads, cranberry sauce, and stuffing. Turnips, soda bread, and scones provided a tasty Irish accent. Conor sensed no tension in the room, likely because everyone save Liam had steeled him or herself for whatever blows or bullets might fly between insults and accusations.

Brendan told stories; Flynn told jokes and Gimpy told lies. Not a soul asked who really killed Wellborn and Ruffulo. When it was all finished and any danger of fisticuffs extinguished, Viviana asked quietly if she might address the gathering.

Standing up, she reached across the table and handed Flynn an official-looking document. "This is your passport," she announced, "authorized and issued to you by The State Department in consideration for service to your country in wartime. Your list of factories has led to the breakup of a major spy ring, essentially a nest of traitors, Americans who worked for years to sabotage

Allied weapons. The State Department has imposed a new temporary moratorium on local and state action against both of you in the murders of Wellborn and Ruffulo. The passport is valid and only requires a photo."

Flynn stared at the documents, gaping. "I don't know what to say."

"This moratorium under The Espionage Act will not be permanent. There may be a change of administration or change of policy. The war is over so we can maintain this moratorium only until the Bureau of Investigation arrests these traitors. It could happen at any time so there's not a minute to lose." Then Viviana smiled. "Where would you like to go?"

Flynn said, "I still have family in Ireland. It's my dream to die on the old sod but not until I do my last bit for the struggle." He went silent for a few seconds, then added, "What about the lad?"

Viviana smiled and handed an identical looking document to Gimpy. "This is your passport if you want it. Unfortunately, we had to change your name again. This time it's Emmett Flynn." Then she handed Flynn two steamer tickets from New York to Queenstown and added, "We needed a first name to go with Flynn, something that wouldn't stand out. Titus Freeman wouldn't make the grade. Best you hold onto both passports until you get to Queenstown, assuming Gimpy wants to go. Pack one bag each and be ready to move in two days. Oh, one last thing. They may challenge your police pension at some point. My department maintains a fund for spy business if you will. We pay informants, move witnesses, bribe double agents, all very sneaky stuff. I'm happy to say they asked me to give you this bank draft for 5,000 dollars to help you get started over there."

Emmett Flynn would make a fine Irishman. With the fair skin and dimples, the lad might have been Flynn's actual nephew. Conor had no doubt the boy would make a go of it, especially teaming up with the sly old detective.

"Ireland? Do they have newsboys in Ireland?" Emmett asked.

Flynn smiled, turned to Emmett and said, "Now wouldn't ye rather own a pub in the West of Ireland, son, and live the country life of a gentleman?"

Toad looked as if he'd lost his best friend. "What about me?"

Conor said, "I doubt you'll have time to hawk papers much longer. Maureen or Missus Schmidt will be ordering your new business cards. They'll say Chief Investigator. But you'll need a real name now."

The newly named Emmett Flynn offered the perfect solution. "You can have your old name back, Toad, if you want it. Titus Freeman is a good name, and I was proud to borrow it."

THE END

Robert W. Smith

ACKNOWLEDGMENTS

I was able to bring this story to life only through the collective efforts of the best independent publisher in the business, Meryton Press, and its tireless staff of dedicated professionals. From Janet in graphics and marketing to my powerhouse editing team of Elizabeth and Brynn, the Meryton staff pulled out all the stops to help make this novel a labor of love—for the second time.

But what is a book if no one reads it? My hard-core readers will always power this journey; folks like June, James, Herb, Beep, Patti, Carl, Mary, Maureen, Bobby G., George, Pam, and many others. Thanks to all of you for the support over the years.

To the book clubs that have proven to be my most anticipated and fun events, especially the Paperback Book

Club and the Naperville Book Club, never hesitate to invite me. "Have Books Will Travel."

Finally, thank you to the Berkeley Public Library, where I once served on the Board, and the wonderful folks there who have embraced my novels, tolerated my insufferable stories, and helped increase the visibility of my humble literary efforts.

ROBERT W. SMITH

ABOUT THE AUTHOR

Bob was raised in Chicago, enlisting in the Air Force in 1968. Following four years of service as a Russian Linguist in the Security Service Command, a branch of the NSA, Bob attended DePaul University and The John Marshall Law School. With over thirty years of experience as a criminal defense lawyer in Chicago, Bob brings a lifetime of understanding and experience to his novels. His Running with Cannibals is the Grand Prize winner of the CIBA 2022 Hemingway Award for best 20th-century wartime fiction. The author lives in the Chicago area.

http://www.robertsmithbooks.com

Also by Robert W. Smith

A Long Way from Clare

https://mybook.to/smithalwfclare

Made in the USA
Middletown, DE
07 July 2024